Praise for *Stealing C*

"Whether it be science fiction, . McAllister story is a marvel. 1 ...s here will fascinate and intrigue, and some or them will break your heart."

- Ellen Datlow, multi-award winning editor and anthologist

"In these wide-ranging, beautiful short stories, readers will feel the characters' emotions as their own. McAllister's well-imagined settings can range from the past to the future, from Arcturus to a small town, and each one captivates. When I reach the end of one tale, I can't wait to turn to the next."

- Sheila Williams, editor, *Asimov's Science Fiction*

"You might think you're getting just a collection of short stories here, but you're not. They're also love letters to the places and curiosities that fascinate us as children; ransom notes, from half-remembered nightmares; and sometimes both at the same time: a warm embrace that ends with a shiv to the spine. It's science fiction, yes, but also poetry, fantasy, and faith. Whatever you think you're about to read, you're wrong - it's far more."

- Trevor Quachri, editor, *Analog Science Fiction and Fact*

STEALING GOD
AND OTHER STORIES

BRUCE MCALLISTER

AEON PRESS BOOKS

First published by Aeon Press 2022
All stories © 2022 Bruce McAllister

Introduction © 2022 Paul Di Filippo

ISBN: 978-0-9934682-1-6

Cover image: Dominic Harman

Cover design by John Kenny

Text design and typesetting by John Kenny

Typesetting Fonts: Book Antiqua and Perpetua Titling MT

To Amelie and to Liz, Ben and Annie
for the love that every story needs
And to my parents, James and Bernice,
for a life full of wonder

My thanks to all of the editors who first published these stories; and
to my editor at Aeon Press, John Kenny, without whom this book
would not have been possible.

Acknowledgements

'What We Forget' was originally published in *Analog Science Fiction and Fact*, Nov/Dec 2021

'The Blue House' was originally published in *Cemetery Dance* #74/75, 2016

'La Signora' was originally published at *Tor.com*, Aug 2014

'Sandy' was originally published in *Analog Science Fiction and Fact*, Oct 2018

'Blue Fire' was originally published in *The Magazine of Fantasy and Science Fiction*, Mar/Apr 2010

'The Messenger' was originally published in *Asimov's Science Fiction*, July 2011

'Ink' was originally published at *Lightspeed*, Aug 2017

'Hit' was originally published at *Aeon Thirteen*, Feb 2008

'Bringing Them Back' was originally published in *Asimov's Science Fiction*, Feb 2016

'The Voice' was originally published in *Asimov's Science Fiction*, May/Jun 2020

'Stamps' was originally published in *Asimov's Science Fiction*, Aug 2012

'Stealing God' was originally published in *Albedo One* #46, 2016

'Don't Ask' was originally published at *Subterranean Online*, Summer 2013

'My Father's Crab' was originally published in *Analog Science Fiction and Fact*, Oct 2015

'Frog Happy' was originally published in *Analog Science Fiction and Fact*, Mar 2018

'The Courtship of the Queen' was originally published at *Tor.com*, May 2010

'Sidha' was originally published at *DreamForge Anvil* #6, 2021

'The Witch Moth' was originally published in *Fearful Symmetries* (ChiZine Publications), 2014

'Sun and Stone' was originally published in *Image: A Journal of Art, Faith and Mystery* #59, 2008

What We Forget
by Bruce McAllister

What is the most haunting color
in your life? Is it the blue of
Christmas lights, your parents
placing you by the tree on your first
blanket and you gazing up at the blue
light until it became the universe? Or
the blue of a landing field's lights at night
as you, no longer crying, set down with your
father after your mother's long funeral in a city
where the sky was not blue. Or the eyes of
the first girl you ever loved, and her sweater
and even the perfume she wore, which
smelled blue to you. And the blue that you became
when things did not work out. This is how we explain
such things when it just isn't true. It is the blue of a
small, hot star not long after the birth of the universe,
which you remember, though you say you don't,
and how you stared for an eon at the heart of creation,
looking for the tiny blue ones, your favorites.
The blue of the very first supernova, and the next,
filling you, as you watched, with a love of all things.
and the blue of the metal that wasn't metal,
of the starship that brought you, little and staring,
to this world, to be born again and to try
to pass as human, as so many of us do.

Table of Contents

INTRODUCTION

HE IS *HEAVY*, AND HE'S MY BROTHER
by
Paul Di Filippo

Being the oldest of four siblings, I never had a big brother. But I often used to wonder what it would feel like to have that relationship with a fraternal comrade who had passed through many of life's initiations ahead of you, and could offer wisdom and advice.

I don't think I am exaggerating when I say that as a teenager and young adult, I came to see Bruce McAllister as my virtual big brother.

Born eight years prior to me, McAllister is nonetheless of the same generation, part of my like-minded Boomer cohort, and consequently possesses life experiences that resonate generationally with mine. Except that his small but significant chronological advantage saw him treading the territory I wanted to tread earlier than I could. Thus, while I was still in high school in 1971, McAllister was publishing his excellent first novel, *Humanity Prime*, and I was snatching it up as part of my mad lust for SF paperbacks, and enjoying the hell out of it, and learning about new modes of SF writing that differed from the Golden Age stuff I loved. And in subsequent years, I would encounter McAllister's short fiction in various magazines, such as *F&SF* and *New Worlds*, and once again feel that here was a sage comrade, relateable to my ambition and attitudes, who could show me the way. A talismanic, totemic trailblazer. As we used to say back then, "Heavy, man!"

Now, I must hasten to affirm that McAllister bears no actual responsibility for my current warped condition. Big brothers can only do so much through leading by good example. His influence was spiritual and artistic, and he never actually stood bail for me, or loaned me his sports car or favorite necktie for a hot date. Also, he was not alone in this unilateral status. There were a whole bunch of men and women just a tad older than I who stood by me in similar stances. George Alec Effinger (born 1947). Ed Bryant (born 1945). Arthur Byron Cover (born 1950). David Gerrold (born 1944). Vonda McIntyre (born 1948). And the biggest, oldest big brother, not quite a Boomer, Chip Delany (born 1942).

These folks were certainly not of the Asimov-Heinlein-Bradbury-Clarke Golden Age generation, whom I adored. They were even too young to belong to the Silver Age Sheckley-Silverberg-PKD-*Galaxy* magazine crowd that I admired. They were, dare I say it, a "New Wave" of SF writers who blazed a path I desired to follow.

Once I became a professional author myself, of course, I entered into a new relationship with these "big brothers and big sisters." Now we were peers. I met some of them in the flesh. (I've never had that pleasure with Bruce, alas.) I often had to examine their works with a critical eye, for purposes of review or blurbing. But in the back of my mind and deep in my heart, they always retained something of the status of worship-worthy elder siblings.

And so nowadays, when Bruce McAllister releases a bold, brilliant new story collection, full of marvelous gems in the patented McAllister mode and style, I can only experience a feeling akin to watching your elder sib stride across some stage to accept a lifetime achievement award. Without, I think, being blindly uncritical of the work—none of us are perfect, though McAllister comes close—I can affirm the unique value of this book wholeheartedly, on a more-than-literary basis.

You, as a reader who might not have had as long an acquaintance with McAllister's fine fictions as I, can of course judge the worth of this volume for yourself. I don't believe you will come away any less enthusiastic than I am.

What awaits you in these pages? A "wealth of fable," to borrow a title from Harry Warner. McAllister works in many modes, and is proficient in all of them.

'The Blue House' is a creepy ghost story equal to anything by Robert Aickman, dealing with family longings and lust. 'La Signora' is one of a semi-series of tales that deal (autobiographically, I think) with expatriate days in Italy, and features a sea monster you'll never forget. Aliens on Earth is the focus of 'Sandy,' which unprivileges humanity from its arrogant perch. Vampires are the focus of 'Blue Fire,' while 'The Messenger' gives us tragic time travel.

A miraculous health cure—via stamp collecting—is center-stage in 'Ink,' another of those quasi-autobiographical pieces. "God wants you to kill the oldest vampire." Such is the novum around which 'Hit' accretes. The saddest tale in this volume, 'Bringing Them Back' wrings deep Anthropocene emotions from its most subtle and understated presentation. Readers might find 'The Voice' slightly reminiiscent of the hit film *The Shape of Water*. Philately returns, with an alien twist, in 'Stamps,' one of the stories that best showcases McAllister's wry humor. The title story deals with the occult aspects of Native American culture in a sensitive and compassionate manner. McAllister-style Military SF? Yes, that's a fine thing, as we see in 'Don't Ask.' And father-son dynamics lie at the heart of 'My Father's Crab.'

Every day, as school was ending, I would get so excited I'd start to shake. Kids would notice it and say, "What's wrong with you, Marcus? You're shaking." Even the teacher noticed, but my parents told her I was fine, it wasn't seizures — "He's just 'frog happy .'"

How could anyone fail to be seduced by a story titled 'Frog Happy' when it contains sentences like that? Has any other writer ever discerned the magic in exotic seashells? If so, they still probably failed to match the wonder found in 'The Courtship of the Queen.' McAllister does Cordwainer Smith? Again, you will be a believer when you encounter 'Sidha,' about a doomed love among the stars. A last encounter with McAllister's juvenile stand-in hero delivers us to 'The Witch Moth,' as our boy learns about the true nature of death. And our compendium of wonders concludes strongly with 'Sun and Stone,' wherein Nature gets its revenge.

What a rich tapestry of terrifying, traumatic, tender, and tantalizing tales!

When I had occasion to review *The Village Sang To The Sea: A Memoir of Magic*, McAllister's most recent novel (search that one out, and I guarantee you will be well rewarded), I said: "McAllister's book radiates an elegaic and meditative aura, as of puzzles that continue to perplex even after their solutions seem conclusive. It charts the slippery interfaces and interstices between the quotidian and the supernal, a realm most of us shut out and pretend does not exist." I think that description embraces his short fiction as well, and proves that, like all the best big brothers, he is willing to bare his scars for our edification.

THE BLUE HOUSE

I don't want your lonely mansion
With a tear in every room
All I want's the love you've promised
Beneath the halo moon
— "Silver Threads and Golden Needles"

Maybe it was my uncle's cigar — maybe it was bad bullfrog legs he'd cooked up for us — or maybe the blue house on the hill and its weirdness — but that night I dreamed the strangest dream I'd had since I was little and scared of things under beds and in closets.

I dreamed my uncle Wes was dead. It was years from now, and he was dead, and he'd left me the house, the little blue one that looked like a children's book. I was married — not to Diane, his best friend's daughter, or my on-and-off girlfriend in San Diego — but to someone else. I couldn't see her face in the dream, but she was older — a lot older than I was, though still a girl — that part made no sense — and we were living in that house together. We were happy. It felt like love, and this was all my uncle wanted.

Then the dream changed. I was outside painting the little blue house with its fruit trees and the tame rabbits that lived under them, never leaving. Why dogs and coyotes didn't get the rabbits, I didn't know. Why the trees were always so full of fruit, their limbs touching the grass where the rabbits lived, I didn't know either. All I knew was that I needed to paint the house *another color* and do it quickly because at any moment she was going to catch me. That was the scary thing: *she'd catch me.*

15

Which she did.

I turned and there she was, mouth open like she was going to scream. She'd screamed before. I remembered that—she was always screaming—but she took the brush from me calmly. It was yellow, a pale yellow paint, and when I'd put it on our house the rabbits disappeared one by one, stroke by stroke, the fruit trees too, then piece by piece the house itself—everything disappeared as I painted. But before I could finish she took the brush and said, "Why, Ken?"

I still couldn't see her face, but now I knew why—in the dream I knew why. Because I didn't want to look at her. I didn't want to see what she really looked like.

"Don't you love me?" she asked and the voice was a girl's, a young woman's, but frightening. "I love *you*, Ken."

I had a gun in my hand.

"What are you going to do with that?"

"Shoot myself," I said. "If you won't let me paint the house, I'm going to shoot myself."

"No," she said. "You're not."

The gun was gone, the rabbits and trees and house were back, the house was bright blue and we were sitting on the porch together, holding hands, rocking on a porch swing. "I've waited so long," she said, "to be happy again."

In the dream my uncle was there on the porch smiling. "See?" he said. "See why it needed to be *you*, Ken?"

ॠ

When I had a chance, I asked Darrell about the house. He was one of my uncle's ranch hands, a little wiry guy who'd lost two fingers to calf-roping. We'd cut the cattle for the vet's visit—the pregnancy testing—and were about to head back to the house.

"The blue one?" he answered, looking small but tough on his quarter horse.

"Yeah."

"That's been in your family a long time."

"You're kidding."

"No, I'm not kidding. Your mother never mentioned it?"

"Absolutely not. She didn't talk much about the Valley when I was growing up."

"Or Wes." It was a statement, not a question, and I didn't know what he meant at first.

"No," I said finally, "she didn't talk about Wes either."

"And Wes hasn't mentioned it?"

"No. He just takes me there and sits in the truck and looks at it."

Darrell smiled oddly then. "I bet he does."

I pressed him, but that's all he would tell me. "Not my place to say," he added.

৯

Two days later I caught my uncle by the ranch house's porch sink and, big man that he is, he jumped, nervous. I didn't know why at first, then saw it. He was washing his hands with turpentine, trying to get paint off. He'd missed a spot on his elbow. The spot was blue.

৯

I tried to tell Diane. She was a beautiful girl, even if (as she liked to put it) "just a plumber's daughter." Her dad had been Wes's best friend for years. We'd gone to catch a movie at the Winton drive-in, one of the last ones in the Valley, and always talked or made out if it was a really bad one. But I wasn't making much sense.

"What are you trying to say?" she asked. "Do you mean there's something wrong with the place. Like someone died there?"

She sounded annoyed, like I was telling her a ghost story just to scare her. I'd never heard her sound that way.

"I don't know what I'm saying. It's just weird. No, I don't think anyone died there."

She didn't answer, just sat there annoyed, like she was mad. But about what? I'd mentioned the dream — I probably shouldn't have done that (there was another girl in it). Still.... How could she get jealous of a dream?

Then it hit me.

"You know something about that house."

She wouldn't look at me. She said, "Not really."

"Yes. You do."

"Just what everyone knows."

"Jesus, Diane. *What*?"

"That your family — your family on your mom's side — has owned it for a long time."

"I know that. How long?"

"How the hell would I know?"

"Why are you so bitchy tonight?"

"Why do we have to talk about that house?"

"I was just making conversation. I thought you'd be interested."

"I already know about it."

"Okay. Okay."

We sat for a while not talking. It was a movie about a blind woman being stalked by a killer and you'd have thought we'd be interested. We weren't. We didn't even have the volume on loud enough to hear. Finally Diane said:

"I'm sorry."

"So am I."

"It's just that — "

"What?"

"I don't want you going to that house anymore."

"You don't want *what*?"

"I don't want you going there anymore."

I told her that sounded crazy. She didn't answer. She stayed quiet all the way home, and nothing I said made a difference.

এ

18

That was the summer I worked on my uncle's ranch for the first and last time, dehorning and castrating and branding calves, shoveling silage, stringing barbed wire, the things that cowboys in the Central Valley did, waving to each other from their pickups with their gun racks. I fainted the first time from the smell of smoke from the burning hide and blood. Just keeled over on the split rail fence of the corral and lay there like I was sleeping, they said later. Darrell just laughed. I woke up to his laughter. It was the summer I was supposed to become a man.

It was also the summer I took a girl to a county fair for the first time — a real country fair — and a rodeo. Diane's black hair was long and gorgeous, like that TV commercial, and I wanted to kiss her the first time we went out, but didn't. I felt — and I know this came from what my mother said to me when I was fourteen, about kissing being "dangerous" — that you didn't kiss a girl unless you wanted to live with her, in her world, forever. It was crazy — the kind of silly thing parents told you then to keep you from having sex — though her words stuck with me like an old whisper. But I'd kissed girls before — girlfriends and girls at parties — and I got over it with Diane fast enough. We'd been kissing for weeks before I saw the house on the hill for the first time.

It was also the summer when my father — a civilian inventor for the Navy who, gentle and bookish guy that he was, was no "man's man" and would be the first to admit it — had decided I should work on a ranch. And because my mother's brother — whom I'd never met — kept inviting me, it should be Wes, his ranch in Atwater, California, in the great San Joaquin Valley. My father wanted me, he told me one day, to have "models" other than just him. "I'm not a very physical, guy, Ken." He said, "You have a right to know what other men are like, men who've married or not, men who work with their backs and arms as well as their brains." It was a strange speech, not like him, but he was still crying some nights from the grief of my mother's death four years before. It embarrassed him, I know, to cry like that. He couldn't stop himself, and he wanted something better for me, I know, than a father's weeping in the night.

My dad thought we were more alike than we were. I'd been on the football team one year and still ran track. If I was gentle around him, not physical, and talked ideas like he did—didn't ask him to throw a football, didn't wrestle with him on the floor—that was because *he* was gentle, liked being in his head, and I did love him. That didn't mean I didn't know how to give grief as well as take it. If that summer made me a man, it wasn't the ranch work that did it. It was the little house on the hill and what I needed to do about it.

ॐ

The next time my uncle took me to the blue house we got paint, and he said, "Yeah, I own that house. I thought you knew that."

"First time we were there, you said you needed to find out who owned it."

"You heard me wrong. Your mom never told you about it?"

"If she did, I'd know you owned it, right?"

I was pissy. He should've called me on it, but he didn't. He was trying to be pleasant that morning—not the hard-ass ranch owner he was to most people—and that was also strange. The house made him this way, I thought. Humble. Nervous. Something else....

"I want to keep it fixed up. I'm thinking of selling it."

"I thought you were going to give it to me when I got married."

"Maybe I still will if you stop giving me so much lip."

He was lying, I could tell. He wasn't going to sell it, and if he wasn't going to sell it or live in it or let anyone else live in it, why was he painting it?

"Paint protects the wood," he said, reading my thoughts.

We rode along in silence for a while, and I said, "Those rabbits—"

"Yeah?"

"Why do they hang around?"

He didn't answer for a mile. Then he said, "We need to start with the back porch. It's going to hell."

Neither of us said a thing for about five miles. We just gave the cowboy wave to the other pickups — some with bales of hay, some with machinery in their beds.

"You see anything last time we were there?" he asked suddenly.

"Like what?"

"Sometimes a girl plays there — a girl about your age. I think she's a painter. I think she likes to paint pictures of the house."

I didn't know what to say except, "No, I didn't see her."

ॐ

We painted the back porch, and it looked good, that bright blue, like the bluest sky in a dream. It was someone's favorite color — my uncle's favorite colors were brown and black — ranch colors — so this was someone else's, maybe his mother's, maybe one of his wives (he'd had three), who knows?

We pulled out some of the picket-fence posts, creosoted new ones, and got them into the ground before sunset. A full day's work. The entire time, I swear, my uncle was looking around.

"Expecting someone?"

"Rodney said he might show up with some new faucet pipe. Too much rust in the old ones."

Rodney was Diane's dad, so it was possible, I guess. But the way my uncle was looking around that day, it didn't feel like Rodney he was expecting.

ॐ

I wanted to get a look at the house by myself — who wouldn't have? — and I couldn't lie that I had a date with Diane. You don't have daytime dates in the Valley — daytime is when men do their work — so I made up a story about how I wanted to build a bridge across the irrigation canal in the northeast end of the ranch, a bridge Wes really needed — he'd said so — and I wanted to scout the cheapest 6X12's. He said he knew where the best deal was — Frankie's — that he could get them for me, so I got testy and said, "I'd like to do this for you, Wes. The ranch needs a bridge there. Will you let me do it, use the truck?"

It worked. And if I took longer than he would, even a couple hours, he wouldn't think twice about it.

I should've just asked him if I could go to the house alone. He wanted me to — to go alone — but I didn't know that then.

ॐ

I got there just before noon. I sat in the chair again eating a peach and glancing at the house, nervous until I realized I was acting just like my uncle — wanting to be near the place, but nervous as hell. *Why?*

I walked around the house twice, saw two holes under it where the rabbits might go at night to sleep. There were cobwebs over the holes, so maybe not. I looked in all of the windows, glancing back at the road, feeling idiotic.

When I was good and ready, I climbed the stairs to the front porch. There was a chair there I hadn't seen before, a wooden one, with paint fresh as yesterday. Had Wes been out here since our last visit?

The chair was the same blue as the house.

But there weren't any footprints on the porch, and if he'd been out here, there should have been.

I tried the door and the knob just twirled. Didn't matter whether it was locked. You couldn't open the door with the knob spinning like that.

I looked through the door — the glass, the lace — and when the lace moved a little, like by a breeze, all I could think was draft — there was a draft. It was windy on the hill and chimneys — this house had two — were funny things, and so were floor heaters, if it had them. You could get crazy drafts moving through an old house like this on a windy day.

Inside I could see furniture. It wasn't covered with sheets. It was just sitting there, antiques. Where sunlight hit the floor through the windows, you could see dust, but not as much as you'd think there'd be. Someone cleaned it occasionally. Wes? Probably. He seemed to want to do the work that needed doing on the house by himself.

I turned back around. The grass was untrampled except for my prints around the house.

Then I heard the singing. At first I thought it was a machine — something in the distance — a siren maybe. But it was *singing*.

I went down the stairs and looked to either side of the house. Nothing. The singing was coming from somewhere, and it wasn't a radio.

I almost passed her without seeing her. If she'd fallen asleep, I'd probably have walked around the house again, never looked under the tree, assumed it had been my imagination, and left.

Her eyes were closed. She was lying back in the chair, and you could barely hear her voice:

"...*the fair maid arose...*," she sang quietly.

She wore a white dress, a summer dress — that's what I'd seen the other day — and she was lanky and pretty. Whether she knew I was there or not, I didn't know. If I hadn't seen her, maybe she hadn't seen me.

An easel sat in the grass a few feet from the chair, an old box of paints and some brushes and a square palette with it — just like my uncle had said. I thought he'd been lying, covering something up, but here she was. A girl who liked to paint.

Eyes still closed, she sang a little more:

"...*and hurried on her clothes...and she bid....*" Her voice sounded so faint I didn't know whether to bother her or not. She was so close to sleep.

"Hello," I said.

"Good day," she said, eyes still closed. She'd known I was there, I realized.

She looked pale and, as I said, pretty — my uncle had left that out — and I didn't know what to say.

When her eyes finally opened, they were blue, too — not like the house, but like those flowers — you know, cornflowers. She smiled. She was missing a tooth, the way old people miss teeth, but it didn't make her look less pretty — just funny.

"*Don't leave me,*" she said suddenly, as if quoting someone, and for a moment that was funny, too.

Then her smile disappeared, and she looked at me so hard, with such seriousness, I flinched and stepped back.

All I could think was, *Why didn't Wes tell me she was crazy*?

And whose fault was that? He hadn't known I'd be sneaking back here alone.

"Where do you live?" I asked gently. "Can I take you home?"

"I'm home," she said. "I'm always home. *I've hurried on my clothes to bid you, my dear — to bid you welcome home.*"

She smiled again at me and her eyes looked blind. I mean, there was nothing wrong with her eyes — they were blue and normal and she could obviously see — but the way she looked at me, it was blind. Like she could see me, but also not.

I heard tires on the road then and looked around. It was Darrell's truck.

But it wasn't Darrell. It was Wes. The window rolled down on the driver's side and his head poked out. He didn't shout. He didn't looked surprised to see me here. He didn't wave at me to come over. He just waited.

I looked back at the girl, who was singing again. I didn't care about that — I didn't care about the words — I just wanted to make sure she was all right.

"You stay here," I said to her. "I'll be right back."

"*Don't leave me,*" she said, but I wasn't sure she was talking to me. And the way she said it was like a song, too — musical notes.

"*When little fishes fly and the seas they do run dry,*" she started singing, "*and the hard rock do melt in the sun.*"

Jesus, I thought. *What is **wrong** with her?*

I trotted down to my uncle and said, "Who the hell is she?"

"Who?"

"You know who!"

"What is she wearing?"

"A white dress—why does that matter?"

"Does she have a missing tooth?"

"Of course she's got a missing tooth. What are you talking about?"

"Do you want to go back to her?

Jesus. "Of course I want to go back to her. I want to make sure she's okay. Shouldn't we take her somewhere?"

"She's okay."

"What do you mean she's okay?" He was looking at the house. He took a deep breath and didn't answer.

I ran back to the peach trees expecting to find her asleep and stopped dead. She was gone. The easel and paints were gone. The blank canvas on the easel was gone.

I looked at my uncle's truck. I looked back at the empty chair, and then ran back to the truck.

"She's gone!"

"Yes...."

"We've got to help her, Wes. She's crazy."

"She's okay," he said again, calmly.

"No, she's not! What's wrong with you?"

He didn't answer, started up the truck, put it in gear and said, "See you back at the ranch. Stay as long as you want, but I don't think she'll be back today. She likes the sun."

It was late afternoon and the sun was leaving.

I stayed for another hour, looking at the grass around the white chair, looking for anything she might have left. Then I headed back. My uncle didn't say anything over dinner—which was "eggs on horseback," which he loved any time of day—and I didn't either.

ॐ

I'd rather have gone to the drive-in again that Friday, but Diane said her lips were still sore from all our kissing, so we went instead to the Pine Cone Branding Iron in Merced for dinner (we split it—it was expensive) and a local country band, the Valley

Boys. Too much kissing? That wasn't Diane. She was acting like an ice queen. I didn't know why. I kept trying to find out and she kept saying, "It's nothing," but of course it was something.

Finally she said, "You went to that house, didn't you."

I didn't know what to say. "Well…yeah…I did. Is it on the TV news or what?"

"Your uncle told my dad."

"So? Should we break up over it right now? I go to that house and that's the deal-breaker in our relationship, and this is it—a 'Dear John' dinner?"

I wasn't going to get her to laugh. I could see that.

"Did you see her?"

"Jesus, does my uncle tell your dad everything? I wear Jockey shorts, too. My uncle knows that. Does your dad know it now, too?"

"Did you kiss her?"

"Of course I didn't kiss her, Diane. She's crazy or slow or something. Why would I kiss someone like that? I'd feel like a pervert."

"Is she pretty?"

Yes, she's pretty, I was thinking. *So pretty I've been dreaming about her. She's crazy or slow and I couldn't possibly kiss her – a guy just doesn't do that – but she's so pretty in that white dress I'm dreaming about her, Diane.* "I guess so," I say. "If you call a missing tooth pretty and you like girls who act crazy and talk to you like you're not there. Sure."

She didn't move for a full minute. She was staring at me, fork in her hand, and the band was getting ready to start. She closed her eyes, took a deep breath just the way my uncle did that day, and opened them.

"Please don't kiss her, Ken," she said.

She said it so forcefully—as if my life—or someone's life—depended on it—that I jerked and sat up straight. "What?"

"*Don't ever kiss her,*" she said, but more quietly this time, eyes dropping to the table, fork nailing a piece of prime rib—the Branding Iron's specialty—and pushing at it for a moment.

"Okay, okay. I won't."

I tried on the drive home to ask her why, but she wouldn't answer. No one in this town answered your questions. She was acting just like my uncle and Darrell.

I thought I'd heard jealousy in her voice, but it wasn't jealousy, I realized.

It was fear.

Please don't ever kiss her.

I thought of my mother, the crazy thing she'd said out of the blue when I was fourteen. *Kissing can be a terrible thing.*

What the hell was going on?

ༀ

I'd have stayed away from the house—just to make Diane happy—but my uncle suddenly had all sorts of errands for me to run to the house. Paint to take. Two by fours. Food for the rabbits, though they sure didn't need food. The errands didn't make any sense, and they were in the middle of the day, the sunniest time, in his truck, and he obviously wanted me to do them alone. He made me wear his hat—one passed down from his grandfather. "You'll get more respect if the sheriff stops you," he explained. "Maybe not get a ticket."

He was lying again, I could tell, but about what? It was just a hat, for God's sake, so I went ahead and wore it. Maybe he really was having a life crisis. Maybe his life was falling apart and no one knew it—or everyone did except me—and if that were the case, I should be kind and respectful to him, my dad would say.

ༀ

She wasn't there the next two times I went, even though it was sunny. The first time I found her easel, but not her. I checked the porches, walked around the house a couple of times, looked in the windows, but nothing. The second time there wasn't even an easel, though the rabbits were acting funny, grouped around a spot on the grass in a way that made me think she'd left food for them. There were footprints in the middle of the spot—as if someone had been standing there—but no food. Just a perfect circle of rabbits, facing each other, noses twitching, unafraid.

There was a half-eaten peach—a fresh one—on the arm of a white cane chair, and I couldn't remember leaving one there myself.

Someone had been here. Today even.

On the third errand there she was, standing on the front porch, watching me arrive. I stopped the truck, turned off the engine, and sat for a moment. She was definitely waiting for me—that was the feeling—so I got out of the truck and walked toward her.

The closer I got, the bigger her smile got and the more her missing tooth showed. When I was in front of her, she stepped to me. I guess I was thinking she was a dream—how it had all been a dream, even if Wes thought she was real—because when she put her arms around me to hug me, it was like a kid, the way a kid would hug you, and I let her. I was supposed to let her—that was the feeling, too. She wasn't a *danger*. Everything was fine—beautiful, in fact. Even the feel of her body against mine, her thin arms, her breasts under her white dress—just made it more beautiful.

"You didn't leave me!" she said, laughing, and her laugh sounded like cool water. I sighed. What was the harm in holding her, in being in the dream, in the story she was telling?

"No, I didn't," I said. "*And I never will.*" I tried to give it some melody—to sing it a little, but it came out so badly she laughed, poked me with a fist the way a cowgirl would, and took my hand as if we'd known each other forever.

The doorknob opened for her, no trouble, and before I could check to see why, she was pulling me inside the house. Dust rose from our footsteps and the sunlight made certain places in the living room and hall too bright. I looked around for switches, but knew there'd be none. The house was too old. *Older than almost any other, and unchanged*—that was the feeling.

She was pulling me up the stairs.

It was awfully dark at the top, but she seemed to know where she was going. She found a door in the darkness, a knob, turned it, and pulled me in.

I was blinded by the light.

The window curtains were apart, so that sunlight filled the bedroom. The sun lit the bed like fire. The bedcovers had been pulled back and she was pulling, pulling me toward them.

This wasn't what a guy should do, I remember thinking. She was a child, innocent, and everything about the world was too beautiful to ruin it in a bed — *where she might bleed, where she might cry from the pain.*

I pulled back — and she let me, coming toward me with the force of my pull — big smile and wide eyes and outstretched arms. She wrapped them around me again, and what harm was there in this, a voice said again? The bed was safely away... *though she was weary of lying alone....*

Her eyes looked blind again, but that would not have been enough to save me if she'd simply done it — kissed me then without waiting or warning. Settled it. *What could not be undone by lover or maid....*

It was what she said that saved me.

"I want to taste your lips!" she cried. She said it deliriously, blind eyes imagining the kiss, her whole body feeling it as her mouth came toward mine, as it had in two weeks of dreams I could never tell Diane about.

And because she spoke — instead of finishing it in silence, I heard Diane's voice say:

Never kiss her. Ever....

And another voice, a woman's, whispered too.

I pushed her back hard.

Her mouth came again at me, as if on air, without a body, and my arms flailed, unable to find her.

Her mouth was so close I brought my right arm — sleeve rolled to the elbow — up to block it, and when I did, she bit me, tore at the flesh with her teeth, snarling, a child but an angry one.

"*Kiss me, you son of a bitch!*" she screamed.

I stumbled back. She lunged toward me again and this time my hands found her, shoving her toward the bright bed as I slipped out the door and down the stairs. Behind me a voice that was a siren, an animal in grief and rage, sang and wailed, wailed and sang, spoke of loving me, needing me, *her Johnny*, and how could I do this—how could I leave her?

Outside, I looked up at the window. The sound had stopped. *You don't want to leave*, a voice said. I wanted to stay, yes, and that scared me more than anything else.

ॐ

At dinner Wes kept looking at me. I was rubbing my arm where she'd bitten me—covering the mangled skin with my hand as I did—and he asked me if I was okay.

"I'm okay."

"You sure?"

"Yes, I'm sure." I wouldn't look at him. If I looked at him, I'd say something I shouldn't.

After a moment he said, "You go to the house today?"

"You know I did."

"Did you see her?"

It was how easy his concern—which for a moment felt real—could turn to selfishness that sent a chill through me. I could hear it in his voice—the calculation. *Had I made happen what he wanted to have happen? Had I done what he wanted me to do?* Nothing else mattered.

"I'm going to see Diane," I said. "I need the truck."

"I don't think so, Ken."

He kept the keys to the truck on the mantelpiece over the fireplace. He knew I knew they were there.

I pulled my hand away and showed him my arm. "I think so, Wes. I think I'm taking the truck—unless you want to drive me, but you don't want that, do you. You'd rather drive me to the house and have her—have her bite me again, right? Or, even better, kiss me—?"

He stared at the marks on my forearm, started to say something, didn't, and then did — and it was again how easily he said what he said that told me I could never trust him again, and that I needed to leave as soon as I could.

"*Did* you kiss her, Ken?" I could hear the hope in his voice. "I know she bit you. She was frustrated and sad. You've got to understand how long she's been waiting for a boy like you, for family."

But I do, I wanted to say. *I do know. It was in her eyes. She's been waiting longer than anyone should....*

"You should definitely get a shot for that bite — get it cleaned up by Pete at least. But did you...did you kiss her?"

"Jesus!" I said, standing up, knocking my glass over and stomping toward the mantelpiece.

"Did *you*, Wes?" I shouted at him without turning. "Did *you*?"

I wasn't sure what I was saying, but I knew it was the right question:

"Did **you** kiss her, Wes?"

ॐ

I didn't bother doing anything silly like tossing a rock at her window. I knocked hard on the front door. Rodney came to it still in his plumber overalls. I barreled through with Rodney saying, "Well, hi, Ken — we're still eating, but if you'd like something to eat, I'm sure Miriam can — "

I turned on him and said, "Are you going to tell me?"

"Tell you what, Ken?" He sounded calm at first, but I changed that.

"About *her.*"

"Who?" He knew. You could see it in his eyes — which were a paler blue than the house.

"The girl at the house on the hill, Rodney. Don't be an asshole. My uncle's the only asshole I need right now."

"Ken!" his wife said from the hallway. "We don't talk that way in this house. Rodney, tell him — "

31

"I can handle this, Miriam," I said. "Rodney has something he wants to explain to me, right, Rodney?"

Diane was standing in the hallway too.

Rodney had regained his composure. "Young man, we do not talk to our elders like that in this house, in this town. You will *not*—"

I held up my arm. The bite mark was puffy and red. My uncle had been right. God knows how dirty the mouth of a crazy girl was—*a girl who wasn't a girl, who'd been waiting longer than anyone should*—

This was crazy thinking. *A girl who wasn't a girl?* What did that mean? It had to be the bite. Blood poisoning moved quickly. Infections could make you crazy.

But it wasn't crazy thinking. I knew that too. Something I couldn't explain—that no one could explain—had happened at the house, and only words spoken by two women who loved me had saved me. Crazy or not, that was what I believed—*because it was true*.

"Look at this. She bit me, Rodney, because you didn't have the balls to warn me. Diane had more guts than you did. What is wrong with you people?"

"Who bit you?"

He was going to hold onto the lie. He was going to back my uncle up.

"Diane, let's go."

Diane didn't move at first. "Where are we going, Ken?"

"Does it matter? We need to talk."

She looked at her mom, then her dad and back to her mom. Her mom, with a glance at me—an understanding look, a kindness—gave Diane a nod. Her father saw it and shouted, "Miriam!" His wife answered back with a "Yes, Rodney?" and then it was too late, Diane was at my side and we were heading toward my uncle's truck.

૪

32

"You've got to get that attended to," Diane said as we drove toward nowhere.

"What would have happened if I'd kissed her, Diane?"

She didn't answer.

"I think you know," I said. My arm was beginning to throb. Finally she said:

"Your uncle was drunk. It was one night at the ranch house. That's where he told my dad. Your uncle was drunk and sad. My dad said it was hard not to laugh—a big guy like that crying like a baby in his beer and talking crazy."

"I've never seen my uncle drunk."

"My dad hadn't either, but he was. My dad was laughing when he told us. He didn't believe it and that's why he told us. It was just a story—a funny story about Wes—"

"Believe what, Diane?"

"—but then my dad saw her himself one day up at the house—setting a new faucet for the house. He still didn't believe it, but there was something odd about her."

"Believe what?"

"That she was Wes's great-grandmother."

"His what?"

"Great-grandmother. A girl like that—crazy and disappearing when you weren't looking—being that old. Why would my dad believe it?"

"He told you this?"

"No, my mom did. He told her and she told me."

"Why—why would your mom tell you?"

"Because she didn't want me around your uncle if he was that crazy. Even if he was just that way when he was drunk, she didn't want me around him."

"So she didn't believe it either?"

"No. Until my dad came home one night and wouldn't talk to her. I was there. I saw it myself—my dad so upset. It was the second time he'd seen her at the house, I found out later. He wouldn't look at my mom and then he did look at her and he said, 'She tried to kiss me, Miriam. She came up behind me and when I turned around she reached up, ready to kiss me, but then got this look on her face. It wasn't a girl's face I saw, Miriam — it was something else — and it was angry, really angry, and she let go and screamed at me — she screamed, 'You're not *him!*'"

ℵ

It would be another fifteen years before I found out the rest. It was a strange day. I don't know what he actually said, how much of it was Wes's words, I mean — spoken out loud, given the pain he was in — and how much was what I'd somehow already figured out, though it was impossible.

Wes was dying and I hadn't talked to him all those years, and he was dying of stomach cancer. It was all through him by that point. My father — I'd lied to him about what had happened that summer (I'd told him Wes treated his ranch hands badly — which wasn't true — and how he and I had had a knock-down argument about it) — said, "You ought to go see him, Ken. I know you two had a falling out, but you don't want to regret not seeing him before he dies. You don't want to regret something like that at the end of your own life." My father had no idea.

I wish I could say I went out of compassion or forgiveness. I went to get the rest of the story and, though this sounds pathetic, maybe an "I'm sorry, Ken," too. Wes knew it. Looking up from his bed in the hospice, the morphine tube in his arm, the little trigger in his hand so he could administer it himself, he wasn't the big bear of a man I remembered. His broad face was gray and soft and wrinkled, as if were being eaten away slowly by something just under his skin. His eyes weren't the dark bullets I remembered. They were milky, like an old blind dog's.

He was quiet for a while when I said, "I'd like to know the rest, Wes."

"Of course," he said finally, and took a breath. I don't know how he had the energy, but no one wants to die alone, no one wants to die with regret. He told it, and, when his breath just couldn't manage the words, I filled it in myself. I'd been thinking about it for years.

His great-grandmother was born in 1855 in Ohio, he said. Her father was a Protestant preacher (there weren't many in those days) from Londonderry — Londonderry, Ireland — and her mother a farm girl from County Cork who didn't mind leaving Ireland either. Tired of Ohio winters, and dreaming of a congregation on the California frontier, they brought their pale, pretty daughter to the Valley when she was ten. Their name was Kelly, and they were a pioneer family by Valley standards here, but they liked "culture," too — the kind simple people understand. The girl liked seashells, had a little collection in her dresser drawer, and her father, a bookish man, told her their common names. She liked to paint, too, though she wasn't very good at it, and she'd set up her easel in the yard, among the willows. There hadn't been peach trees then, wouldn't be for another fifty years. She put out vegetables — ones her mother grew — for the cottontails, which were safe in the yard and knew it. Coyotes wouldn't come in that close if people lived there. The Valley was wheat and beef then, just starting up, people spread out with miles between them, but churches brought them together. Her father had a congregation in no time — just as they'd prayed he would — and the family was happy. Her parents were protective, of course, and there'd be no gentleman callers for her until she was eighteen.

The girl would sing to the rabbits, people said. She loved them, and she'd sing the old songs. Ones from the old country. Songs like "Ghost Lover" and "The Twin Sisters" and "The Terrible Stone" — which she'd been hearing her mother sing since she was a baby. The rabbits like it, the girl told everyone, or at least this is how the family legend went. She sang, she painted, she was tall and lanky and pretty — like clean bone, bone china — and she was waiting, like all girls were in those days, for a man to take her away or at least settle down with her, have children by her, take care of her.

When she fell in love with a boy from the other side of the

river — a Smith — her parents didn't approve. He was a little wild and a year younger than she was. He couldn't take care of her, they insisted. She needed to wait for someone better, they said — someone they approved of — but this was not something she was willing to do. She loved him.

Her parents hassled her, sure, but they hassled him even more. Her father got him out by the barn one night. The boy had come unannounced, trying to get the daughter to come out to the trees for a kiss — a very un-Christian thing for a young man to do — and her father had hit him, in the jaw. That wasn't very Christian either, but the father was angry and the boy was surly, insubordinate, as if his own father had never taught him respect, and so the father hit him. The boy looked at him with hatred, and something else. Her father should have seen the vengeance in it. If he had, he might have been ready when the boy came for him, which he did one night a week later — with a pick.

The boy she loved — his name was Johnny — found her father putting tools away in the barn and killed him. He took things from the barn — things a thief would take — so that people wouldn't know it was him. And when word went out that the girl's father had been killed by a thief — one of the first killings of this kind in the Valley — the boy had the gall to go over to console her and her mother, who was weeping disconsolately.

That night, out among the trees, in the grass, by her easel, which she'd forgotten to bring in because she too was hobbled by grief, they made love, and she got pregnant. When she was showing and her mother was crying again from the second crisis in less than a year, the boy told his parents that he wanted to help them; and his parents consented because it was a Christian thing for them all to do.

The boy moved in practically. He stayed the night once, and then two more nights, and then it was pretty regular. No one thought it odd. It was the boy's child, after all — everyone knew it — and the girl and he would be married soon as her mother regained her strength. The mother was grateful. There were so many things the house and yard and land around needed done—that only a man could do.

When the baby was born, the boy saw his future and didn't like it. Two nights later he was gone—for the Bay City, people said.

The girl's mother died a month later, of a quiet heart attack in the night—the "broken heart" of those days—and of course despair. The girl didn't understand it all until one day she was out by the barn and found the locket she'd given the boy, the chain broken as if yanked. It was covered in old blood. The barn eaves had protected it from the rain, so blood was still on it. It was the exact spot where they'd found her father, the blood pooled from his body on the earth.

She saw it then, and it was fury that saved her. It's fury that can get us out of grief and despair. It was fury, and for the rest of her life all she could think of was getting Johnny back. *Don't leave me*, she would sing. She would turn the songs her mother had sung when she was a baby into new songs—songs that hid the fury in their beauty, but the message was always the same: *Don't leave me, Johnny. Don't leave. Don't leave.*

The boy's father—a member of her father's congregation, and full of a good man's guilt—brought her into his family's home to make sure the girl and her infant son (their grandchild, after all) had shelter and food. But when she tried to kiss him and more than once—the father—he threw her out in horror, denied the baby could be their son's, and sent the girl back to the blue house with her child. With his wife's consent (she knew whose baby it was), he gave her money when he could, as did other members of the congregation, who missed their pastor's presence.

Even when she died, an old woman, her fury didn't stop. A few weeks after her funeral, a girl appeared in the house on the hill. Just appeared. Living alone somehow, but how? No one knew who she was at first, but when older members of the congregation went to see her, hear her voice, see her face, her gestures, they *knew* and hurried away. *It was an un-Godly thing—* that was how they put it. Word spread. Only her son, the grown-up baby now, who'd married years before, had a wife and children and grandchildren, found the courage and heart to live (his wife refusing to join him) in the blue house with the girl. But he, too, left when her attentions became inappropriate, and he re-joined his wife, though he was never the same.

She was going to be that girl, Ken, until she got her Johnny back…and she did to him what needed to be done to make him stay.

༄

"I didn't believe it at first…," my uncle was saying slowly, trailing off now and then as if he were somewhere else. "I thought my grandmother…who was pretty feisty…was telling me a tall tale…to jerk my chain."

He fell silent. It had been a very long speech for a man who was dying. Without the morphine he'd have never made it, and I knew he'd made it because he felt he owed me, and what else was there to give?

"Her son had two sons and two daughters," he started again. I sighed, wanting to hear, but wanting him to stop, too. "Some of the men warn their sons. Some don't. After her son died… and the grandsons were getting the house ready to sell…one of them met a girl with an easel under the willow trees and, though he was married…and old enough to be her father…he kissed her. He changed. He wanted the house. He was determined to live there…. He left his wife and two kids, a son and daughter… and lived in the house until the day he died. He willed the house to his son — which had always been her plan — and his son didn't know he'd need to find someone to take his place…or he would be hers as well."

I took a deep breath, wanting it to be over. It was grueling hearing him work so hard to tell it. It didn't matter anymore. "You don't have to do this, Wes."

"I do."

I sat down in the chair by his bed. I saw him finger the pump again.

"This went on for two more generations.... Son after son. If a man had more than one, it was the son who kissed her first that she got...and that couldn't get away. Some took their own lives to end it. My own father...."

"Yes?"

"My own dad.... You don't remember him?"

"No, I don't."

"He thought he'd broken it. He'd stayed away from the house his whole life...but he went that day. My mother said he had matches. He fell asleep on the porch.... She did that to him. She can do things...but you know that, don't you?

"He woke up feeling lips on his. She was standing there... grinning. It was terrible....

"He needed to live there on the hill now. That...is how it always went. My mother wouldn't move in with him. She didn't...know the stories.... He'd never told her. He kept me away from the house, too.... But she'd seen him — seen him change overnight...heard him talk for hours about a girl. One that...that might have been real.... And she could feel the love was gone...in him. The love for her, I mean.... She stayed in Winton while he lived at the blue house.... But they never saw each other. I was ten.... Three years later he was dead. Fell from the roof of the house. He knew...how to walk on roofs.... It was his decision.... I know that now...."

I could tell he was trying to decide. He could do it if he wanted — tell me what it had been like for him, the girl and the house — he wasn't feeling pain now — but did he really want to?

All he said finally was:

"I've been married three times, Ken.... No kids.... I'm still alone. I can't...leave the valley.... I can't live...more than ten miles from that hill. And, yes.... I kissed her once."

He'd simply wanted to be free, and I was blood family, and young, and if I kissed her he'd be free to really love a woman again — maybe even his fourth wife — maybe have kids and not have to worry about them.

But he'd kissed her.

There was another way, I wanted to say to him. *You could have done what other men did. You could have ended things.*

But he would have answered, *I know, Ken. I'm a coward. I know that....*

I wasn't going to be that cruel. He was dying, after all, and he was family.

Besides, I knew he'd already had that conversation with himself. Any man would have.

ৰ

"I've got to leave," I told Diane that night forty years ago.

"I know."

"I'll probably not be seeing you again—unless you come down to San Diego."

She forced a laugh. She was trying to make it easier on me. She loved me, I know now, and wanted me to be safe. "I doubt it. I'm a Valley girl and I'm probably going to marry a plumber like Dad and take my own kids to the rodeo and country fair, and that'll be fine. We live our lives the way we're supposed to."

I didn't know what to say.

"Will you write?" she asked.

"Sure."

"Will you ask how your uncle is doing?"

"No."

"If he asks for your address—I mean, when you're not living with your father —when you're away at college and he asks my dad to ask me for your address…?"

"I don't think so, Diane. It's going to be hard to forget."

"I know."

"Thank you for telling me these things tonight," I said suddenly.

She was on the edge of tears. I was almost there too—which was not very manly.

"You're very welcome, Sir," she said back, which made us both laugh. It was an old joke—from our first date—when I'd been nervous and absurdly formal with her dad.

I don't know if an infection is supposed to spread that fast or make a person so crazy, but Diane had barely finished saying, "You're very welcome, Sir," when I started seeing people behind her. Old-fashioned dresses and old-fashioned suits, faces of skin and bone, looking at me, *wanting something.*

I started up the truck and somehow got myself to the emergency room of the hospital in Merced. Diane was looking at me funny as we sat there in the lobby, and I knew I'd been talking about those faces behind her. I shut up until the doctor came to clean the bite, stitch it up, and give me two shots — one to make the red streak on my arm stop growing.

When we were in front of her parents' house, I started to kiss her — she wanted me to, I could tell, and I wanted to, believe me — but I couldn't.

ॐ

I left a week later and never saw her again. I wrote to her a couple of times. I didn't get back together with my on-and-off girlfriend in San Diego and Diane didn't have a boyfriend. Then, when I was in college in the Northwest and she was seeing this guy from Snelling, the letters got fewer and finally stopped.

I met a girl in Seattle. Was it hard kissing her? Not really. It's easy to when you know who you are and aren't afraid.

ॐ

I married that girl. What amazing eyes — a blue like fractured glass, a little speck of orange in one — and what a laugh. Like water over falls. Her name was Cheryl, and I liked that, too. We've stayed married. It seemed important to do that — not in the usual sense of faith and commitment — which are good enough reasons — but to prove something else. I don't need to say what that was. We've been married for twenty-eight years and have three kids — a son and two daughters — and they're

41

starting to have kids, too. But I haven't worried about them—
my son and grandsons—ever going to that house.

It burned down that summer. It happened just before I left,
and my uncle looked at me, started to say something, thought
better, and in two days I was heading home. I could hear the
screaming and the singing—I could hear both sounds in the
flames—as I was driving away from it. Sometimes you've got
to stop thinking, stop being in your head so much, and just do
it: *Make the darkness go away.* That's what being a man is
sometimes, I used to tell my son when he was younger, and it's
what I told my dad too when I got back that summer. I think it
helped him at night, when I was away at college. When the
darkness was a little too much.

We've lived, Cheryl and me, in all sorts of houses. Little ones,
big ones. More than most people have, I think. We've moved
even when we didn't need to. The house we live in now that the
kids are grown is yellow. It came that way. Cheryl keeps asking
whether we should try another color—"just for variety's sake."
"We've still got a lot of life left in us and we don't want to get
too stiff and comfortable, do we?"

"No," I say. I've never told her about that summer and never
will.

She says, "Well, if you don't want to paint the house, let's do
some traveling. Let's run away together for a little while...."

"Sure," I tell her. "I've never had a problem with that."

"I know...," she says with a smile, and for a moment there's
a look in those blue eyes of hers—as if she knows—*really* knows
and always has—in the way that women sometimes know such
things, even when they shouldn't.

LA SIGNORA

I have heard the mermaids singing, each to each.
I do not think that they will sing to me.

—T. S. Eliot

As a boy of thirteen, bookish but very American, I lived for two years in an ancient fishing village on the Ligurian Sea, a village of myths and superstitions that had no intention of dying. It was the Cold War. My father, a naval officer, had been assigned to a submarine-warfare research center twenty minutes north, in the big port there. My mother, a teacher and a lover of other cultures, was not going to have me attend school on the American navy base to the south. She wanted me to get to know the people of Lerici, and so (she announced one day) I would need to attend the village school. You don't argue with a teacher. "Sure," I said. Besides, I didn't want to attend school with the crew-cut, tackle-football sons of navy enlisted men.

I studied Italian hard the summer we arrived, helped by a tutor the research center had recommended—a little man, *Dottore* Stoi, who held his cigarettes oddly and came down to the village on a bus from the port. With his oversight I learned enough to be admitted to the middle school that fall and to survive it. Studying in my room all day, I made no friends that first summer; but when school started, I found them quickly. I wanted to learn soccer, and they wanted to learn basketball, which I played well enough for a book lover. When you're young, you make friends even if you have no more in common than a gray classroom with a single light bulb and an old iron heater that barely works in winter. But we had more than that:

We had ball games, the olive groves' bright green lizards that were fun to catch, and *fishing*.

They were the sons of fishermen, my friends. And I—navy kid that I was—arrived in the village already loving fish. In the ports we'd lived in, on the bases there, I'd caught black sea bass, yellowtail, and big halibut—huge fish by local standards; but the fish here, smaller, were brand-new and charming: the *branzino, cernia, ricciola*, and sometimes, yes, a huge *tonno*. You couldn't catch these from the wharf or jetty; but the fishing boats, the old *lamparas* and a small *paranza* or two, would bring them in to the wharf, to the fish stands run by the wives of the fishermen. My friends wanted, of course, to be with their fathers on the brightly painted boats; but except for the weekends, they had to be in class, which got out just as the boats returned.

To catch our own fish after school—the big-eyed *occhiata* and the silver *paraghino*—we would sit, the four of us, on the rocks of the jetty that ran from the foot of the old fourteenth-century castle out into the Gulf of the Poets. We would fish there with our hunchback teacher, *Professore* Rigola, who loved the water and its creatures as much as my friends' fathers did. He'd never be able to go out in their boats with those men, given his curved back and unsure legs, but he managed to take us all to sea when he taught us geography, Roman history, and literature... especially Homer. Both *The Iliad* and *The Odyssey*: *Cantami o diva del pelide Achille! Sing to me, o goddess!* and *Pass these Sirens by, Odysseus — listen not to their songs!*

You could tell by how he taught us Odysseus and that sailor's fantastic adventures that he loved Homer's *wine-dark sea* as much as any poet or seaman did. Sometimes, in his excitement, our teacher would shake, make funny sounds, and have to hold himself up at the edge of his desk. My friends—and not without affection (because our teacher did have a kind heart)—would titter, saying, "It's the *Signora*. She makes him like that."

I had no idea know what they meant. He was a hunchback and also had a lisp; and if he should shake and make funny sounds when he recited great stories that excited his nerves, why not?

I had no idea who the *Signora* was, or why, if I understood my friends' tittering, she would make a man shake, get weak, or make funny sounds. No explanation would have made sense to me. My father was an officer, my mother a teacher — one with a master's degree in psychology, in fact. Their world was one of civilization, science, and reason, not legend and myth. They would not have condemned the villagers for their beliefs — they would not have held them in contempt for such things — but they would not have entertained superstitions. And I was their son.

ॐ

Fishing from the jetty wasn't enough for my friends, and it wasn't enough for me. But they were the sons of *pescatori*. They could go out on the boats on Saturdays. They needed to learn their fathers' trade, and they needed to help with the fishing if their families were to make enough money. But what could I do? They had invited me more than once to go with them, leaving at first light. They wanted to share with me the waves and changing light and devious nets and glorious fish as they were pulled from the sea. I'd always said no. I knew my parents wouldn't let me go.

It was not because either of them was afraid of the sea. In an irrational sense, I mean. My father had served on a famous battleship in Hawaii during World War II, during the bombing there, and my mother had grown up in Long Beach, California, and learned to swim at six. It was simply (they explained) that things could happen on small boats given the moodiness of the sea, rocks and reefs, unreliable motors, and sudden swells; and that though I was a decent swimmer, I was no Olympian. It was not (they said) that I would drown. It was that I might be injured, and the fathers would feel terrible. That, as my mother put it, would be "no gift" to them...or, she added, looking at my father, a good thing for "relations between the two countries" either.

"Better safe than sorry," my father said. "If you want to go out into the little bay, that's one thing. We'll get a ten-footer—put an engine on it—from the navy club in Spezia if you can find a mooring for it here; but out in the Ligurian Sea, where storms can come up with no warning, we just don't think it's a good idea."

"You could take your friends out in the little boat," my mother added brightly. "They'd enjoy it, wouldn't they?"

I didn't answer. I just nodded.

ৡ

So I fished from the jetty. My father put in a requisition for a dinghy with a ten-horsepower motor; but it would take time, and I kept thinking how embarrassing it would be: inviting my friends to ride in such a tiny thing, in a tiny bay, when they'd grown up with vessels that could handle, if the men were skillful, the big swells and violent storms of the Ligurian Sea and travel so far—boats they would inherit themselves if they chose their fathers' trade, which most would.

My father had once sailed on ships, but not since I was little. I remembered those ships, how huge they were—steel and rivets and thick paint, towering above the wharfs—and how the sea, which smelled like a wet animal, kept them floating somehow by magic.

I missed those ships and I knew my father did too. He dreamed of them—and the sea—almost every night, he'd told me once.

ৡ

It was in the cove just south of the great castle, a minute or two from it, that the women dyed the fishing nets in big iron pots. They dyed them with the ink from three kinds of sea snails that crawled across the floor of the bay and that their husbands, fishing in deeper waters, brought up in their nets by the thousands. I'd watched the women coloring the nets more than once. I'd seen how dark the liquid was in the pots, and how they stirred the nets with great sticks, and how, after a day's boil, they dragged the nets out onto sand to dry them in the sun for days before washing them in the sea. The water of the cove would turn red — a dark red that was almost purple — and I thought of Homer's seas.

It was the ink from those snails that the Etruscans, Greeks, Romans, and Phoenicians had used for their "royal purple" dye — their royal robes, which had, like Homer's seas, been red, not purple at all. Or so Rigola explained to us one day in our little classroom. Looking at me for some reason, he added that in Ligurian villages like this one, the dye was often used for the fishing nets because, people believed, the Woman of the Sea — frightening though she was — could bring a fisherman good luck if she liked your nets. And she did like that color, he insisted — the wine-dark red that made the cove look as if some beast had been butchered there long ago. And so in every fishing village in this province three women — the *streghe* — the witches — blessed the nets, hoping to receive *La Signora*'s blessings.

I had seen the three women. I'd stood in the cove with two of my friends, skinny Maurizio and wide-eyed Gianlucca, that first winter, watching the women in their black peasant dresses move from net to net, muttering and blessing each with a gesture that looked both Christian and not. The nets had been arranged on the sand for the three, under a dim sun, and looked like ropy hair, the dye bleeding into the sand. At one point the three women turned as one and stared at us, but then went back to their business. For a week I dreamed of blood-red seas that churned in the night with endless schools of fish, and of a presence — a presence in the darkness — that filled me with both a terrible love and a sweet terror.

ॐ

The next time my friends — not just Maurizio and Gianlucca, but Perosso, whose father was considered the best fisherman in the village—invited me to go with them in the boats, it was not for a Saturday fishing adventure, back before dusk. It was for a nighttime trip—something I'd never heard of.

A few weeks earlier, my father, who was never moody—who was what a military officer should be like—strong and calm and even-tempered—had started crying (yes, crying) after he returned from work in the big port. He would come home, eat dinner, and then go to his bedroom, where we would hear him weeping. It made no sense. I didn't even know that's what the sound was at first. It wasn't one I knew from our family life.

"Does he miss the sea?" I asked my mother. Twice the previous summer he and I had gone down to the wharf together and stared at the bay. I didn't know why we were staring. "Do you ever wish you could live in the sea—just swim there, not caring whether you could breathe or not?" he finally asked me the second time.

It scared me a little. I didn't know what to say, so I said, "I guess so." The week before, I remembered, he'd eaten a fish from the market and gotten sick. Not my mother or me, just him. The way he talked on the wharf, I thought he was still sick. It didn't sound like my dad.

"Does he miss the big ships?" I added.

"I think he does, Brad, but he's missed them for a long time. You don't say no to the navy when it asks you to work on land and help run research stations, but a man doesn't cry over that. I don't know why he's crying, Brad."

"Is he still sick from the fish?"

"Oh, no. You don't stay sick for months from that...."

"Oh."

I would stand by the bedroom door listening to it. He was trying to be as quiet as possible, but it was a small house, so you could hear it.

I kept trying to understand. If he wasn't missing something—and, by missing it, feeling sad—what would make a grown man cry?

Sometimes when I stood there I thought I could hear singing.

There was no radio on in the house, and the Lido far below us in its own little cove wasn't playing music.

There were no houses in the olive groves with loud radios.

Maybe I was imagining it. Maybe I was listening so hard to his crying that I was imagining singing.

One night I heard my parents, in their bedroom, talking.

"Can you ask Dr. Lupi for medication?"

"I'll talk to him about it."

"I thought you were going to two weeks ago."

"I haven't had a chance. I thought it would pass...."

My mother's voice softened. "Of course. I'm just worried about you, Jimmy."

"I know."

I was worried, too, but what could I do? I couldn't ask him about it. I'd be too embarrassed. All I could do was stand by the door listening, because that way at least I was near him and could try to feel what he was feeling.

Sometimes I thought, standing there, that something was calling to him. The sea, sure, but something else, too. And that because he couldn't go to it— couldn't leave the land and go at night to the bay to find it, which it wanted him to do—he was filled with terrible sadness.

I could almost hear its words as it called to him. *You don't love me, James. I thought you did.*

That's what I told myself anyway, and when I did, I felt it too: that something was calling to me as well. Not enough to make me cry, but enough to make me feel what my father was feeling, a sadness, a longing...and enough to make me want to *answer* it.

ॐ

"We think you should come fishing Wednesday night with us, Brad. It is a special night." It was Maurizio talking, and it was after school, the four of us together on the sidewalk that led to the *passeggiata* and the sea. "It happens rarely, Brad, at the proper phase of the moon and the planet-star Venus. *Disegno sacro.* The best fishing is that night, so you should come. Our fathers' boats meet down the coast, only four coves away, where the water is deep and all of the boats can make a sacred circle with their nets. The light of the moon helps the fish come, but other things come too."

I'm not sure I believed everything Maurizio was saying, but I so wanted to do it. I wanted it more than anything. I wanted to steal away on that special night with my friends, on their fathers' boats. But I knew my parents would say no, and I felt I shouldn't leave them, leave my father, with his crying. It was selfish of me to want to go, wasn't it? It was selfish when my father was so sad. A son should stay, even if he didn't know how to help, even if there wasn't anything he could really do.

Then Perosso—who was tall and dark and had kinky hair because, he said, his mother's people were from Sicily—spoke:

"If your father is crying, you should come. He ate a fish she touched, people say—that is why he got sick, why he hears her and still suffers—and he needs another fish, one prepared the right way, to set him free, my father says."

I stared in astonishment.

Had I told him about my father? I'd told Gianlucca, but I hadn't told anyone else. And yet everyone seemed to know. All three of my friends knew—it was clear from their faces—and they all wanted me to come with them Wednesday night because my father was crying.

"You can stay overnight with my family," Perosso said. My other friends were looking at him, then me, then him again, and nodding. Perosso lived in Vecchia Lerici, the ancient part of the village, with its dark alleys and ghostly cats. "You can tell your parents that my family wants you to stay the night so that we can go night fishing from the jetty with lights. You can tell them that my parents will make sure we all go to school the next morning."

"Will we?" I asked.

Perosso smiled "No. *Professore* Rigola—and the administrators—

know what that night is, so they will not be expecting us to be at school."

"Won't my parents hear about it?"

"These are not things," Gianlucca broke in, always serious, "that teachers and administrators talk about. There will be nothing for your parents to hear..."

"Is that true?" I asked the others.

"Yes," Maurizio said.

"*Va bene*," I said at last with a sigh, and headed home to lie to my parents.

ॐ

When Wednesday came, I packed some clothes, my toothbrush, toothpaste, and comb, and took them in a bag to school with me. My father hadn't cried the night before, which made me feel better about going. My mother, still worried about him, said, "Yes, you may spend the night with Perosso's family, but be sure to thank them for their hospitality and to help with any fish cleaning. Be a good guest and a good friend." She said all of this looking distracted, her eyes on my father at dinner. My father, distracted too, was staring out the dining room window at the night. I looked for tears, found none, but could tell from his eyes that he was hearing something.

ॐ

When night fell, we went to the wharf, where the boats were tied to the old iron cleats.

"What will happen?" I asked Perosso. We were wearing windbreakers. My friends weren't going to wear life jackets, I knew — the fishermen never wore them — but my friends were better swimmers than I and knew these waters, so shouldn't I? I wasn't planning on drowning, but if I did, my parents would feel it was their fault even if it wasn't. Parents were like that. And I didn't want to drown.

"It will be very good fishing," Perosso explained. "We will use the newly dyed nets, the ones blessed by the three. We will meet in a cove not far from where the great English poet drowned, and the fish will come because it is the night of *La Signora.*"

Did he mean *Mary*, mother of Jesus? Who else would *La Signora* be? *La Signora dei Pescatori*? Our Lady of the Fishermen? You heard countless names for Mary in this country, especially in the villages, where each village loved her in a different way.

"You mean the mother of Jesus, right? *Her* night?"

I thought Maurizio and Gianlucca were going to smile, maybe even laugh, but a look from Perosso — who was older and wiser than the rest — stopped them.

"No, another *signora*," he said.

"It will be good fishing in any case," I said quickly — simply to say something, afraid that my friends were going to fall silent, that the only sound I would hear was the lapping of the water against the pilings and the hulls of the boats. "I was thinking... maybe I should wear a life jacket." *An English poet had drowned....*

"You won't need one," Perosso answered quickly. "We'll watch over you, as will our fathers."

We were looking out at the little bay, its inkiness, the light like silver coins on its surface. The fathers were doing what they needed to do. First Maurizio, then Gianlucca left to help them. The nets needed to be coiled the right way, the weights and floats attached in the right places, the net booms wired correctly, the engines checked and rechecked.

Perosso waited with me. I knew he needed to help, too, but he would want to take me with him. It would be on his father's boat that I would watch the night's events. *The night of La Signora.* The most successful fishing night of all fishing nights, everyone agreed. "There will be, in fact," Perosso explained as we stood there, "too many *pesci* for one village, and our village will share the catch with San Terenzo and Palormino to the north and Germana and Todesti to the south." "Why don't boats from those villages join us?" I asked. "Because," he answered slowly, "*La Signora* chooses the village. One of the *streghe* dreams it. It fills her dreams for many nights. Other villages must wait. Their turn will come, though it may be ten years or a hundred before it does, my father says. Patience is important with the sea, he says — with its fish, its *woman*...."

I knew he wanted to say something else, but what?

"If you wear a life jacket," he added at last, "she will think you are afraid of her and will not bless a fish — to set him free. You must not love her too much — for if you do you may want to touch her, and that is a mistake. But you must also not be afraid, for it is love, not fear, that she demands of us tonight." He paused. "That is what they say...."

Though it made no sense, this terrified me. How could it not be at least a little frightening? *La Signora* was not only real, Perosso was insisting — and if he believed it, how could I not? — but there were also *rules*; and if you didn't follow them, if you felt the wrong feeling at the wrong time, horrible things might happen out there in the night....

"I know you cannot believe me," Perosso was saying, "but I hope that you will — for your father's sake, *gentiluomo* that he is. My father hopes it too."

He touched my shoulder with his hand, and in a moment we were scrambling aboard his father's boat.

א

I was so happy I could have cried. I'd wanted to be sailing on one of the fishing boats for two whole years, and here I was at last, in the darkness, on a calm sea, the engines moving us through the night. Our trip was uneventful, as if nothing was supposed to get in our way, as if what waited for us in the cove wanted us very much to be there this night.

The moon rose as we traveled. The boat smelled of fish, and I could see fish scales glistening on the deck. Even the wind was mild, offering nothing for the men to complain about. It smelled of salt and seaweed and something sweeter, something that made my mouth water, but when I asked Perosso what it was, he just looked at the darkness ahead.

When we reached the cove, the moon was above us, and you could see, really see now. The seven boats from the village bobbed in quiet swells, in a circle, just as Perosso had promised, their bows facing the circle's center. The waves lapped at the hulls. Now there was no wind at all. Two men standing near me were silent, heads down, as if praying. We were waiting, but for what?

The swells calmed. Perosso, I saw when I turned, had finished helping his father unfurl the great purse-seine nets so that they could be dropped into the sea when the signal came. Figures on the other boats had done the same. They would drop the nets soon, wouldn't they?

I heard Perosso's father say something to another man, and the man answered, "It is this cove, yes. La Bianca is sure. It was a dream like the others."

"It is late," Perosso's father answered. "I simply want to make sure. She drinks more these days."

"*Si, beve molto,*" the other man answered, "but she was not drinking that week."

Perosso's father nodded and in a moment was waving a lantern. Boat by boat, the nets were released, soon becoming a great hand cupped and waiting under the center of the circle the bobbing vessels made.

ॐ

When the cove's water began to move, it was indeed at the center of the circle. The sea bulged, as if a head were appearing, and the light caught its shape. It was not a head. It was a body, and what sounded like a song that could not have been a song began to fill the night air, making me dizzy. Was I hearing it with my ears or just my mind? I didn't know, and it didn't matter. Like everyone else, I was hearing it.

It was the same song I'd heard that night I'd stood listening to my father's crying. I was sure of it.

The sea rose again, the shape revealing itself once more. It was a body, one the size of small whale—twenty feet perhaps—dark as the sea, but with its own color. Even under the moon you could tell. The color of wine and old blood and nets blessed by three women—those nets that now floated below it, waiting for the fish to come. Its thick body—which bore a tail, or more than one, and a bulky head with no neck, and a face as round as a plate—was covered with what looked like seaweed, the kind they called hag's hair.

When the body surfaced again in the moonlight, the face—the features not quite clear—opened its mouth and *sang*, this time with sounds, real sounds.

The sounds hurt my head, and I put my hands on the gunnels to steady myself. To my left and right men and boys were doing the same. They had heard the voice before, but they were feeling it, too. They knew they needed to steady themselves.

I thought suddenly of the story we'd studied all year—because our teacher wanted us to—because he knew it as well as if he'd written it himself: of men—Odysseus and his crew—warned to tie themselves to masts and put wax in their ears...to be safe from what sang to them.

No one was tying himself to a mast or boom on our boat, but the men were cautious.

To love her – which she requires – but not too much.

And then the fish came.

The sea boiled behind us and then in front of us, as impossible schools of big-jawed *cernia*, *pesce serra* the size of dogs, and other fish larger than anything my friends and I would ever catch on the jetty appeared. They made endless, slick, bright ribbons in the water around us, heading, because of the song or something else entirely, toward the body that continued to rise and fall with the swells at circle's center.

The creature was nearer now, the moon a little brighter, and I could see its mouth: round as the face, and bigger than it should be, like a hole in the night. The mouth had jaws, and the bright, sharp teeth in them had no trouble taking — without the help of arms or hands, which might or might not have been there in the water — a fish that surely weighed forty pounds.

The jaws tore at the fish, eating half of it, then moving on to take another as the poor *cernia* jumped in panic and landed too close.

You could hear the men doing now what needed to be done — winding the pulleys to bring the nets up, to pull them tighter, to catch what could be caught.

Then something hit our boat. It was a shock that made me fall to one knee and did the same to others on the deck — those who didn't have more than gunnels to hold them up.

The boat shook again. I looked down at the water. A great fin moved by, upset, hungry, heading toward the creature. It too had come because of the song, and yet it was not an animal the fishermen wanted. It was too big, too violent. Yet it had been invited — by the creature feasting on a fish that had also heard its song.

One of the men near me grabbed a spear gun, another a harpoon, but Perosso's father shouted, "No!" The men stopped.

We waited.

The shark moved toward the creature with seaweed hair. *She can't blame the squalo, can she?* my mind babbled. *It came at her calling, didn't it? It came because it loved her, didn't it? But this isn't the love she wants.*

The *squalo* — a big-bellied *longimano* from deeper waters — surfaced at last. It was no longer than the creature, but just as heavy. It was nearly to her when it rolled, and rolled again.

The song had grown even louder in our heads, and all of us were holding on for dear life to gunnels, masts, and booms.

The shark curled up like a child, and the creature did nothing but watch it, even as the huge animal drifted toward it.

The song was enough to still men and fish, but a shark is another kind of beast. This one rolled again suddenly, teeth flashing as its jaws opened only a few feet from the creature's face.

Men around me were whimpering from the creature's sound. I was, too, but it was the moonlit scene in the water that held me.

If love is not enough, then death....

The creature lunged.

The shark — breaking from the song — arched its back, flipped backward, and struck our boat again with its full, thrashing weight.

I was at the gunnels still, leaning over to see it all, and this time fell in — to the rolling, boiling mass of fish that was trying to reach the *One Who Sang*.

As I fell, I remember thinking: *Is she the only one? Were there ever others, or was it always just her, living forever?*

I could hear shouting, but it was far away. The song — like teeth on glass, like cicadas in a forest we'd once lived near in Washington, DC, like a machine that could make whatever music men desired — was so much closer now.

I smelled a terrible smell, and turned. Paddling as best I could to stay above the frantic fish around me, I saw the *face* three feet from me.

How ugly it was — the tremendous, slitted eyes, the open mouth and rows of teeth, the gashes that were nostrils. The ugliness of an old witch whose face had been twisted by time and pain and spells gone wrong.

As I looked — the song filling me like the sea — I saw the face change, becoming beautiful: the face of a pretty girl, a cameo the color of wine, smiling at me, wanting me, as I'd wanted her for eternity.

I am beautiful, am I not? a voice said. It was not mine.

My hands grasped and grabbed, sliding off fish bodies, unable to look away from the eyes and the mouth that opened and closed.

It was the smell of death — that breath — but it was wonderful, too, a perfume I remembered from long ago, rocked in a cradle as safe as the sea, feeling loved.

Do you love me, Bradley? the voice asked, as if it might be hurt—as if it might weep in sadness—if I did not.

Yes! I shouted, though it couldn't have been with lips, which were spewing water.

Will you ever have another?

No....

Never?

No...never. You are my one and only...and always will be.

I meant every word of it. The song was everything, she was everything, and I loved her completely, as so many men had.

Then live, the voice said, and the body it belonged to slid a long arm that was not an arm under me, holding me up so that I could breathe, so that I could stop my flailing. I saw the shark, its belly torn, floating like an overturned boat not far away, and, in the lullaby she sang for me and me alone, I slept.

৯

When I woke, it was on Perosso's father's boat, and human faces were looking down at me, backlit by lanterns.

"He is fine," Perosso's father was saying. "*Bagnato, ma vivo.*"

I spat a little more water. "*Please*—please don't tell my parents."

I thought they might laugh, but no one did. The men looked sad—that is how their shadowed faces looked to me—and I didn't understand. Why sad? I was alive, wasn't I? And they would not tell my parents. That was what really mattered. And who would believe it anyway? That a huge shark had struck the boat—the boat I wasn't supposed to be in? That I had fallen in and been saved by something that could enchant anything with its song?

When I stood up, I was weak-kneed, but why wouldn't I be? My knees gave out twice, and both times I dropped to all fours and heard myself make little sounds. Still no one laughed.

Perosso's father had put his hand on my back, with affection, and was looking at me as if he understood something and wished he didn't. "Be careful with him," he said to everyone.

"I still have water in my stomach," I proclaimed, wanting this to explain the sounds.

The men looked at me. Some nodded, but were, I know now, only being kind.

ॐ

When the boats were back at the wharf, the men unloaded the nets. There were fish everywhere, though fewer in Perosso's father's boat because of what had happened to me, the distraction of it, the shark, the net it had torn.

When I took my first step on land, my knees buckled again.

Standing in front of me was wide-eyed Livia, Maurizio's sister, whose untamable hair curled in every direction and who had come with the women and other girls to the wharf to wait for us. I liked her. I wanted her to be my girlfriend, though I'd been too shy to ask before. Such a thing, I told myself — an American boy and a Ligurian girl — wasn't possible in a village like this, was it? Would it be good or bad for 'relationships between the two countries'?

When I thought of her this way — a girlfriend, one I very much wanted to kiss — my knees collapsed, and I dropped to my hands and knees.

I made the little sounds again, too, and this time they sounded like an animal's.

No one seemed to notice. A few of the grown-ups wouldn't look at me. Others exchanged glances. Two men helped me up. Livia was smiling at me — but when I looked at her I couldn't see her.

I wasn't supposed to.

ॐ

In school the next week, I saw another girl—one with green eyes, blonde hair, and a braid. Her mother was German, I'd heard. I stared at her because she was pretty, and my knees went weak. This time I fell down on the hallway floor.

Professore Rigola asked me if I was okay, and I lied. "Yes."

He helped me up. His misshapen back made him unsteady, so we had to help each other to stay upright.

"Thank you, *Professore*."

"Of course, *ragazzo*."

I looked for sadness in his watery eyes—what I'd seen in other faces—but found something else: *He understood.*

I remembered then that he was not married, how people said something had happened to him when he was young and he would never marry.

ॐ

The night after the events of the cove my father stopped crying.

"How is he?" Perosso asked.

"Better."

Perosso nodded. "That is how it goes, my father says. *One man for another*. Your father is free...."

He should have sounded happy for me, but did not. He wanted, I know now, to tell me he was sorry—about what had happened in the cove, which no one had wanted—but he was just a boy, like me, and did not know how.

ॐ

Even in high school, when we returned to the States, I sensed what path my life would take—what it would have to take. Though I learned to hide it, to claim with a smile "a mild epilepsy," my knees did weaken and strange sounds did come from me when I met—or even thought of—a girl or woman I might want in my life, or, in lust, just for a night. No one knew what the sounds were, though I did: They were the sounds men had always made when they'd come under her spell. They were the sounds men made when they broke their vows to her...

In college I read it again, understanding it better — that book *Professore* Rigola knew so well, the one he was thinking about as he looked down at me that day when I lay on the hallway floor. The one he thought about every day of his life.

And I, Odysseus, answered her: How, Circe, or should I address you as Scylla? — whatever name and form you bear — can you ask me to be gentle to you when you have turned my comrades into swine, and you keep me here, and with terrible guile you invite me to your chamber, to your bed, that when you have me naked you might render me an animal as well, weakling, no man at all?

None of this mattered really. How other men had once acted and what people had thought of it, what stories they'd told to make sense of it, legend and myth and epic poems. What mattered was simple: The closer I, Brad Lattimer, got in body or heart to any woman, the weaker I became, because, when you belong to her, she *knows*.

א

Perhaps he had been swimming as a child, at night, in a cove, before his curvature appeared, heard her song, and touched her by accident. Or, when he was a young man, he heard her singing at night in his room and, lonely as he was — misshapen and despairing of ever having a woman to love him — he promised himself to her. Perhaps she had even done this to him when he touched her — given him his physical malady — that he might be unfit for a woman's bed. I would never know what our teacher's story was, but I knew he understood. He had learned to hide it well in his kyphosis, his unsteadiness, his lisp, and the terrible moments when, in his longing for love and a woman's touch, human speech failed him.

My parents found out, but weren't angry with me. They were just glad I was okay, though my father would look at me after that night as if he, too, understood something, but something he could not quite put his finger on. An understanding that knew no words. When I didn't date girls in high school or even in college, they explained this to each other, I'm sure, as a shyness and bookishness — a boy lost in his mind, too distracted for the opposite sex. And when, a few years later, I joined the clergy, it all must have made sense to them.

It was difficult — because even the celibate may know lust in their hearts — but I never lost my resolve. I started attending the church I hadn't been to since I was little, finished college and then seminary, and have been a priest (a Benedictine so that I might be devoted to the Blessed Mother in my contemplative life) for thirty years. I still hear the song, and it is beautiful. Like the word of God — or the song His Son might have sung had he been a singer — it is enough for a man's life if he wishes it to be. I have not dropped to my hands and knees other than in supplication for more than a decade now, and I am happy — happy as any man promised to something beyond this world can be.

SANDY

Because she had four arms and a six-fingered hand on each arm, Sandy could look for four-leaf clovers faster than I could. I also understand now — because I'm older and know what you do if you like someone — that she found more of them than I did at the bus stop, but never told me she did. She'd show me only as many as I showed her, probably hiding the others under her big feet, which were more like hooves, though you couldn't see them in the clunky shoes she wore.

Why did I think Sandy was a "she"? Because she had long blonde hair like human girls I'd known, wore the clothes that human girls wore, and had big beautiful eyes that stared at me and made my face get hot. And her voice was higher than mine, too. I don't know if she really was a *she*. It's more complicated than that for the Tacuz, I know, but she was a *she* to me; and I don't think she minded that I thought of her as the same gender as my little sister and mother — both of whom she knew I loved.

I called her "Sandy" because I could tell without touching it that her skin, so much paler than mine, was like sand. I'd heard a man — a friend of my father's in the apartment building where we lived (he worked on the monorails too) — say, "Their skin is like a shark's." I didn't know what that meant — sand was sand — but I knew it wasn't a compliment. Sharkskin must have been ugly. He didn't like them — Sandy's kind.

We exchanged glances at the bus stop that first time and didn't sit together on the bus, but looked at each other a lot across the aisle. Those big eyes!

The next day, I got to the bus stop early — I lied to my parents about why — hoping. She didn't come early, though, so I sat on the grass and looked for four-leaf clovers. I'd found one before. Just one, and I'd thrown it away when it dried up. If I found another, I'd give it to her. But I didn't.

The day after that, she did come early. I got there first, knelt in the grass, and finally, when I looked up, saw her walking from the big apartment building we both lived in toward the bus stop. She was looking at me, smiling, and I was smiling back. She was making that rolling motion of her body that the Tacuz make when they walk—something about the way their hips are built and something that disappears when they start to run, running faster than any human can.

I'd found a four-leaf clover. I'd certainly had time, getting to the stop thirty minutes early (you do this kind of thing when you're young and hopeful)—and as she came up to me, I gave it to her. She cocked her head, as if puzzled, but took it with her inner right hand, twirling it in her two index fingers. She didn't have a thumb, but she didn't need one. The bowed index fingers Tacuz have are like magic.

"Thank you," she said. Her mouth twisted a little with the words, working hard to say them and making a whistling sound as it did. It was wonderful.

ঽ

So we got there, both of us, early—really early—every morning after that and looked for clovers together, stopping and standing up only when the other kids, humans and Tacuz both, started to arrive.

And we sat together on the bus. We weren't the only ones. Carlos and a Tacuz—a "boy," I remember thinking, because its hair was short—sat together, too, and a human girl sat with a Tacuz with long hair, just like Sandy's. It was nice to have it this way—not like first grade, when we'd sat separately, the Tacuz at the back and humans in front, and the human bus driver (at least that's how it seemed) meaner to the Tacuz kids.

Sandy

ૹ

I don't know why it happened. There was a boy named Kirk. He wasn't big. He'd never acted like a bully. But one day on the bus, coming home, he grabbed Sandy's hair and pulled. He pulled way too hard. He was laughing and looking at the boy beside him, showing off, and that other boy, human, was laughing, too. He pulled so hard Sandy made sounds I'd never heard her make, and something like saliva — a lot of it — came out of her mouth, which had only two teeth on top and two on the bottom. Her four hands clenched, and I thought she might be crying. But then she did something I'd never expected. She turned around and hit Kirk in the face with both of her outer hands, which she could swing the hardest.

Kirk's nose started bleeding, but he didn't cry. He hit her back. He was ferocious, angry in that way that makes you think someone is mad about something else. He hit her in the face, hard, and when she looked over at me, I could see blood — the clear pink blood the Tacuz have — running down her face, oozing from the slit of her nose, covering her thick lips, one of her teeth gone.

I didn't play sports. I didn't have older brothers I roughhoused with. I'd never hit anyone or been hit, but I knew I had to do something. After all, Sandy had *looked* at me. I was part of it now.

I climbed quickly over the seat and onto Kirk, and it was pretty silly. He was punching and not connecting, I was punching and not connecting — we were too close to do damage — and his human friend was hitting me on the back, which didn't hurt. But then Kirk went limp under me. I pulled myself back, looked down and saw that Sandy's four hands were around his neck and that he wasn't moving.

"No, Sandy!" I shouted. "No! Don't!" I tried to pull her hands away, but couldn't. They were like stones. "Please!"

When she finally let go, it was because the bus driver, a big guy, human, with muscles and tattoos on his arms, was towering over us, his face white as a sheet. He was shaking, and

65

I wasn't sure why. I thought maybe it was because Sandy had killed Kirk, and I just didn't know it yet.

But Kirk wasn't dead. He moaned in his seat and squirmed to sit upright. I got off him. The bus driver was still white, looking down at Sandy's face, at the pink, honey-like blood dripping from her chin.

"Please sit up front with me," he said gently to her, and his voice was funny. It sounded scared. "There's a seat up there right behind me. Please sit there until we get to your stop."

Sandy stood up. I stood next to her. I knew my nose was a little bloody, too, because I could see a red smear on the back of my hand where I'd wiped it. When she took a step, it was unsteady on her big shoes, but she headed toward the seat just behind the driver's, and I followed her. The driver looked at me as if to say "No," but Sandy glanced at him, and he backed off.

We sat down where we were supposed to. Behind us, way back in the bus, Kirk wasn't crying. The other kids were talking, but quietly. Someone said something to Kirk, and he said, "Shut up!" I was watching the back of Sandy's head, her long hair, worried about her face. But I shouldn't have been. "Tacuz are tough," my father always said. "They heal faster than we do."

When the bus was moving again, Sandy turned to look at me with those big eyes of hers and said, "You are a wonderful human being, Argun. I will tell my fathers."

ॐ

A few months after that, we were all—all human beings on Earth—and just ten years since the Tacuz had arrived to "colonize kindly," as they put it—rounded up and put in camps behind fences. The Tacuz had had enough, my parents said. My sister was still too little to know what was happening, but I wasn't. "Enough what?" I asked. My father was quiet and then said with a laugh that wasn't really a laugh, "They don't want to share anymore." I was only eleven, but I knew what he really meant: *We don't play well with others.*

Sandy

ℵ

My father said that one day after The Separation, when he and I were standing inside the fence — one taller than two men, coils of razor-sharp wire on the top of it shimmering with some kind of electricity — and looking out at the endless suburbs we'd once lived in, abandoned, and the endless groups of Tacuz, some official, some not, that every day passed by the fence, looking at us but saying nothing. I was thinking of Kirk, why he'd done what he'd done that day to Sandy's hair. Why would you do that?

Six months after that, when my little sister was sick, and we were worried she would die, we were moved to a better camp, one with more doctors, equipment, and supplies. I knew Sandy had made it happen. My father had no idea what I was talking about, but when the envelope arrived in the camp mail, I was sure. At first I thought it was just grass in the envelope. Then, looking more closely, I saw it was dry, curled-up four-leaf clovers. Thirty-six of them. (I counted.) "I know," the note said, as if she were still talking to me on the bus that day — and in that strange, angled handwriting Tacuz fingers make — "that you think I am wonderful too, Argun. Sincerely, Sandy."

BLUE FIRE

At the end of his remarkable long life, Boniface XII, *Dodecimus Episcopus Romanus*, once and forever known to Christendom as "The Child Pope," lay dying in his favorite bed — the one in the Papal Summer Palace in Grossetto, and the one he had slept in even when he was child, just after his uncle, the Cardinal Voccasini, had performed his political magic and arranged to have the boy, only eight, elected Pope. His uncle had done this, Boniface knew, not only because it would consolidate power in the Voccasini family and its friends — which was important if the Holy City were to function — but also because his uncle had... well, to put it simply, because his uncle had *cherished* him. The man had believed his nephew possessed a rare spiritual purity and an equally rare, especially for his age, devotion to truths greater than worldly affairs and glib distortions of faith. That, at least, was what his uncle had told everyone for decades, and with apparent sincerity, before his own death at fifty-two from liver problems that seemed to run in the Voccasini family.

Boniface hoped his uncle had been right, for the boy in question, Boniface himself, had reigned for nearly seventy years, a very long time for a Pope-maker to be wrong, especially when the secular condition of the Holy City and Christendom itself, not to mention tens of millions of souls, was at stake. Right or wrong though his uncle may have been, it was over now, and the fog that made the bedroom harder than ever to see in would take him soon. He was grateful that the cardinals had moved so quickly to transport him by carriage, with his doctors, to Grossetto, where he could pass from this life more peacefully than he ever could in the Holy City. In Rome — in addition to the

68

politics that had often numbed his heart — the Drinkers of Blood had, sixty-five years ago, almost won in their onslaught against the Holy City, with far too many souls (and far too many priests among them) lost to Darkness, to the bites and the infections of the soul, and the dark immortality of those infections.

The Oldest Drinker, a man without a name but with many names, had been born, so legend said, on the same night as God's Son, and in Jerusalem, too, though in a bloody, violent darkness where his own mother died even as he entered this world, without a star to shine or angels to sing for him. Without milk from a mother's breast, he had only his mother's blood to nourish him; and that night, as a squalling infant, he drank for the first time.

Fifteen centuries later, deciding at last that the time had come, he had led the onslaught on the Holy City himself, his minions trailing like an endless cloak of night behind him; and only by God's grace had the Light won, using three hundred priests hand-picked by Boniface's uncle to be trained by the Holy City's best archers, and arrow tips made by the city's best arrowsmiths from the wood of The Cross, which had taken five years and a third of the Holy City's treasury to locate at the eastern border of the Empire, ten days' journey from Jerusalem itself, in a cave that was barely a rumor.

Though it could — and did — disturb his sleep in the Vatican, all of that — the dreams of teeth at his neck these many years after the battle had been settled — did not disturb his sleep here. Here it was safely in the past, in a fog as great as this room's; and like Christendom itself he was, for a while at least, safe here from what might, had history and spirit and God's will danced differently, have been.

But if he was safe, what was this figure before him now — standing in the warm summer light of the bedroom, backlit by the sun through lace curtains? How had the figure entered the room, and why had the figure not been announced?

The figure was of average height, and thin — young perhaps, and perhaps a woman. Was it the Angel of Death, come to him as a youth, which would only be appropriate irony? Or had Satan come for him, to tempt him one last time with dreams of a woman he had, as a young man, loved at a distance for a month in Umbria, never quite sure whether it was love or merely lust, when of course, as he understood now with no little amusement, it had been both. In life, as God designed it, rarely was the truth as simple as "black or white," though Good was certainly very different from Evil—if one could see clearly enough and not be fooled into thinking one was the other.

"Good morning, Your Holiness," the figure said.

It was not the Angel of Death, nor was it Satan, nor a woman. It was a young man who, as he stepped to the old man's bedside and let the sun's light fall on his face, revealed himself to be serious of expression, with an earnest look—perhaps, Boniface imagined, the kind of young man who believed that time stole things and that a man's duty, if he were truly devoted, was to save what could be saved before it was indeed stolen.

"*Buona mattina a te, ragazzo,*" Boniface answered, giving the young man the smile that had served the old man well in making others feel at peace. "*Posso aiutarti con i miei ultimi respiri?*" May I help you with my final breaths?

It was meant as a joke, a *scherzo*, yet the young man looked as if he had been slapped.

"Do not be so serious, *ragazzo*," Boniface added. It took an effort to speak; and yet the more words he spoke, the more he felt the very energy, the *sanguinity* of blood's life, that he needed to keep speaking, as if words held life and could, if he simply used them, keep him here a little while longer. He wanted to thank the young man for this, but he was not certain how to do it. How to thank one he did not know for a few more minutes of life, or clarity? How even to phrase it, in the Papal protocols of speech? He could not remember. There were many matters he could not remember, and no doubt that was because, so close to the end, they were not important. And yet he wanted to thank this young man, and had no idea how to do it.

"I have lived a good life," Boniface heard himself saying,

finding it almost effortless. Why he was moved to say it, he did not know — unless it was the look of concern on the young man's face. "I have seen Darkness nearly reign victorious, and yet I am free now, and blessed, to die in the Light of the days we live in. What more could a man of God possibly want, my son?"

The young man cleared his throat, started to speak, held his tongue, cleared his throat again, and, finally, his voice shaking like windblown leaves, said:

"We want to be certain, Your Holiness, that those who come after us in the Holy City fully understand that Darkness you speak of...."

What a strange thing for a young man to say, even a very serious one. Boniface did not know how to answer.

"And who is 'we,' may I ask?" he said at last.

The young man look flustered now. "Forgive me, Your Holiness. I am Niccolo del Pagano, a recorder in the Office of *Verbum Dei*."

"I see. A 'recorder'?"

"Yes, Your Holiness. A kind of archivist — one who saves the past from mortal forgetting."

"That is a lovely expression. Is it yours, your superior's or someone else's?"

"It is mine."

"Lovely.... And what is it that you and your Office do not wish to forget?"

The young man looked flustered again, but not so badly. Boniface was tiring from holding his smile — a much more demanding physical act than words, which flowed of their own volition — though the smile did seem to be calming the young man.

"We have heard that you met the Youngest Drinker once," the young man said boldly.

Could this be true? Years after the battle, which lasted seven years and stretched from Lombardy to the north, Gaulle to the west, Greece to the east, and North Africa to the south, as the Drinkers struggled both physically and spiritually with those of

71

the faith, there had been stories about a young Drinker, one no older than Boniface had been at the time, and how different his fate had been from the others'.

Boniface lay back in his bed and closed his eyes. He had heard those stories, but had one of the stories been about *him*? Had he really met the Youngest Drinker himself?

Then, perhaps because a little more sunlight filled the room at that moment, or because the young man was so sincere in his desire not to lose what death takes from the world, the room's fog did part and Boniface did remember. Clearing his own throat now, he began to tell the story; and as he did, each word made the memory of that night long ago more vivid. The young man, who held paper and pen in his hands, would transcribe it as Boniface told it; but would he also clean it up when he made of it a final document—removing the tics of speech, eccentricities, excesses, asides, and whatever else? Boniface hoped so, for old men were notorious for their sloppiness.

ॐ

It was a week (Boniface began) when my uncle was away from the Vatican, in Parma, to meet with the Alexian and Augustinian Archbishops to discuss the rumors of "those who drink blood and can turn a man or woman into one of them, and for eternity," and what that might actually mean. The great onslaught on Rome led by the Oldest Drinker was yet a few years away, and so the rumors, it was felt, were just that: the insane whispers of those who feared Darkness more than they loved Light. I was recovering from a fever, a minor one but one that made me distrust what my eyes showed me, especially at night. I was seated in the Apse of the Basilica of St. Peter, in what people claim is St. Peter's chair (because it is ancient and made of acacia), as I often was when I sought aloneness in illness or self-doubt. A little table made of cedar, ancient too, sat beside me empty except for a goblet of water, for I was never hungry when I was ill. My attendants had left me alone, as I had requested, and the Basilica was empty. No sounds echoed in its great Nave or Transepts, for the only one who could make a sound was myself, and I sat quietly, my feet dangling above the floor, not quite able to reach it.

Then sounds did begin to echo. Footsteps. I stared into the shadows of the Basilica, where the sounds seemed to originate, and watched as one of them, a very small one, broke away and moved toward me.

When the shadow became a beggar child, a boy my own age, I assumed that I was dreaming a fever dream.

The figure approached slowly, his face hooded, one hand out as a beggar's would be, his feet shuffling on the marble floor and hidden by the rags he was wearing.

When my eyes, despite their blinking, could not make him go away, I startled at last, my heart leaping with fear or excitement or both. He was not a dream—he was not a shadow on the floor I had mistaken in half-dream for a beggar child. He was indeed a boy like myself, though a beggar, and how he had entered the Basilica without being challenged, I had no idea. He was nearly to me when I said:

"Blessings upon you, my child. Who are you?"

Was I afraid? Of course. A beggar child, and, given how he walked, probably sick, wandering somehow into the Basilica — should I not be concerned about contracting what ailed him? Did the child even know where he was? Did he, in his sickness, even recognize me, dressed though I was in my vestments? When he finally realized where he was, he might be more afraid than I, and what might he do then?

And yet behind the vague fear—for it was only that, a vagueness—was another thought, the kind I often had when I was young:

What if this were a miracle—the kind my uncle spoke of— the "miracles that illuminate our lives, whether we are saints or sinners"? Do the scriptures not tell of Christ and his disciples traveling as beggars? Does Christ himself not speak for the meek and weak and poor—of how we must look in their faces to find

Him if we are to forget the lies that riches and fine clothes and the body itself are, blinding us as they do to the Truth, which needs no finery?

Was this beggar perhaps not mortal, but His Son returned? Or if he were indeed just a beggar, did he not carry with him a child's innocence and therefore grace?

Head still bowed and hidden by his cowl, the beggar child said:

"I am a Drinker of Blood."

I did not know what to say at first. I was shocked by the child's words, and yet they made a strange sense to me.

"All who seek eternal life through Him are drinkers of blood."

The child laughed, which shocked me, too. To laugh at the solemn words of a Pope, even if he were a boy?

"I am not sure I am comfortable with your laughter, my child."

"I am no one's child," the boy answered, and it was not with hostility, but sadness.

At that moment D'Orgoglio, one of my attendants, appeared in the doorway just behind me to check on me.

"Your Holiness!" he exclaimed, seeing the child.

"I am fine, D'Orgoglio. The boy and I are simply in conversation."

The child had not turned to look at my attendant, and this made D'Orgoglio even more concerned. He was thinking (as I had thought and should still be thinking): How had the child gotten past the guards? How had the child even known where the Pope would be?

"A conversation at this hour, Your Holiness? Are you—"

"Please do not worry yourself, D'Orgoglio. I will call if you are needed."

D'Orgoglio seemed attached to the floor, unable to move his feet. How could he leave and at the same time obey my uncle's orders that he watch over me with his life?

"Your Holiness—"

"This boy is my guest tonight, Pier. We will be speaking of spiritual matters and so need privacy. As I said, I will call for you — I will ring the bell on this chair, in fact — if I need you."

After what seemed an eternity, D'Orgoglio moved at last, nodded once, stepped back through the doorway, and closed the door. He would send for a Papal guard or two, of course; and when they arrived, though they would all respect my wishes, they would also all listen, out of fear for my safety, on the other side of the heavy door. The child and I would need to speak *sotto voce* if we wanted privacy.

I turned back to the boy.

"Step closer, that we might converse quietly."

The child took two steps and stopped.

"You are *someone's* child," I answered him.

"I was *once*," he said, and, as he did, glanced at the doorway. Seeing that the door was shut, he let his cowl drop at last, so that I could see his face.

I jerked back. He was a boy, yes, but not a normal one. His skin was paler than the whitest marble inlays on the floor. His eyes were sunken, his lips thin. The dark slit of his mouth glinted with teeth, and not in a way that teeth should glint.

"You are God's child," I finally said, struggling for words. "And you will always be."

"I think not."

At that he raised his arm. The sleeve fell from it. His arm was as pale as his face. And then he did the most amazing thing: He bit into his own flesh. He raised his forearm to his lips, opened his mouth, and bit into himself.

It felt for a moment as if he had bitten *me*. I squirmed in St. Peter's chair from the sensation of it, looked down at my own arm, and calmed only when I saw no mark of mouth or teeth on my sleeve.

His arm was of course bleeding. He had bitten himself more than once, and his teeth had both punctured and torn his skin. Blood oozed from the wounds.

And then he did something else.

He licked the blood from his arm, paused as if to taste it, licked his lips to clean them, and looked back at me again.

"Would God have His child do this?" he asked bitterly, and I could see that his eyes were not what eyes should be. The pupils were too large, occupying all but the white. There was no color to his eyes, only the pupils' darkness.

He laughed again, amused at my astonishment.

"You still do not know what I am?"

He was correct. I did not. What could he have been, other than a child who seemed to have no blood in his body — pale as marble — and yet could bleed and drink his own blood happily?

Then the most disturbing thing of all occurred; and as it did, I stood up from St. Peter's chair, ready to rush from the Apse.

As I watched — and as he held his arm out to me so that I might do so — the wounds on his arm began to heal. They tightened, puckered, and slowly began to fill with fresh, smooth skin, until soon there were no wounds at all.

For a moment I thought of His Son again. Perhaps (I told myself, wanting to believe it) I was witnessing the kind of healing spoken of in the Holy Book; that I had been right — this was His Son come again, disturbed perhaps, doubting God, but had he not been in this same state, for a moment anyway, on the Cross of Golgotha?

But then the child said:

"It is not what you think, Your Holiness."

It was, yes, as if he had heard my unspoken thoughts; and was this not proof, too, that he might be the Son come again?

"All of us — the Drinkers of Blood — can hear the thoughts of mortals, like voices in our skulls, if we wish to," he said, performing the miracle again.

"But that does not mean," he continued, the bitterness there again, "that we are holy."

"I — I do not understand."

"We heal so that our damnation is ensured," he answered.

"But if you heal, you are immortal in flesh as well as soul."

"That is our damnation, Your Holiness."

"How can this be?"

He paused and the pause was like damnation itself.

"Because," he said at last, "we do not exist in God's grace."

"Everyone exists in God's grace—simply by being God's child."

"Not those cursed by the bite of the Oldest Drinker and his children, grandchildren and great-great-great grandchildren. The Oldest Drinker is the son of the Fallen One, born to graceless starvation, misery, and eternal damnation."

I remembered something from my eighth year of life: Adults speaking in a corridor, their voices low. My uncle and two others. Phrases like "those of the Dark Communion" and "a thirst that never ends." When one is eight years old, the words of adults belong to adults, for adults to understand, and I had thought nothing about them. And as I remembered the event, I remembered the fear in the whispers—and the mutterings of prayers that had followed. Later, when the Drinkers began to take the Holy City, I would learn what these phrases truly meant; but at that moment, faced with a beggar child who could heal from his own bite, I remembered only the whispers and the fear of that corridor.

"I am not old enough," I said at last, "to know of what you speak, my child."

"Nor was I," the figure rushed to answer, his voice made brave by what was clearly anger and despair, "until I was bitten three years ago and my body told me, as it changed, what I now know. As I met others like me, damned as well, I learned the words to describe it. The Curse. The story of the Oldest Drinker, who has lived for fifteen hundred and seventy-six years when perhaps he should have died in another man's place, on a cross, on a hill that day. Had I not learned these things from others like me, but older, I would not, at ten years of age, stand before you able to speak of anything other than my own misery."

"I still do not understand. But you are here because you wish something of me. This I understand."

"I do wish something of you, Your Holiness, and yet I do not know whether you understand enough of the world to grant it."

"We do not need to understand everything to do what should be done."

The child laughed again, and, though perhaps a little less bitterly, with the same despair.

"Those are the words of a man, not a boy," he said. "Where did you learn them?"

I saw no harm in answering, and, in fact, felt that only honesty would take us both where we needed to go this night. "From my uncle, the Cardinal Voccasini, and from the holy texts I studied under his guidance long before I was elected Pope."

Tears had appeared suddenly in the child's eyes, and I did not know why. He had been bitter and hopeless before, and angry before that, but the tears told of something else.

"I am not accustomed to the caring your honesty implies," the child said, sounding like a man even older than my uncle. When you were cursed in his way, did you become old before your time?

But the question that possessed me more than any other was this: Why would God curse a child when His Son had so loved children?

"I do not believe," I began, "that God has damned you or those like you."

"You do not know," he answered.

"I believe that you have damned yourselves by choosing to believe that God has forsaken you."

Where these words issued from, I do not know. They were almost heretical, and certainly not my uncle's. They were not from any holy text I could remember, and yet they felt very much like the word of God. I sometimes think that they were the first words I *truly* spoke as Pope; and by that I mean that they were the first real words of the Holy Spirit speaking through me; and that, had the beggar child who drank blood for reasons I did not understand not appeared before me that day, I would never have truly become Pope.

More tears had appeared, and the child was now embarrassed by them.

"How could God," he asked, "not have forsaken us if we are so miserable? Is it not God's wish that we suffer for our sins, though our sin is only that we are the children of the Oldest Drinker?"

"You are damned only by your bodies, just as I am," I heard myself say, a voice somewhere telling me to say it, "and bodies mean nothing, for they are a lie. They tell us that we are not eternal, when we are. They tell us that God must want us to suffer, when of course He does not. We suffer simply because we are here in this world and in bodies for but the briefest moment, after which we will return to Him."

Again, whose words these were, heretical as they sounded, and yet true, I did not know.

"We will certainly *not* return to Him," the child said.

"You will."

"But we are damned."

I sighed. What more could I say?

Fighting tears, he said, "Do you wish to hear my request or not?"

"Yes."

"It is this: Will you give me communion? And confession?"

My breath stopped. To grant communion and confession to one about whom my uncle and the other cardinals had whispered in fear should have been unthinkable; but as I looked into my heart I saw that it was not my love of God that made it "unthinkable," but a fear of what might be "Godless." And as my uncle had taught me, there is nothing that is Godless. And fear, as my uncle also taught me, should never be the reason for a Pope's action. A love of God should be; and if the words I had just spoken to the child—my first real words as Pope—had indeed come to me through the Holy Spirit, I should listen to them and not to fear.

"Why do you wish this, my child?"

"Because...," he began, but seemed unwilling to finish.

"You must tell me, if I am to decide whether to grant your request or not."

"Because I want to *know*."

"To know what?"

"Whether I am damned."

"My words of assurance to you as your Pope are not enough?"

"I wish that they were, but how can they be?"

It was true. How could they be, when I was but a child, too, and they were conversation, not sacrament.

"Did you also think," I asked, "that because I am a boy, too, you might persuade me more easily?"

"Yes."

"That I would be weak and so persuading me might be easier?"

"No. Only that because you are a child, too, you might understand and have more compassion than any priest, bishop, or cardinal."

He was speaking the truth, and I was moved.

When I rang the bell to call D'Orgoglio, it was not without doubt. What if what I was about to do was wrong in a manner I could not foresee? What if the child were playing me like a musical instrument for his own purposes, or, worse, the purposes of a greater darkness, the Oldest Drinker's? What if my performing the Sacrament of Penance and Reconciliation, with Communion, provided strength to Darkness?

What if, even if the consequences of my actions were not so grand, I nevertheless compromised the Voccasini family position by doing this? A Pope must remain sensitive to politics, too, that faith not die from the onslaught of worldly matters.

Once doubt fills us, it finds reasons everywhere for itself; and my doubt soon found more than I had ever imagined possible, and with the speed of hunting dogs.

When D'Orgoglio appeared, his face was full of alarm, and two guards were with him.

"I am still alive, Pier," I said, with a little laugh to calm him. "I wish to perform the Reconciliation for this child. Please bring me the Body and the Blood and leave us when you have. Thank you, and thanks to you two as well, who guard the Papacy so well."

Their astonished looks held them where they stood, but D'Orgoglio moved at last, turning and leaving. Because the two guards remained, the boy and I waited in silence. When D'Orgoglio returned, he placed the goblet of wine and the bread plate on the table by my chair, and then, at an insistent nod from me, departed with the guards, closing the door behind them.

"Step closer, please, my child."

Was he afraid? Was that why he did not take a step? Or was it something else?

"Do you wish to confess?"

"What might I confess," he answered, "that I would not repeat by my actions every day hence?"

"It is no different for all of us," I heard myself say. "And yet we all confess."

It was difficult—nearly impossible, in fact—for him to say what he said next, I know now; but he found the courage or will or desperation to say it; and I was again moved, and for a moment could not see through blinking eyes.

"Bless me—" he began, stopped, closed his eyes, and, eyes closed, began again:

"Bless me, Father, for I...." Again he stopped, and I could see him struggle with himself as if with a demon. "Bless me, Father, for I have sinned."

"And what is the nature of—" I began, also stopping, for the words that should have come to me would not come either. I heard only the voice that had spoken before with words that were neither mine nor my uncle's. "*And what is the nature,*" I heard myself say then, "*of what you believe has lost you God's love?*"

His eyes opened in surprise. These were not the words he had expected.

"I—I have taken into darkness too many souls to count, Father."

"Whether they are in darkness now," I heard myself continue, "is not for you to judge, but for God, for whom there can be no Darkness, for He and all that He has made lives in

Light beyond Darkness."

"But I have *sinned*."

"That is not for you to determine, my child," I went on, "but for God, who does not need to forgive what needs no forgiveness."

The boy, squatter of body than the boys I had grown up with — as squat as a Southerner, and just as long-armed, with eyes graced by the lashes of a girl — looked at me in confusion. How could a boy, even if he were a Pope, change the very words that every priest spoke and had spoken forever in this sacrament? Every sacrament was holy and beyond even a Pope's revision.

I was as confused as the boy was, and now frightened. What was this voice that spoke through me, changing what should not be changed, even if its words felt like Truth? Was I an instrument of the Lord of Lies now? Had I become it simply by accepting the boy's presence, a Drinker's?

And yet below the fear was a strange peace, one that let me say:

"So that you will know the peace in your heart that you deserve as God's child, I, your Pope, ask only that you say, when you have left this place tonight, and as you lie down to sleep, no matter how restless your sleep may be, a hundred Our Fathers. Utter them in joy and sincerity, as if your fear that God has abandoned you were but a terrible dream from which you have now awakened."

Not knowing what else to do, the boy nodded, but I could see the doubt in his eyes: *Forgiveness and salvation could not be so simple.*

And then the voice was gone, and I was free to begin, if I so wished, the Sacraments of Reconciliation and Communion, which the boy had requested and which, I remembered, might be combined in a single rite if a Pope saw wisdom in it. My uncle had never performed such a ritual, and yet such a ritual was what I would perform. I would even, because of what the boy had become, give him Blood before Body. Heresy or not, this is what I would do because it was right; because a voice somewhere insisted that it was.

I stood, picked up the goblet of wine from the table beside me, and held it out to the boy's lips. But when I said, "*Misereatur tui omnipotens Deus,*" a blue light appeared on the goblet's lip, and I stopped until it had faded. I had never seen such a light. Was it my fever, a trick of the eye in the candlelight, fatigue? I did not want to believe that it was real, for that would have meant something more frightening.

Blinking, I thrust the goblet out again toward the boy's lips; but when I said "*Et dimissis peccatis tuis,*" the blue light not only appeared once more but danced frantically on the rim of the goblet. I returned the goblet to the table, where the fire faded again, tore a piece of bread from the loaf, and tried once more. I handed him the bread first, so that he might partake of Body before Blood, that it might discourage the flame.

As if afraid it might bite him, the boy merely nibbled on the piece—

And then it did indeed bite him: The blue flame leaped from the bread, and the boy jerked back, as if burnt.

"It is as I feared!" he cried.

Doubt was taking me as well. What could I do against blue fire? And yet there was something odd about the flame. It did not feel like God's anger. It did not feel like damnation. What was it then?

"Let us continue, my child," I said, not knowing what else to do.

"No!"

"We must." Quickly I said, "*Perducat te ad vitam aeternam,*" and held the goblet to his lips once more.

The boy did not want to obey, but he touched his lips to the goblet's rim at last and even took a sip.

Again the blue flame stirred on the goblet, rearing up to leap from the metal to his mouth; and this time I reached out to put my hand in its way.

The flame did not burn me, but instead danced around my hand like a snake until it broke free and leaped to the boy's mouth again.

Again, the boy jerked back as if burnt.

"I cannot do this!" he cried, and the door started to open behind me.

"Do not come in!" I shouted. "We are doing what must be done for this child, Ser D'Orgoglio. We are not to be interrupted."

"But Your Holiness," the man's voice said, as if he'd seen the blue light himself—which perhaps he had though a cracked door—"if this is demonic possession, you are perhaps too inexperienced to attempt—"

"It is not a possession, D'Orgoglio," I said, wondering why I felt so certain, "and I am not accustomed to being interrupted by my attendants in the middle of a sacrament."

It was unkind of me to speak like that—especially to a man like D'Orgoglio—but rudeness was the only way I knew to make him leave. The boy would certainly not continue the rite in the presence of the man, and the manner in which this strange mixture of communion and reconciliation was proceeding would certainly excite D'Orgoglio too much for him to allow its completion.

"Yes, Your Holiness," D'Orgoglio's voice said, and the door closed once more.

"What is your name, my child?" I asked, turning back to him.

"Taddeo—Taddeo da Casta."

"We must continue, Taddeo."

"I cannot."

"You say this and yet you are here. You wish this. Why do you claim you cannot continue?"

"Because I am damned," he answered.

"As you have said before." I was growing impatient.

As he said it again—*because I am damned*—the blue flame danced higher, not only from the goblet, but from the plate of bread as well, as if fueled by the very words he was repeating. And a voice I knew well by now whispered: *Yes, that is the reason.*

"It must burn me because I am damned," the boy was saying yet again, and yet again I was answering, "You are *not* damned."

"But you can see the flame of God's anger?"

"It is your flame, *filius Dei*. It is yours, for you to use as you wish." This I now knew, and it was certain.

"No!"

The boy shook his head violently. The two places on his lips where the fire had indeed burnt them were healing, of course.

"And in your self-loathing you use it this way — as no loving God ever would."

"No!"

He was stepping back, and, as he did so, the blue light reached out for him from the goblet and loaf. The flame was larger now, as tall as a child, hot and blue, and a figure was taking shape within it.

"See!" he exclaimed. "That is no loving God!"

"I see a boy in the flame, Taddeo. I see *you*."

It was indeed the figure of a boy, his face shapeless but somehow familiar.

The boy screamed, unable to look, and, turning, began to run. He ran toward the distant shadows of the Basilica's Nave, and when those shadows took him, I listened to his footsteps until they too faded.

The flame had hesitated for a moment on the goblet and bread, but then had followed him, becoming a wisp and a whisper and then nothing at all.

ॐ

Two weeks later, after my uncle had returned and reprimanded me for allowing a beggar child to visit me in the middle of the night (and without proper security during the visit), I heard a story from one of my tutors. I had not told a soul what had actually happened that night. It would be a secret I would keep for years. The tutor in question was one responsible for keeping me aware of news in the city; and the story he told me was of a child who had been killed at the Travinia Gate of the Vatican, and under strange circumstances. The child, my tutor explained, had run menacingly toward the guards brandishing a torch, one with a mysterious blue fire; and, though the guards, their bows raised and arrows nocked as was proper, had shouted warnings at him, the child had continued toward them, shouting demonically and screaming heretical oaths, all of which the guards found frightening. What ensued, then, is understandable, is it not, Your Holiness? Release their arrows the guards did, in their fear of the blue flame and the demonic noise; but strangely, the first five arrows, though they struck the child, did not stop his forward rush.

It was the sixth arrow, a particularly stout one, striking the child in the heart, that stopped him mere steps from the gate itself. The child looked, in the words of one guard, like Saint Sebastian, full of arrows, which no child should be because no child should have to be a martyred saint; and the guards did feel the tug of conscience and compassion. But stranger still, Your Holiness, was what happened then: Although the torch rolled away from the child at his collapse and could therefore not have set his robe on fire, the child did catch fire, and the fire was blue, as I said, and it burned intensely until only the child's bones remained, even as the astonished guards looked down on this miracle and crossed themselves in protection.

"Do you have any idea," my tutor asked when he finished, "what this might mean, Your Holiness? Is this related to the rumors of those who drink blood, who can heal themselves and can only be brought down by arrows to their hearts?"

Of all my tutors he was the one who most believed I would indeed serve Christendom well as Pope, and for this I loved him and would always be grateful for him in my life.

"No," I heard myself answer. "It means simply that a child is free at last."

My tutor was silent, trying to understand. And then he said: "So that he might return to God?"

"Yes. So that he might return to God."

Boniface stopped talking at last, and with a great sigh fell back. The young man was still standing where he had been standing throughout the telling. Had Boniface not told him to sit, to conserve his energy for the transcribing? But no, the young man in his earnestness had stayed upright, scribbling frantically with a quill in one hand and parchment and an inkwell somehow in the other. How difficult he had made it for himself.

The young man stopped writing, but did not look up. He was staring at the sheaves of parchment he had used, some where they had fallen on the floor, slipping from his hands, others still clenched in them. He had trembled more than once during the story, the old man knew. Boniface had seen him tremble, but had not stopped his tale. Who knew when the words might exhaust themselves, leaving the story unfinished — which would have grieved the young man terribly.

"I do not wish to leave you, You Holiness," the young man said suddenly. Still he would not look up.

"You are afraid that I will die if you do, am I correct?"

The young man's silence answered for him.

"Thank you for your concern, but I am not a story," the old Pope said. "I am a man whose time has come. If I die, I will be forgotten in time by the living; and if not forgotten, my boy, then transformed by the flaws of public and private memory into something I was certainly not. But the true world itself, where words are not needed, nor stories, will not forget what I have touched in this life, just as it will not forget what you touch in your life, *ragazzo*. What we touch is of the world forever because we ourselves were once of it. As the world remembers, so does God, and the forgetfulness of mortals matters not in the slightest."

"Yes, Your Holiness."

"I told you my story not because I wish to be remembered, but because you, by asking, helped me to remember it, that is, to remember how important that night was to me; and so we have spent, you and I, some time together in this life; and that matters more, though you may not believe it, than any archive."

Boniface stopped. The words were tiring him at last, perhaps because these words were not really necessary.

The young man was nodding. He was confused, Boniface could see. He did not know what to do, standing there. He did not know what to say. He was not sure he understood, though years from now he probably would. And was this not the plight of all mortals — every day of their lives?

"Stand where you are," Boniface said with compassion, "a little while longer, *ragazzo*. Soon we will need neither words nor memory...." He heard the young man make a small choking sound, as if from an emotion; and then, as the old man had predicted, none of it mattered, for the fog had completely filled the room now; and somehow it was the young man, no longer a shadow backlit by the familiar sun beyond the window, that had become the brightest of lights.

THE MESSENGER

I go to see my parents yesterday. They're thirty-five. I'm fifty. This kind of thing is easy with the Non-Paradoxical Time Channel you subscribe to if you've got the money for a portal and don't mind spending real-time in the past. I just haven't done it before. When you've got your own kids, you prioritize: Your parents already raised you, and now your children need you to raise them.

They're living in a house I don't remember. I don't remember ever seeing stills or video of it either — because that's where it probably happened, and my father didn't want reminders. A big Spanish thing — a century old at least — two stories, courtyard, fan palms, terracotta tiles. The kind my mother would have loved, I know, and that my father, a successful partner in a big product-liability law firm, could have afforded. He did love her, I tell myself.

Don't know why the big pots on the travertine patio by the front door catch my eye, but I'm leaning over, trying to figure out why someone's let the flowers in them die, when I look up and there's my mother walking up the steps toward me in slacks and a red blouse. I've seen the pics from their wedding, one vacation video from a little later, and all sorts of childhood and college shots of her (in those bright red dresses she loved); so I know her even if I don't remember her.

I stand up, nervous. I smile. There are lots of people around, going up and down the steps, grabbing things from vans and trucks — as if they're getting ready for a party or fixing the house to sell it. She glances at me. Just once. No reason she should recognize me — I haven't even been born — though maybe she'll think I look familiar, like the men from my father's family. But, no, she glances at me once and walks by.

As she passes, time slows a little—just a little—and I see that distant look in her face, that unhappiness you could see in those snapshots from college. (I'm thinking of one where she's sitting on a park bench in winter, not looking at the photographer; and another, on the deck of a boat owned by her father, looking into the distance too.) A look you'd only know the importance of if you could see the future.

Remember, this is my first time. Some people who've had the channel for years—they get good at it. They have fun with their parents—who don't recognize them (since they haven't been born yet)—socializing, getting drunk with them, even pulling childish pranks on them for the hell of it. They have fun because they know it won't change anything. It can't. It's Non-Paradoxical. Anything they do is already in the temporal loop.

Or they visit for weeks, even months if they can afford it, become neighbors, close friends, or just strangers watching from a distance, trying to get over grievances and hurts, feeling whatever love they can, understanding better the two people who brought them into this world. And they always come back wiser, make conversation of it in the present, even art, write about it, publish the writing, or at least carry it back it to their children as the miracle it is—the wonder of it.

All in the loop, of course. Pre-set.

If you actually went to *change* things—say, to tell your mother lies about your father so she'd marry someone else, so you wouldn't be born because you hate your life in the present—you wouldn't be able to do it. Something would always get in your way no matter how many times you tried.

Time is ingenious.

ॐ

But this is my first time, and I've got something I need to do. Loop or no loop.

I head up the stairs and into the house. It doesn't feel like a dream at all. It's real, and I'm seeing it as I never would as a child. It has to be preparations for a party, I tell myself. Workmen are fixing a mantelpiece in the living room and oh-so-perky men and women in black-and-white uniforms, who've got to be caterers, are setting things up in the dining room.

In the kitchen a man I know — I know his back even in a shirt I've never seen him in — turns from a workman he's talking to and looks at me, wondering what I want, who I am if I'm not in a uniform and don't have tools in my hands.

Those brown eyes and long lashes. I see them in the mirror every morning, but the face before me is thirty-five, not fifty. It's not mine.

"I —" I start, but don't know what to say, so I blurt out a stupid: "I just saw Mom."

When a 50-year-old man — one you've never seen before — maybe there's something familiar about him, maybe not (he looks like your Louisiana uncles?) — stands in front of you and says, "I just saw Mom," you don't hear the word. He couldn't possibly have said it. He must have said, "I just saw *Don*?" or "I just saw *Tom*?"

"What?" he asks. Not annoyed. Always his calm self. Just a little puzzled.

I think fast and say, "Sorry to intrude like this, but I need to talk to Theresa about a school matter."

He's looking at me like he should know me, but doesn't, but should pretend he does. I know her name, after all, and I've said "school." I'm someone from where she's teaches, down at St. Mary's — isn't that where she taught the year before I was born?

"Sure," he says.

He's decided he doesn't need to recognize me. I'm new to the school. He's never met me, and if I'm rude not to introduce myself, so what? He's busy. If I've driven over instead of calling to talk school matters with her, it's because teachers are that way. "Touchy-feely," as he always put it. "About as far from attorneys as you can get, Tim."

"She's not feeling well," he says. I know what this means. I can

91

hear the weight of it in his voice. "But you'll find her upstairs probably. I'm Jim, Theresa's husband," he adds, holding out his hand.

I take his hand as I've taken it so often, and I say it — my real name. "I'm Timothy."

I wait. Nothing. I turn to leave as he turns too — back to the workman.

It will be the name they use, yes, but he'll forget this meeting. I'll ask him when he's old and dying, and he'll say he doesn't remember, and he won't. Maybe it's my saying it that does it, maybe not. Maybe the name is already in him — in them both — a name they love — so they use it. However it happens, it's set.

ॐ

I find her in the hallway upstairs, looking dazed. Someone is leaving her when I approach — another workman with paint on his pants, looking puzzled, as if she's said something that made no sense.

I stand in front of her, and, sure, I'm making her look at me. I want her to look at me even if she doesn't understand why, even if she'll forget this moment.

She looks pretty in her red blouse, vulnerable with eyes that won't stay still. The faint Asian fold of her eyelids — those from her mother. I understand now why he loves her. Always did and always will. I wish I had her eyes.

"Do you love him?" I say.

"What?" Her eyes stop on me now, though it's difficult. They've always needed to be somewhere else. The old photographs don't lie.

"Do you love him, Theresa?"

"Who are you?"

"I think you know." If anyone could see the truth with those flitting eyes, it would be her. I've known this for a long time. It's one of the reasons I'm here.

She cocks her head, peers at me, touches her collar nervously, drops her hand in self-consciousness, and takes a breath.

"Perhaps I do...," she says at last.

She stares at me. A faint smile appears on her lips, passes, and she says:

"When I look past things around me...."

"Yes?"

"When I look past things around me, I see people. People like you."

"I know, Mother."

She doesn't jerk at the word. She *knows*.

"I don't know whether they're real or not, but I see them...."

"Yes, you do."

"It's difficult to be here...in the way I should be here."

I nod.

"With him, I mean...."

"Yes...."

"How can you be real?" she asks suddenly. "You aren't here yet, and perhaps you'll never be...."

"It doesn't matter, Mother. I'm here and I'm sorry, but I've got two questions...."

"The one you just asked?"

"That's one."

"Do I love him?"

I nod.

She closes her eyes. "Sometimes I think I do.... And sometimes I think I can't love anyone, not here in this world."

"But that isn't his fault, is it." I don't say it as a question.

"No. It isn't."

I take a deep breath and ask the harder one:

"If you do what you're thinking of doing—"

"Yes?"

"—it won't be because you don't love him, right? That won't be the reason, right?"

"No, it won't, Tim."

I do it—I jerk. Of course I do. She knows who I am, and to hear my name from her voice is like an old, old dream.

"He loves you," I blurt.

"I know….. I just don't want to be here anymore. Can you understand that?"

I can't, but I nod.

They'll have me in the hope that it will make her happy — happy enough not to leave this life — but it won't.

"I have a favor to ask of you, too, Mother," I hear myself say. "Just one.

She finds this funny and smiles. "Yes?"

"That you not do it — that you not do what you're thinking of doing — until I am born…."

It's a silly thing to ask. I was born and am talking to her now, so it was already done, in the loop, settled; but I say it because it feels good to — as if we both have the power, we both can decide it together — that I should be born. Something that lovers would decide.

Her eyes aren't dancing away. They're looking at me as if I'm really here, and there's a kindness in them — one that's not in the photographs — one that is unbearable.

"Of course not," she says, almost laughing.

"I'd never do that," she adds.

For a moment I want to step to her and take her in my arms — because I never have, though she must have held me those first six months. But that would be awkward. I'd want to stay, which would be impossible.

I kiss her on the forehead — that's all I do — and as I leave she's already gone, looking at the window's bright light at the end of the hallway.

ॐ

That evening, instead of having dinner with Daphne and our daughters, then whisking them away to the Halloween carnival at the school where I teach, like I do every year, I go to the hospital to see him. We'll be taking him to hospice care the next day (there are some things money can't buy, and he'd be the first to say it — and often does), but I want to spend the night with my father, just him and me, the way it's always been.

"Well?" he says, IV tubing rustling at his wrists like toy snakes, his voice no louder than the thing growing in his chest, stomach and liver will allow.

Those brown eyes again, and the lashes. She'd have loved them the first time she saw them.

I take a breath.

"You weren't the reason," I tell him.

He nods, but he needs the other too.

"Of course she loved you," I say.

He looks at me, and it takes a great effort. He isn't sure—I can tell from his eyes. It's hard to give up a fifty-year-old fear, one that feels just like the thing eating at your body now.

"Would you lie to me, Tim?"

I look at him and hold his eyes. "No, I wouldn't. You just feel bad that she did it, felt it was your fault, which it wasn't, feel bad that you lived on when she couldn't, and so you doubt what I'm saying because you've doubted yourself for so long."

"Nice speech."

I manage a smile. "I've been practicing, Dad."

"You were always good at that." He coughs. He's always coughing. "Making people feel good, I mean."

He's right, of course. I'd have lied.

I keep smiling. What else can I do?

"I'd have gone myself, you know," he says. "But I couldn't."

He means his body, that he can't walk, but he also means—and he wants me to understand this—that he couldn't stand seeing her *alive*—he just couldn't. But he's forgotten the other thing, too, because he wants to—because he wanted it to be his choice: You can't visit a time after you're born. There can't be two of you. The portal won't let you through.

"I know, Dad," I tell him. And I do. It's hard thinking all those years that you weren't important enough to keep someone in this world. And it's hard thinking you're the only one who can see past the things around you to people who aren't there, but might be some day.

95

He lies back, tired, and doesn't close his eyes. When I come back from the nurse's station with the little folding cot, so I can stay the night, his eyes are still open, but they're no longer unsure. He's remembering what she was like when she was here—*really* here—and it does feel like love.

And isn't that the point? To do what we need to do to help them. To help them believe, I mean.

Before they leave.

Whether it's in the loop or not.

INK

The American boy, whose name was David, had always collected things. Coins, minerals, seashells, insects, and even house-brand bars of soap from hotels in his family's travels. His collections helped him know who he was when so much of life did not; and the things he collected did not make him bleed, when so much of the world—the sharp, angular things of it— did. When you bought an old coin in a store, the coin didn't bruise your skin or scratch your fingers. You just needed to make sure you didn't bump against the display cases. When you picked up a *gastropod* or *pelecypod* on the mud of a bay, it didn't hurt you. You just needed to make sure you avoided tripping on a piece of cement from an old dock. You took them home, these things you collected, because they were safe, and put them in neatly organized boxes or jars or trays or books and, when you wanted to, took a deep breath and looked at them in safety. If you did this, your dreams of blood—of bleeding wherever you walked—stopped for a few nights, and were instead about bruises, just that, not skin that leaked out what kept you alive.

The disease was called "severe hemophilia A." Neither of his parents had it, so it was, the doctors said, a "spontaneous mutation," common enough, and one that the treatments of recombinant FVIII—paid for by the Navy everywhere his family went—would help, but only if he didn't miss them.

॰

When his family moved—because of his father's military assignments—to a new city every two years, they had to find a

97

new doctor for his treatments, sometimes nearby, sometimes not. He also had to learn the new dangers—the new ways he might bleed both inside and out. But he also always found something new to collect or additions to what he already collected. It was a way to tie it all together—life and the world and himself. It was a story, and the story continued, which was important. Without it, who was he, and why was he in this world bleeding this way? Was he only a shadow, bled dry, or was he a boy whose skin glowed like the sun?

His father's new assignment was a smoggy port in Northern Italy. Just south of that port, his family would live in a fishing village with a little cove, a castle above it, and clean air and the very sun he wanted to be bright like. When he learned that all of the boys his age in the village had a stamp collection, he began one, too. They were happy with theirs, and he would be happy with his. Sometimes the drives to the base at Livorno for his infusions—to keep him from bleeding so much—took him out of school in the village, where he was learning the language and Roman history and the pig production of Calabria and Tuscany. But he could work on his stamp collection in the car—in his stamp album, with its neat rows of slips.

Stamps were the safest of all collectible things, weren't they? You didn't have to put pins through them or struggle with drawers or wooden boxes. And having a stamp collection was important in this village. If he wanted friends, which he did—friends at the school where he would be for three years—he would have to fit in, wouldn't he? They were kind boys, he'd discovered, rarely asking about his bruises or the careful one-foot-after-another way he walked; and when they did ask, it was gently, not the way kids did back in the States.

Besides, it was a collection—and he knew how to collect things, didn't he?

Yes, you could *buy* new stamps at post offices and old stamps in philatelic stores and by mail. That was easy. But that wasn't how his friends had made their collections. Theirs had been started by their grandfathers in Liguria or Tuscany or Umbria, even their great-grandfathers, and continued by their fathers, and now by the boys themselves. His friends might purchase stamps to grow their collections, but the heart of those collections were *people*, people who gave you stamps whether they were relatives or friends or strangers. That kind of collection was the best, he knew.

The boy's family was soon living in a little stucco house the villagers called a villetta. He would walk carefully, looking for holes and rocks, on the dirt road that ambled from their villetta through shady olive groves, out into the sun, then down to the waterfront, to its colorful boats and crumbling castle, and the school building with its stern façades. None of the trees' branches hung low over the road from his house, so he was safe. No dogs were ever loose that might break the skin if they tried to bite him. He would pass a convent whose walls were covered with lichen and whose courtyard was almost as dark as night from the trees that had grown unpruned for an eternity there. He would also — right where the sunlight broke through — pass the massive wrought-iron gate of the Perotto family villa and the endless path that led from that gate up, like a rose-bush-decorated snake, to the front of the Villa Perotto, which no one in the village had ever been inside. It was rumored that witches — *streghe* — lived in little shacks in the olive groves all around, poisoning cats and talking to the green wall lizards, and he had come to believe it himself. Even his friends believed in spells — ones that came from the shadows of the trees, the darkness of the convent, the sea in moonlight, and, in turn, in miracles that came from the *light*. Ones that came from the kindness of the people, their lack of cruelty, and what mattered most to them and always had: *family*. But the magic didn't touch him directly — he still bled every day and always would, world without end — and so he did not think much about it. Why should he? It was *their magic*, the village's, not his, wasn't it? He was an interloper and would be gone from its blue cove and green hills and people and sun soon enough. He would return to the shadows.

Besides, he had *real* things to do. He had, in fact, decided this morning to do it, and he did. He went ahead and stopped beside the black gate of the great villa, looked down to make sure there was nothing he might trip on—a step, a stone, a brick—and took a step toward it. He was an American, but people would have been kind to him even if he weren't. They were different here. Perhaps the people who lived in the villa wouldn't mind if he asked. He would be courteous, of course. There had to be envelopes, old ones—with old stamps on them—somewhere in the countless rooms of that villa, and maybe they would help him with his collection. Someone in this villa might even have a stamp collection himself and would understand why he, David, needed one, too—so that he might know who he was in this new place. Men who collected stamps had once been boys who'd collected them, known who they were by collecting them, and so...

ༀ

He put his hands cautiously on the iron design—a hawk or eagle with wings outspread—and checked for any metal that might tear his skin. Then he looked again up the path that led to the villa.

He rang the doorbell, which was black and smooth and as safe as a seashell worn by the waves and sand. He was nervous, but that, he told himself, was only because he wanted to ask his question correctly, in the right way, respectfully.

He could see an old woman in a simple black dress—the kind so many old women here wore—coming down the long path from the villa. It took her ages. She had a bad leg and wobbled a little, so the path was even longer for her. When she reached the gate, she did not open it, but asked him gently what he wanted. "*Che vuoi, ragazzo?*"

"I am the American boy who attends the middle school in this village." His family, he went on, lived down the road in the villetta La Lupetta, the little house just below the Villa Lupo, which belonged to Dottor Lupo and his family. She nodded. Everyone knew the doctor, whose name meant "wolf."

He collected *francobolli*, he said, and was sorry to bother her; but wondered whether the family had any old envelopes with stamps on them that they might be willing to give him for his collection, which (he explained) needed more brightly colored stamps. It was unreasonable that he should ask, he admitted — *"Mi dispiace, Egregia Signora"* — but he would appreciate her consideration of a boy's request.

He had red hair, blue eyes, and freckles. His face was round like a moon. He had been teased for these things at his father's other assignments — these and his bleeding and the fact that he didn't like sports — but here he had not, and he didn't know why. He knew he stood out and that the old woman probably knew, even without his saying it, who he was, and his family's story.

The old woman looked at him oddly, as if she knew him, blinked and said very gently, *"Si, capisco, ragazzo mio.* Please wait a moment."

My boy, she had said, and it wasn't just an expression here, he remembered. You said it only to family and friends, people you knew and cared about.

He watched her ascend the path slowly back to the villa and, reaching the dark portico, disappear inside. He waited for what seemed like an hour. He felt bad that he was making her, with her bad leg, do all this walking. He shouldn't have asked.

When she reappeared in the sunlight, she had something — no, many things — in her hand; and as she grew closer, he could see they were exactly what he had asked for: envelopes — and postcards, too. Postcards were even better because the postcard itself was often beautiful. As she handed them to him through the gate, she was smiling because he was smiling. His happiness for some reason made her happy.

It was then that he saw she had only one clear eye. One was brown, the other cloudy, as if blind.

"You may have these, *ragazzo mio*," she said, again gently. "I wish you the very best of luck with your collection. Stamps are a wonderful thing. Boys should always collect them." She paused, and a shadow passed over them both; or perhaps it was only the sadness in her voice as she said: "Many years ago the man of this villa collected *francobolli*, too, as did his son, but their collections are no longer here..."

"*Moltissime grazie, Signora.*"

"*Prego, ragazzo mio...*"

Her happiness at talking to him — that's how it felt — seemed to win over the shadow, and her one good eye was dancing with light now.

He continued to thank her — he did not want to leave — and he wished he knew the language better than a year of tutoring and school allowed. She would not move either, he saw, unless he moved first. And so — though the step he took seemed to make her a little sad, and that was the last thing he wanted to do to her — he was the one to leave first, looking down again to make sure it was safe to walk, but also stopping and turning once to look back at her as she, too, turned and began to ascend the path again, her black dress like a shrinking shadow beyond the dark iron of the tall gate, the windows of the villa suddenly dark, too.

৯

In his bedroom, on his bed, after checking his body for bruises, and thinking of the old woman's pale, bloodless eye, he didn't remove the stamps from the envelopes and postcards. He would never remove them, he told himself. You just didn't do that when the envelopes and cards were old. The stamps were from the Second World War. He could tell from the pictures on them. The handwriting was wonderful — the sevens with their crossed trunks, the ones that looked more like capital A's without a bar, and the floweriness of the handwriting. He saw now that the postcards weren't picture postcards at all, but simply letter-cards. He was disappointed, but not really. The ink was ink — but instead of being perfectly black it was a dark red, sometimes a brown that was almost black. Was this what people called "sepia"? Two of the envelopes — the smallest — had little cards in them, with exquisite, tiny writing, the cards bordered in black. He remembered from reading that stamps bordered with black meant death — that the person on the stamp had died. The black borders were like a little funeral for the person.

He tried to read the letters and cards, but gave up. The words were those of grown-ups writing to each other, not to a boy of twelve, and, even when he could read the words, they were hard to understand. It was enough to have the old war stamps — some with Victor Emanuel, the King, some with old airplanes or Roman busts, some with the man they called Mussolini. It was enough to smell their mustiness, something else that couldn't hurt him, and know that they'd been written in another time. A time when the men in the village had received their wounds in that war — bleeding more than he ever had — and become crippled. A time when the women who now wore black had lost their husbands to a bleeding that couldn't be stopped, and started to wear their black dresses, like the old woman from the villa. Like a funeral, that dress.

ॐ

Not long after he was given the envelopes and cards, the boy's father threw himself on his son, knocking him out of the way of an oncoming car near the doctors' office on the Navy base in Livorno. His father — a tall, gentle man, an officer — broke an ankle saving him, and the boy felt a strange mixture of gratitude and guilt. At least the broken ankle didn't bleed. At least it was just a bruise. "That is what fathers do for their sons," his father explained, his eyes as blue as the boy's and his skin just as pale.

ॐ

A week after that, the boy's bleeding stopped. It stopped suddenly, and it stopped completely. He didn't bruise anymore. His cuts bled only for a moment, the blood clotting as it was supposed to. He no longer needed the infusions, the doctor visits, the drives to and from them. He no longer had to walk carefully.

His Navy doctors in Livorno — and specialists from Genoa that they brought it in to try to understand it — could not explain it. There was, of course, no connection between the car episode and this, and no one even suggested it. Only the boy wondered, and then he stopped wondering.

Bloodwork over the next three months showed the impossible: The FVIII deficiency had disappeared. The clotting protein was now suddenly present.

The adults talked on and on about it, but what mattered to the boy — the only thing that could possibly matter, miracle that it was, and a miracle, he felt sure, that was somehow tied to the village and that old woman — was that he didn't have to be careful anymore, didn't have to check every minute of every day every inch of his skin for scratches, cuts, and bruises.

It took him months to learn how to walk differently, touch things differently, be *different* in the world, not afraid. Sometimes it was frustrating, how long it was taking, because it seemed silly — how breaking a painful "habit" could be so difficult. He also, he soon saw, had to give up a big piece of who he was — a boy who *bled* — and perhaps this made the breaking even more difficult. But by the end of summer the new feeling — that he was like other boys now — told him who he was. *A boy who didn't bleed*.

He continued adding to his stamp collection, yes, but it felt different. It was not desperate. He didn't do it nervously, with a dread whose face was never quite clear. He collected stamps simply because the other boys did, because it was fun, and it was fun because the dread was fading, and with it, the shadows.

Over the years, he would start to bleed again, but stop within minutes. His doctors back in the States could not explain why — it made no sense because the deficiency was still gone — but when he did bleed, brief though it was, he would dream that night of something small and mysterious bleeding in the darkness forever, no one knowing it was there. Was it a heart, dead but alive somehow? Was it a tiny baby, dead at birth? Was it something else in his dream?

As the years passed, the episodes finally stopped. The dreams stopped, too. He was a man now and could forget how much blood there had once been in his world.

ঽ

When the boy was a man of forty-five, living in his own country — his own father long since retired from the military, and the bleeding of his youth a memory that sometimes felt like someone else's (though the day his father had saved him he would never forget) — he found himself teaching high school history. He loved history as much as he'd once loved stamps, and weren't they alike? Every stamp was history, and every country knew what it was by its stamps. He had been teaching history for years, had been married twice — the first time far too young — and now had three grown children whom he loved, but who had never been interested in stamps, or any collection, for that matter. It was a silly feeling, he knew — feeling a little sad about that — because he was no longer interested in his old collections either and hadn't been for years. People were what mattered. In fact, he often said that to his students, who weren't quite sure, he knew from their faces, why he was saying it.

On a spring day, cleaning one of the two attics of his house, he found in a large trunk the box with the old envelopes and cards. The box was black and sticky with something, and at first he didn't recognize them, those letters and cards, the stickiness so filled the box, leaking from its corner and flaps. Someone had — perhaps his parents, perhaps he himself — years ago taped the box up with masking tape, and that was the only thing that had kept it together as the cardboard grew soggy and tried to fall apart.

The sticky material, as he got it on his hands, felt more like honey than paint or an adhesive, but he couldn't, in the dim light of the attic, see well enough to identify it.

He got rubber gloves from the kitchen, put the damp and

crusty box on newspapers on the porch, and pulled out the envelopes and cards. The stickiness was a mystery, but he was more interested in what the box held. The last time he had touched them, he had been a child.

He wasn't sure, holding the letters — covered as they were by whatever the substance was — that he'd be able to read them. He got a wet sponge and tried to wipe them clean, but the water took the writing away as well. He stopped, sighed, started reading what was readable, and found that there was more than enough.

It was stunning.

It was history, immense history, that he held in his hand, sticky or not. He'd held it in his hands as a boy, but without knowing it.

The letters and cards were condolences — ones from senators, doctors, generals, archbishops, members of Mussolini's cabinet — to the family of the man who had died, and died violently, though not on the battlefield. Or a battlefield of another kind. An important man. A hero of the Great War, and now, in these letters, a man of position in another war: His Excellency the General Giuseppe Perotto, *Ministero dello Stato* and *Senatore del Regno*, and a member of il Duce's Ministry of War. A man important not just to a fishing village in Liguria, where he had been born, but to an entire country and its role in that war. "To the Family of General Giuseppe Perotto. We are aware of the painful travails you are enduring at this time of your incalculable loss. The crazed individual who has taken the General and Ugo from us..." "My dear Margherita — What a terrible surprise I received this morning by telegraph from the Ministry of War. I was, at that moment, overwhelmed with gratitude and yet a sense of terrible loss as well for those weeks my wife and I spent with you, the General, and Ugo in 1930 in Liguria, and can only pray..." "I send to you by words that must fail to capture the human heart my most profound condolences for the loss of the Generale and your son to the insanity of these times. His passing will be felt by all..."

Why had the old woman in black given him such letters? Where had she found them when she returned to the villa? Why were they still there, ready to be given to a boy? Who was she, and was the "man of the villa" she had spoken of that day at the gate, when he was thirteen, the General? If so, what had happened to that man's collection?

He didn't know; but the letters remained, and they made his hands tremble, holding them. He needed to look something up, but what was that stickiness? It was, he found himself thinking — crazy as the idea was — as if the letters themselves had somehow leaked the black-but-red stickiness into that box, all over the letters and cards. But that wasn't possible. He was tired — neither he nor his wife had slept well the night before — and finding the letters had put him in a dreamy place, imagining all sorts of things from the sheer emotion of it.

Tossing the vision aside, he went to his computer and did the quick research he wanted to do, a simple search, and stopping suddenly when he felt the blood drain from his face and hands and the air of his office turn cold.

General Giuseppe Perotto (the entry read) had been killed by a lone "anti-Fascist" revolutionary with his Carcano M91 rifle on August 3, 1943.

The assassin had been stalking the General's family that day in Rome, planning to kill them all; and when the first shot was fired, hitting the General in the chest, the General had thrown himself on his wife and son.

That had not been enough to save Ugo, the boy, or himself. The assassin was a marksman trained by the Army.

"Ugo Perotto was twelve —" the entry went on.

" — collected stamps, and suffered from hemophilia."

ॐ

When he got up from his computer, he was shaking. He went back to the porch, to the box of letters, and brought them into the kitchen, to the counter there, where the light was brighter.

Removing the rubber gloves at last, he touched the substance both where it was still sticky and where it was dry and crusty. He recognized it now. Without a doubt.

To make sure, he smelled his sticky fingers, caught the whiff of rust, and tasted it, too. Saltiness. Metal. After all, it was a sea inside us, wasn't it? — and full of iron.

Black and a near-black brown, but with red. It couldn't escape being red even when it was black. It was blood. Old blood.

The letters had bled for him so that he would not have to bleed. They had bled for him for thirty-five years, and he hadn't known it. He had put the letters away, as if they were not — *could not be* — important any longer to him, the bleeding gone at last. And yet they had been there in his life forever, the reason he was no longer cursed, the reason he'd been able to be a good husband and good father and lived a normal life.

The letters and the blood they bled for him, a boy the Perotto family hadn't even known, could not bring a father and son back to life, but they could keep another boy alive even if it meant bleeding for him in the darkness of a box, one attic after another. For if they did that, an old woman in black could leave the shadow of a villa's portico, enter the sunlight, and begin walking and keep walking, thinking of the grandson she had loved and missed so very much, and might have again, if only for the briefest moment, in the moon-faced boy she was about to meet.

HIT

I'm given the assignment by an angel — I mean that, an angel — one wearing a high-end Armani suit with an Ermenegildo Zegna tie. A loud red one. Why red? To project confidence? Hell, I don't know. I'm having lunch at Parlami's, a mediocre bistro on Melrose where I met my first ex, when in he walks with what looks like a musical instrument case — French horn or tiny tuba, I'm thinking — and sits down. We do the usual disbelief dialogue from the movies: He announces he's an angel. I say, "You're kidding." He says, "No. Really." I ask for proof. He says, "Look at my eyes," and I do. His pupils are missing. "So?" I say. "That's easy with contacts." So he makes the butter melt on the plate just by looking at it, and I say, "Any demon could do that." He says, "Sure, but let's cut the bullshit, Anthony. God's got something He wants you to do, and if you'll take the job, He'll forgive everything." I shrug and tell him, "Okay, okay. I believe. Now what?" Everyone wants to be forgiven, and it's already sounding like any other contract.

He reaches for the case, opens it right there (no one's watching — not even the two undercover narcs — the angel makes sure of that) and hands it to me. It's got a brand-new crossbow in it. Then he tells me what I need to do to be forgiven.

"God wants you to kill the oldest vampire."

"Why?" I ask and can see him fight to keep those pupilless eyes from rolling. Even angels feel boredom, contempt, things like that, I'm thinking, and that makes it all that more convincing.

"Because He can't do it."

"And why is that?" I'm getting braver. Maybe they do need me. I'm good — one of the three best repairmen west of Vegas, just like my sainted dad was — and maybe guys who say yes to things like this aren't all that common.

"Because the fellow — the oldest bloodsucker — is the son of...well, you know...."

"No, I don't."

"Does 'The Prince of Lies' ring a bell?"

"Oh." I'm quiet for a second. Then I get it. It's like the mob and the police back in my uncle's day in Jersey. You don't take out the don because then maybe they take out your chief.

I ask him if this is the reasoning.

The contempt drops a notch, but holds. "No, but close enough."

"And where do I do it?"

"The Vatican."

"The Holy City?"

"Yes."

"Big place, but doesn't have to be tricky." I'd killed men with a wide range of appliances — the angel knew that — and suddenly this wasn't sounding any trickier. Crossbow. Composite frame, wooden arrows — darts — whatever they're called. One to the heart. I'd seen enough movies and TV.

"Well," he says, "maybe. But most of the Jesuits there are vampires too."

"Oh."

"That's the bad news. The good news is they're pissed at him — the oldest vampire, I mean. They think he wants to turn mortal. He's taken up with some 28-year-old bambina who knows almost as many languages as he does — a Vatican interpreter — and they've got this place in Siena — Tuscany, no less — and he hasn't bitten her, and it's been making the Brothers, his great-great-great-grandchildren, nervous for about a month now. Handle it right and she just might help you even if they don't."

"You serious?"

"Yes."

"Why?"

"Because she wants to be one, too — she's very Euro-goth — you know the type — and he just won't bite her."

No, I don't know the type, but I say, "She's that vindictive?"

"What woman isn't?"

This sounds awfully sexist for an angel, but I don't argue. Maybe angels get dumped too.

"Does he really?" I ask.

"Does he really what?"

"Want to be mortal again."

"He never was mortal."

"He was born that way?"

The eyes—which suddenly have pupils now, majorly dark blue ones—are starting to roll again. "What do you think? Son of You-Know-Who—who's not exactly happy with the traditional wine and wafer thing, but likes the idea of blood and immortality."

"Makes sense," I say, eyeing the narcs, who are eyeing two Fairfax High girls, "but why does God need someone to kill him if he wants to flip?"

He takes a breath. What an idiot, the pupils say. "Remember when China tried to give Taiwan a pair of pandas?"

I'm impressed. This guy's up on earthly news. "No."

"Taiwan couldn't take them."

"Why not?"

He takes another breath and I hear him counting to ten.

"Okay, okay," I say. "I get it. If they took the pandas, they were in bed with China. They'd have to make nice with them. You accept cute cuddly creatures from someone and it looks like love, right?"

"Basically."

"If You-Know-Who's son flips—goes mortal—God has to accept him."

"Right."

"And that throws everything off. No balance. No order. Chaos and eventually, well, Hell?"

The angel nods, grateful, I can tell, that I'm no stupider than I am.

I think for a moment.

"How many arrows do I get?"

I think he'll laugh, but he doesn't.

"Three."

"Three?" I don't like the feeling suddenly. It's like some Bible story where the guy gets screwed so that God can make some point about fatherly love or other form of sacrifice. Nice for God's message. Bad for the guy.

"It's a holy number," he adds.

"I get that," I say, "but I don't think so. Not three."

"That's all you get."

"What makes you think three will do it—even if they're all heart shots?"

"You only need one."

The bad feeling jumps a notch.

"Why?"

He looks at me and blinks. Then nods. "Well, each has a point made from a piece of the Cross, Mr. Pagano. We were lucky to get even that much. It's hidden under three floors and four tons of tile in Jerusalem, you know."

"What is?"

"The Cross. You know which one."

I blink. "Right. That's the last thing he needs in the heart."

"Right."

"So all I've got to do is hit the right spot."

"Yes."

"Which means I need practice. How much time do I have?"

"A week."

I take a breath. "I'm assuming you—and He—know a few good crossbow schools, ones with weekly rates."

"We've got special tutors for that."

I'm afraid to ask. "And what do these tutors usually do?"

"Kill vampires."

"And you need me when you've got a team of them?"

"He'd spot them a mile away. They're his kids, you might say. He's been around 2000 years and he's had kids and his kids have had kids—in the way that they have them—you know, the biting and sucking thing—and they can sense each other a mile away. These kids—the ones working for us—are ones who've

112

come over. Know what I mean?"

"And they weren't enough to throw off the — the 'balance.'"

Now he laughs. "No, they're little fish. Know what I mean?"

I don't really, but I nod. He's beginning to sound like my other uncle — Gian Felice — the one from Teaneck, the one with adenoids. *Know what I mean?*

ℵ

I go home to my overpriced stucco shack in Sherman Oaks and to my girlfriend, who's got cheekbones like a runway model and lips that make men beg, but wears enough lipstick to stop a truck, and in any case is sick and tired of what I do for a living and probably has a right to be. I should know something besides killing people, even if they're people the police don't mind having dead and I'm as good at it as my father wanted me to be. It's too easy making excuses. Like a pool hustler who never leaves the back room. You start to think it's the whole world.

She can tell from my face that I've had one of those meetings. She shakes her head and says, "How much?"

"I'm doing it for free."

'No, Anthony, you're not.'

"I am."

"Are you trying to get me to go to bed with your brother? He'd like that. Or Aaron, that guy at the gym? Or do you just want me to go live with my sister?"

She can be a real harpy.

"No," I tell her, and mean it.

"You must really hate me."

"I don't hate you, Mandy. I wouldn't put up with your temper tantrums if I hated you." The words are starting to hurt — the ones she's using and the ones I'm using. I do love her, I'm telling myself. I wouldn't live with her if I didn't love her, would I?

"And I live on what while you're away, Anthony?"

"I'll sell the XKE?"

"To who?"

"My cousin. He wants it. He's wanted it for years."

She looks at me for a moment and I see a flicker of—kindness. "You in trouble?"

"No."

"Then you're lying or you're crazy but anyway it comes down to the same thing: You don't love me. If you did, you'd take care of me. I'm moving out tomorrow, Anthony Pagano, and I'm taking the Jag."

"Please...."

"If you'll charge."

"I can't."

"You are in trouble."

"No."

How do you tell her you've got to kill a man who isn't really a man but wants to be one, and that if you do God will forgive you all the other killings?

She heads to the bedroom to start packing.

I get the case out, open it, touch the marblized surface of the thing, and hope to hell that God wants a horny assassin because I'm certainly not seeing any action this night or any other before I leave for Rome, and action does help steady my finger. Which Mandy knows. Which every woman I've ever been with knows.

When I get up the next morning, she's gone. The note on the bathroom mirror, in slashes of that lipstick of hers, says, "I hope you miss my body so bad you can't walk or shoot straight, Anthony."

ॐ

We do the instruction at a dead-grass firing range in Topanga Canyon. My tutor is a no-nonsense kid—maybe 20—with Chinese characters tattooed around his neck like a dog collar, naked eyebrows, pierced tongue, nose, lower lip. He's serious and strict, but seems happy enough for a vampire killer. He picks me up in his Tundra and on the way to the canyon, three manikins (that holy number) bouncing in the truck bed, he says, "Yeah, I like it — even if it's not what you'd think from a BUFFY re-run or a John Carpenter flick — you know, like that one shot in Mexico. More like CSI — not the Bruckheimer, but the Discovery Channel. Same way that being an investigative journalist isn't as much fun as you think it'll be — at least that's what I hear. All those hours Googling the public record. In my line of work, it's the tracking and casing and light-weapons prep. But you know more about that than I do, Mr. Pagano. Wasn't your dad — "

"Sounds like you've been to college, Kurt," I say.

"A year at a community college — that's it. But I'm a reader. Always have been."

How do you answer that? I've read maybe a dozen books in my life, all of them short and necessary, and I'm sitting with this kid who reads probably three fat ones a week. Not only is he more literate than I am, he's going to teach *me* how to kill — something I really thought I knew how to do.

"Don't worry," he says. "You'll pick it up. Your — shall we say 'previous training and experience' — should make up for your age, slower reflexes, *you* know."

What can I say? I've got fifteen years on him and we both know it. My reflexes *are* slower than his.

As we hit the Ventura Freeway, he tells me what I'm packing. "In the case beside you, Mr. Pagano, you've got a Horton Legend HD with a Talon Ultra-Light trigger, DP2 CamoTuff limbs, SpeedMax riser, alloy cams, Microflight arrow groove, and Dial-a-Range trajectory compensator — with LS MX aluminum arrows and Hunter Elite 3-arrow quivers. How does that make you feel?"

"Just wonderful," I tell him.

The firing range is upscale and very hip. There are dozens of trophy wives and starlets wearing $300 Scala baseball caps, newsboy caps, and sun visors. There are almost as many very metro guys wearing $600 aviator shades and designer jungle cammies. And all of them are learning Personal Protection under the tutelage of guys who are about as savvy about what they're doing as the ordinary gym trainer. They're all trying their best to hit fancy bullseye, GAG, PMT and other tactical targets made for pros, but I'm looking like an even bigger idiot trying to hit, with my handfuls of little crossbow darts, the manikins the kid has lined up for me at 50 yards. The other shooters keep rubbernecking to get a look at us. The kid stares them down and they look away. If they only knew.

"Do the arrows made from the other material—" I begin. "Do they—uh—act…?" I ask.

"Arrows with wood made from the Cross act the same," the kid says, very professional. "We balance them the way we'd balance any arrow."

"When it hits—"

"When it hits a vampire, I'm sure it doesn't feel like ordinary wood. I've never taken one myself."

"Glad to hear it."

"Actually, someone did try an arrow once. Deer bow. Two inches off the mark. I've got a scar. Want to see it?"

"Not really. How would it feel to *us*?"

"You mean mortals?"

"Right."

"It would probably hurt like hell, and if you happened to die I doubt it would get you a free pass to Heaven."

"That's too bad."

"Isn't it."

When I've filled the manikins with ten quivers' worth of arrows and my heart-shot rate is a sad 10%, we quit for the day. It's getting close to sunset, one of those gorgeous smoggy ones. The other shooters have hit the road in their Escalades, H3s, and Land Sharks and the kid is acting distracted.

"Date?"

"What?"

"You know. Two people. Dinner and a movie. Clubbing. Whatever."

"You could say that. But it's a threesome. Can't stand the guy—he's a Red-State crewcut ex-Delta-Forcer—but the girl, she's so hot she'll melt your belt buckle."

He can tell I'm not following.

116

"A job. It'll take the three of us about three hours. You know, holy number."

"Yeah, I know."

"Two Hollywood producers. Both vampires. They've got two very sexy, very cool low-budget vampire flicks—ones where the vampires win because, hey, if you're cool and sexy you should win, right?—in post-production, two more in production and three in development. These flicks will seduce too many teens to the Dark Side, He says, so He wants us to take out their makers. They'll be having late poolside dinner at Blue-on-Blue tonight. We'll be interrupting it."

"I see," I say. I'm staring at him and he beats me to it.

"You want to know what we eat if we can't drink blood."

"Yes, I do."

"We eat what you eat. We don't need blood since we came over."

"Which means you don't—how to put it?—you don't perpetuate the species."

"Right."

"Which can't make the elders very happy."

"No, it can't."

ॐ

By the end of the sixth day my heart-shot rate is 80% and the kid's nodding, doing a dance move or two in his tight black jeans, and saying "You're the man, Anthony. You're the man." I shouldn't admit it, but what he thinks does matter.

When I get there, courtesy of Alitalia (the angel won't pay for Luftansa), the city of Siena, in lovely Tuscany, country of my forefathers, is a mess. It's just after the horserace, the one where a dozen riders—each of them repping a neighborhood known for an animal (snail, dolphin, goose—you get the picture)—beat each other silly with little riding crops to impress their local Madonna. There's trash everywhere. I've got the crossbow in its case, and a kid on a Vespa tries to grab it as he sails by, but I'm ready. I know kids — I was one once — and I nail him with a kick to his knee. The Vespa skids and he flies into a fountain not far away. The fountain is a big sea shell — a scallop — which I know from reading my *Fodor's* must be this neighborhood's emblem for the race. He gets up crying, gives me the *va-funcu* with his arm and fist, and screams something in native Sienese — which isn't at all the Italian I grew up with but which I'm sure means, "I'm going to tell my dad and brothers, you asshole!"

The apartment is not in the Neighborhood of the Scallop, but in the Neighborhood of the Salmon, and the girl who answers the door is stunning. Tall. The kind of blonde who tans better than a commercial. Eyes like shattered glass, long legs, cute little dimple in her chin. I don't see how he can keep his teeth off her.

This is Euro-goth? I don't think so.

"So you're the one," she says. Her English is perfect, just enough accent to make it sexy.

"Yeah. Anthony Pagano." I stick out my hand. She doesn't take it.

"Giovanna," she says. "Giovanna Musetti. And that's what you're going to do it with?" She gestures with her head at my case. She can't take her eyes off it.

"Yeah."

"*Please don't do it,*" she says suddenly.

I don't know what to say.

"You're supposed to want him dead."

She looks at me like I'm crazy.

"Why would I want him dead?"

"Because you want him to bite you — because you want to be one too — and he — he won't oblige."

"Who told you that?"

"The — the angel who hired me."

"I know that angel. He was here. He interviewed me."

"You don't want him dead?"

"Of course not. I love him."

ৰ

I sit down on the sofa. They've got a nice place. Maybe they enjoy the horseraces. Even if they don't, the tourists aren't so bad off-season according to *Fodor's*. And maybe when you're the oldest vampire, you don't have to obey the no-daylight rule. Maybe you get to walk around in the day — in a nice, clean, modern medieval city — maybe one you knew when you were only a thousand years old and it was being built and a lot trashier — and feel pretty mortal and normal. Who knows?

"Why did my employer get it wrong?"

She's got the same look the angel did. "The angel didn't get it wrong, Mr. Pagano. He *lied*."

"Why?" I'm thinking: *Angels are allowed to do that? Lie? Sure, if God wants them to.*

"Why?" I ask again.

"I don't know. That's one of the things I love about Frank—"

"Your man's name is Frank?"

"It is now. That's what he's gone by for the last hundred years, he says, and I believe him. That's one of the things I love."

"What?"

"That he doesn't lie. That he doesn't need to. He's seen it all. He's had all the power you could want and he doesn't want it anymore. He's bitten so many people he lost count after a century, and he doesn't want to do it anymore. He's tired of living the lie any vampire has to live. He's very human in his heart, Mr. Pagano — in his soul — so human you wouldn't believe it — and he's tired of doing his father's bidding, the darkness, the blasphemy, all of that. I don't think he was ever really into it, but he had to do it. He was his father's son, so he had to do it. Carry on the tradition — the business. Do you know what that's like?"

"Yes. I do."

I'm starting to like her, of course — really like her. She's great eye candy, but it isn't just that. The more she talks, the more I like what's inside. She understands — she understands the mortal human heart.

"But I'm supposed to kill him," I say.

"Why?"

"Because of — because of 'balance.'"

"What?"

"That's what my employer said. Even though Frank wants to flip, and you'd think that would be a plus, it wouldn't be. It would throw things off."

"You really believe that, Anthony?"

Now we're on first-name basis, and I don't mind.

I don't say a thing for a second.

"I don't know."

"It sounds wrong, doesn't it."

"Yeah, it does."

We sit silent for a while. I'm looking at her hard, too interested, so I make myself look away.

"Do I make you self-conscious?" she asks gently.

That turns me red. "It's not you. It's me. You look awfully good. It's just me."

"That's sweet." Now she's doing the looking away, cheeks a little red, and when she looks backs, she says, "Any idea why God would *really* want him killed?"

"None whatsoever."

"But you've still got to do it."

"There was this promise."

"I know."

"You do?"

"Sure. If you do it, He'll forgive everything. They offered me that too if I helped you."

"And you said no?"

"Yes."

She loves this guy — this vampire — this son of You-Know-Who — so much she'll turn down an offer like that? Now I'm *really* looking at her. She's not just beautiful, she's got *coglioni*. She'll stand up to God for love.

I'm thinking these things and also wondering whether the angel lied about her because maybe she stiffed him. Because *he's* the vindictive one.

"There's nothing I can say to stop you?" she's asking. She

doesn't say "nothing I can *do*." She says "nothing I can *say*," and that's all the difference in the world.

"Wish there were, but there isn't. Where is he?"

"You know."

"Yeah, I guess I do. He's in the Vatican somewhere trying to convince those Jesuit vampires that it's okay if he turns."

"That's where he said he was going when he left a week ago, so I'm sure it's true. Like I said, he—"

"Never lies. I know."

I get up.

"I'm sorry."

"Me too."

I'm depressed when I get to Rome and not because the city is big and noisy and feels like LA. (My dad's people were from Calabria and they never had a good thing to say about *Romani*, so I'm biased.) It's because—well, just because. But when I reach the Vatican, I feel a lot better. Now this—this is beautiful. St. Peter's. The church, the square, marble everywhere, sunlight blinding you like the flashight of God. Even the silly little Fiats going round and round the circle like they're trapped and can't get off are nice.

He's not going to be in the basilica, I know. That's where the Pope is—that new strict guy, Benedict—and it's visiting day, dispensations, blessings, the rest. I don't even try to go through the main Vatican doorway on the opposite side. Too many tourists there, too. Instead I go to a side entrance, Via Gerini, where there's no one. Construction cones, sidewalk repair, a big door with carvings on it. Why this entrance, I don't know. Just a hunch.

I know God can open any door for me that He wants to, so if my hunch is right why isn't the door opening? Maybe there'll be a mark on the right door—you know, a shadow that looks like the face of Our Lady, or the number 333, something—but before I can check the door for a sign, something starts flapping above my head and scares the shit out of me. I think it's a bat at first—that would make sense—but it's just a pigeon. No, a dove.

Doves are smaller and pigeons aren't this white.

I know my employer thinks I'm slow, but a *white dove*?

The idiot bird keeps flapping two feet from my head and now I see it—a twig of something in its beak. I don't want to know.

The bird flies off, stops, hovers, and waits. I'm supposed to follow, so I do.

The door it's stopped at is the third one down from mine, of course. No face of Our Lady on it, but when I step up to it, it of course clicks and swings open.

We go through the next doorway, and the next, and the next, seven doorways in all—from a library to a little museum, then another library, then an office, then an archive with messy files, then a bigger museum. Some of the rooms are empty—of people, I mean—and some aren't, and when they're not, the people, some in suits and dresses and some in clerical outfits—give me a look like, "Well, he certainly seems to know where he's going with his musical instrument. Perhaps they're having chamber music with *espresso* for *gli ufficiali*. And of course that can't really be a pure white dove with an olive twig in its beak flapping in front of him, so everything's just fine. *Buon giorno, Signore*."

When the bird stops for good, hovering madly, it's a really big door and it doesn't open right off. But I know this is it—that my guy is on the other side. Whatever he's doing, he's there and I'd better get ready. He's a vampire. Maybe he's confused—maybe he doesn't want to be one any longer—but he's still got, according to the angel, superhuman strength and super-senses and the rest.

When the door opens—without the slightest sound, I note—I'm looking down this spiral staircase into a gorgeous little chapel. Sunlight is coming through the stained glass windows, so there's got to be a courtyard or something just outside, and the frescoes on the ceiling look like real Michelangelos. Big muscles. Those steroid bodies.

The bird has flown to the ceiling and is perched on a balustrade, waiting for the big event, but that's not how I know the guy I'm looking down at is Frank. It isn't even that he's got that distinguished-gentleman look that old vampires have in the movies. It's what he's doing that tells me.

He's kneeling in front of the altar, in front of this big golden crucifix with an especially bloody Jesus, and he's very uncomfortable doing it. Even at this distance I can tell he's shaking. He's got his hands out in prayer and can barely keep them together. He's jerking like he's being electrocuted. He's got his eyes on the crucifix, and when he speaks, it's loud and his voice jerks too. It sounds confessional — the tone is right — but it's not English and it's not Italian. It may not even be Latin, and why should it be? He's been around a long time and probably knows the original.

I'm thinking the stained-glass light is playing tricks on me, but it's not. There really *is* a blue light moving around his hands, his face, his pants legs — blue fire — and this, I see now, it's what's making him jerk.

He's got to be in pain. I mean, here in a chapel — in front of an altar — sunlight coming through the windows — making about the biggest confession any guy has ever made. Painful as hell, but he's doing it, and suddenly I know why she loves him. Hell, *anyone* would.

Without knowing it I've unpacked my crossbow and have it up and ready. This is what God wants, so I probably get some help doing it. I'm shaking too, but go ahead and aim the thing. *I need forgiveness, too, you know*, I want to tell him. You can't bank your immortal soul, no, but you do get to spend it a lot longer.

I put my finger on the trigger, but don't pull it yet. I want to keep thinking.

No, I don't. I don't want to keep thinking at all.

I lower the crossbow and the moment I do I hear a sound from the back of the chapel where the main door's got to be, and I crane my neck to see.

It's the main door all right. Heads are peeking in. They're wearing black and I think to myself: *Curious priests. That's all.* But the door opens up more and three of them — that holy number —

step in real quiet. They're wearing funny Jesuit collars — the ones the angel mentioned — and they don't look curious. They look like they know exactly what they're doing, and they look very unhappy.

Vampires have this sixth sense, I know. One of them looks up at me suddenly, smiles this funny smile, and I see sharp little teeth.

He says something to the other two and heads toward me. When he's halfway up the staircase I shoot him. I must have my heart in it because the arrow nearly goes through him, but that's not what really bothers him. It's the *wood*. There's an explosion of sparks, the same blue fire, and a hole opens up in his chest, grows, and in no time at all he's just not there anymore.

Frank has turned around to look, but he's dazed, all that confessing, hands in prayer position and shaking wildly, and he obviously doesn't get what's happening. The other two Jesuits are heading up the stairs now, and I nail them with my last two arrows.

The dove has dropped like a stone from its perch and is flapping hysterically in front of me, like *Wrong vampires! Wrong vampires!* I'm tired of its flapping, so I brush it away, turn and leave, and if it takes me (which it will) a whole day to get out of the Vatican without that dove to lead me and make doors open magically, okay. When you're really depressed, it's hard to give a shit about anything.

ॐ

Two days later I'm back at Parlami's. I haven't showered. I look like hell. I've still got the case with me. God knows why.

I've had two martinis and when I look up, there he is. I'm not surprised, but I sigh anyway. I'm not looking forward to this.

"So you didn't do it," he says.

"You know I didn't, asshole."

"Yes, I do. Word does get out when the spiritual configuration of the universe doesn't shift the way He'd like it to."

I want to hit his baby-smooth face, his perfect nose and

124

collagen lips, but I don't have the energy.

"So what happens now?" I ask.

"You really don't know?"

"No."

He shakes his head. Same look of contempt.

"I guess you wouldn't."

He takes a deep breath.

"Well, the Jesuits did it for you. They killed him last night."

"What?"

"They've got crossbows too. Where do you think we got the idea?"

"Same wood?"

"Of course. They handle it with special gloves."

"*Why?*"

"Why kill him? Same line of thought. If he flips, things get thrown off balance. Order is important for them, too, you know. Mortals are the same way, you may have noticed. You all need order. Throw things off and you go crazy. That's why you'll put up with despots—even choose them over more benign and loving leaders—just so you don't have to worry. Disorder makes for a lot of worry, Anthony."

"You already knew it?"

"Knew what?"

"That I wouldn't do it and the Jesuits would instead."

"Yes."

"Then why send me?"

Again the look, the sigh. "Ah. Think hard."

I do, and, miracle of miracles, I see it.

"Giovanna is free now," I say.

"Yes. Frank, bless his immortal soul—which God has indeed agreed to do—is gone in flesh."

"So He wants me to hook up with her?"

The angel nods. "Of course."

"Why?"

"Because she'll love you—*really* love you, innocent that you are—just the way she loved him."

"That's it?"

"Not exactly.... Because she'll love you, you'll have to stop. You'll have to stop killing people, Anthony. It's just not right."

"No, I won't."

"Yes, you will."

"Don't think so."

"But you will—because, whether you know it yet or not, you love her, too."

What do you say to that?

The angel's gotten up, straightened his red Zegna, picked up the case, and is ready to leave.

"By the way," he adds, "He says He forgives you anyway."

I nod, tired as hell. "I figured that."

"You're catching on."

"About time," I say.

"He said that too."

"And the whole 'balance' thing—"

"What do *you* think?"

Pure bullshit is what I'm thinking.

"You got it," he says, reading my mind because angels can do that.

Twenty-four hours later I'm back in Siena, shaved and showered, and she doesn't seem surprised to see me. She's been grieving—that's obvious. Red eyes. Perfect hair tussled, a mess. She's been debriefed by the angel—that I can tell—and I don't know whether she's got a problem with The Plan or not, or even whether there is a Plan. The angel may have been lying about that too. But when she says quietly, "Hello, Anthony," and gives me a shy smile, I *know*—and my heart starts flapping like that idiot bird.

126

BRINGING THEM BACK

When I was in the fifth grade, I loved snakes, lizards, frogs, and turtles. I was "obsessed" with them, or so my teachers put it. And because we were a military family, we moved a lot, and I saw many kinds.

I loved them so much I caught as many as I could, kept them in my bedroom in wire cages and aquariums, fed them tenderly, and stared at them with wonder. They were miracles. I remember thinking that—how they were "miracles"—even at nine and ten. I wanted them near me, their magic, their miracle.

I had to let them go after a while, of course. I knew that was the right thing to do. They would get sick and die if I didn't, and that would be horrible. So I did it even if I didn't want to. I let them go and then caught others. But I would hold onto those I released in a special way—so that they would return to me.

I would take a simple book like *Hammond's Nature Atlas* or *A Field Guide to Western Reptiles* and on my father's portable typewriter—which I learned to use by hunt and peck (which was slow, but I didn't mind)—type out on small sheets of colored tracing paper the descriptions I found in those books of the animals I loved. I would leave the top half of each sheet empty. There I would trace from the book a picture of the snake, lizard, frog, or turtle.

Even this was magic—the typing and drawing—because, when I stared at the sheet of paper, the animal was there. It was in my room again. It had come back. It lived again, because, in my love for it, I had brought it to life through this magic— the paper and pencil and words and the dance of my fingers on a machine.

THE COMMON TOAD

This common inhabitant of the American East may not be pretty, with its many warts of various sizes; its roughly tubercular arms and hands, legs and feet; its dark spots and dirty olive-colored skin; and its protruding eyes. But it is a most useful collaborator of man.

COMMON WATER SNAKE

Most people chase it or beat it to death when they find it hanging on a tree branch over a pond, calling it "a poisonous water moccasin." But this reddish snake banded by dark brown stripes in front and by blotches on its posterior body, is non-poisonous, harmless, and shy, though feisty when cornered.

I loved birds, too, but never caught them because I was afraid I might break their wings. But I typed and traced on colored paper so that I might have them in this way.

Bringing Them Back

RUBY-THROATED HUMMINGBIRD

This tiny bird weighs only as much as a copper cent, and half a silver dollar will cover its neat little nest that is built of plant down and lichen, spider webs, and silver threads. Its flying capacities are astonishing, its wings vibrating so rapidly that all you can see is a blur and hear the humming sound that gives it its name.

I still have my father's typewriter. I get it out in my little house, which is far from any city. It's time. I need to bring them back—the creatures I loved when I was a kid...and many more I didn't even know about then.

On green tracing paper—which catches easily in the roller, so I have to be careful—I type "THE COMMON TOAD" and the same description I typed when I was ten. But I add at the end "Last seen in the wild: 2035. Last specimen in captivity: 2047."

The amphibian populations, stressed by fungus and other factors, began to disappear early in the century. Total collapse of the amphibian class occurred three decades later, and with inevitable reverberations in classes like *reptilia, aves, arthopoda,* and *mammalia.* This was not, I taught my students in high school, only because of habitat loss, but also—and even more importantly—because of old and new, constantly changing diseases in all animal classes.

When the classes began to collapse, one after the other, it had a snowball effect, geometric, algorithmic, impossible to stop.

I trace the same picture, from the same book—which I've kept, of course—but do it better because I'm older now.

On red tracing paper I type "RUBY-THROATED HUMMINGBIRD" and use the same description I used as a child, but I add "Last seen in the wild 2042. Last specimen in captivity 2053."

The viruses that targeted larger mammals, and not humans at first, took the megafauna in fifteen years. It was going to be a mass extinction of Permian-Jurassic and K-Pg dimensions — we all felt this — so this is what I taught my students, too.

On yellow tracing paper — which is like a sunny African daydream I've had more than once in my life — I type from another book and change what needs to be changed in the text:

THE LION

The Lion (Panthera leo) was one of the five big cats in the genus Panthera and a member of the family Felidae. The commonly used term "African lion" collectively denoted the several subspecies found in Africa. With some males exceeding 250 kg (550 lb) in weight,[4] it was the second-largest living cat after the tiger.

Then I trace it, doing my best because it's important, and because I fill it in, it looks pretty good.

On gray paper I type, making changes too:

Bringing Them Back

THE ELEPHANT

The Elephant was a large mammal of the family Elephantidae *and the order* Proboscidea. *Two species were traditionally recognized, the African elephant* (Loxodonta africana) *and the Asian elephant* (Elephas maximus), *although some evidence suggested that African bush elephants and African forest elephants were separate species (*L. africana *and* L. cyclotis *respectively). The Elephant was scattered throughout sub-Saharan Africa, South Asia, and Southeast Asia.*

I'm happy with this one, too. I'm getting better.

Domesticated animals died in the extinctions, of course. The viruses evolved quickly, as viruses do, built up resistances, found the most protected places in living bodies to thrive in, and replicated. That's what these epidemic and pandemic retroviruses — with their new "envelopes," their ways of handling genetic replication — are so brilliant at. I remember the terrier my brother and I had when I was twelve. His name was Billy. I type:

FOX TERRIER

The Fox Terrier is one of the most curious, intense, and impulsive of the terriers – indeed of all breeds. Untiringly active and playful, it has a special passion for ball chasing – which really helps with exercise – and it seldom walks when it can run.

It isn't him, but it's the same breed, and I trace the picture from a children's book I didn't have when I was a kid – but one my children had because I bought it for them, old-fashioned though books were.

I take a photograph from a frame. Of my wife. I type this description:

Deborah was a woman who loved flowers, but she loved everything, and especially us.

I do a terrible job of tracing it. I keep what I've done – I have to – but I don't look at it.

I take from a scrapbook photographs of our two children, Charlotte and Michael, and on bright blue paper – our daughter's favorite color – I type:

CHARLOTTE

She was a bright star. She lived for twelve years, and each year was a joy for all who knew her.

It's hard to concentrate on her photograph. I'm not doing it well. Then I type:

Bringing Them Back

MICHAEL

He was as curious as a child as I was, and that made me happy. There wasn't anything that didn't fill him with wonder.

He was more handsome than this — I've done a terrible job with his face — but it brings him back.

I would go to my computer for what I need now, for the last piece of it, but the computer isn't working. Nothing is, just the candles at night, the can openers during the day, and the well — the one my great-grandfather dug.

I must go to another old book. On lavender — Deborah's favorite color — I type:

HOMO SAPIENS

Modern humans (Homo sapiens or Homo sapiens sapiens) are the only extant members of the hominin clade, a branch of great apes characterized by erect posture and bipedal locomotion; manual dexterity and increased tool use; and a general trend toward larger, more complex brains and societies. Humans have created complex social structures composed of many cooperating and competing groups, from families and kinship networks to states. Social interactions between humans have established an extremely wide variety of values, social norms, and rituals, which together have formed the basis of human society. The human desire to understand and influence its environment, and explain and manipulate phenomena, is the foundation for the development of human science, philosophy, mythology, and religion.

I add because I have to:

(This species is nearing extinction.)

Instead of using a picture from the book—Cro-Magnon man or the drawing of a naked man and woman sent out into space a century ago—I get dressed in an old jacket, wear the hat that Deborah said made me look jaunty, and look in a mirror. I keep my glasses on. The face looking back isn't smiling. It takes me two hours to draw what I see—many drafts, which I ball up and throw away—but here is what I end with because it just might matter:

I stop and wait. I wait for it all to come back.

THE VOICE

It's not my business to meddle in something like this. I'm an in-house corporate auditor, not a physical guy. I'm not a field operative. I don't confront people. I don't break into facilities, but the *voice* keeps whispering. It whispers in the day. It whispers in the night. It's been whispering for weeks now, ever since I found the files on the Financial Division's system, and I'm sleeping less and less. Sleep deprivation is not a good thing. It can make you imagine things.

The voice whispers: *Come to me, Jude. Do what you didn't do for him — your father.*

The voice knows me well. It knows the pain.

I should be scared — not for my sanity, that I might be hallucinating, but that a voice like this one might indeed be real, belonging to another mind out there and yet visiting mine day and night — but I'm not. Of course, this may be the very thing it *wants* — that I not be afraid, not resist its call to find it — and so, just as it makes me hear it, it makes me feel what it wants me to feel: *unafraid*.

This may indeed be insanity, but it doesn't feel like it. It feels real, like the miracles, sometimes fantastic, that life itself gives us — the second chances — if we will only recognize them and take those second chances.

Because it whispers, because it pleads, I stand in a darkened wing of the city's aquarium, closed for remodeling, and, so local media report, for the installation of new exhibits, with new creatures, some of them bio-engineered, some not. It is night. The building is closed, but I found an open door. I have snuck past three out-of-shape, ill-trained guards, and it was easy, the voice helping me by its whispers to know where to go, even perhaps helping the guards, by whispers, too, to be somewhere else and chatting, not listening for someone who might be moving through this wing.

The water before me, behind a fifteen-foot wall of clearest acrylic, is barely lit. The fish are shadows, barely moving. The dark forest of kelp is still.

The creature hanging in the water before me, taller than any man, floats like wet cloth, its arms stretched out and unmoving, like someone's dream of Christ.

I am glad I can't see the face, and it knows I am glad. It knows everything — or that's how it feels, true or not. It knew I would come if it whispered long enough, and it knew *why* — the soulful eyes, ones I once knew so well, that rise every night in memory, pleading with me.

You've come, Jude, the voice says suddenly. *You haven't abandoned me after all.*

Its jaw, a hole in the night, opens — huge, able to do terrible things with what lies within it — and the voice speaks again without words moving through water or air. *You've come, Jude.*

This is the fourth time I've stood before it. I know what I must do now.

༅

It was the kind of stupidity that can bring down a company. There was a file with the long list of losses to be taken on the "mistakes" — the genetically engineered bioproducts that hadn't worked out and that my company, DreamPet and its subsidiaries, could write off. But someone had, in another file, one encrypted with an old key, used the product codes from that first file, and that second file was a list of sales. Bio-products that had been sold. There were no sales figures, just the list, but anyone with half a brain would realize the bio-products were being written off for design flaws and "unacceptable mortality projections," *and* they were also being sold. The second file also listed, with no secondary encryption, the buyers where the bioproducts had gone; and the P-chain payment anonymity was sloppy. I'd been able to identify fifty of the buyers. One of them was local, and I knew it well.

And there was this: I could tell the executives in Financial, including the CFO, and possibly the CEO, were making more money than they should be. They had smart retro Stutz Blackhawks, self-driving Lambo 700s, and AI-managed superyachts with tenders and aqua-toys bigger than most powerboats. I just didn't know how they were doing it exactly or how far up it went; and I couldn't go to anyone above Financial or the CEO, if he was involved, until I did. How much could you get from the right buyer for a bio-product mistake under a state and federal disposal order? Not as much as a perfect bio-product, but a decent amount. People will buy anything if they feel justified.

The city aquarium where I'd taken my son and daughter two weeks before—before it closed for remodeling—was on that buyer list. It was a good aquarium, or had been once, but attendance had been shrinking because of the bigger aquarium forty minutes up the 405 with its immersive jellies, problem-solving cephalopods, and pressurized "Creatures from the Deep," and because of LA's glorious hologram zoo, which had replaced its live-animal exhibits decades ago.

You couldn't use wild or captive-bred megafauna anymore—larger mammals or even sharks and mantas—because of state and federal laws; but you could use bioengineered ones. They were expensive; but if you could get ones with flaws, ones that should be put down for a spreadsheet loss, you could avoid the expense and stay in the black. If the inspectors from the USDA's Biological Design and Disposal division came, you hid the creatures or bought the inspectors off or, better yet, did both. It happened regularly in the worlds of building inspection, contracting and zoning, so why not the brave new world of megafauna bio-products? Low-level corruption was in the human DNA, even in first-world countries, even where inspectors were paid a livable wage. Human nature and the fear of a zero-sum game. To be afraid of not having enough.

You also couldn't use the human DNA code that differentiated us from other primates. That was a worse felony. You had to stick to the shared DNA, the common primate code. Better yet — if you didn't want inspectors really taking a close look — you needed to use "lesser simian."

What was it exactly that our city's aquarium had bought?

ॐ

The first time I visited the wing, I came home late to find my wife and our kids still up, sitting on the sofa. Cassia, dressed for after-work yoga, was worried about me — where had I been? — and August, who was eight, and Birdie, who was four, had picked up on her worry and wouldn't leave her side. Their pajamas looked innocent, free of fear, but their faces said something else.

"August fed Thor," Cassia said, staring at me. I knew he had. He loved the threefoot Iguana Rex, a DreamPet product, that lived in a terrarium in his room, scales a glaring fluorescent green and its voice engineered to sound like a tiny tyrannosaurus.

I nodded and said quickly:
"Let's watch the nature channel."

Somewhere between wonder and boredom, nature shows always seemed to put them to sleep. Talking wouldn't do it. Sitting with their father, knowing he was okay, and their mother, feeling her calm, was better than words. Cassia knew what I was doing. We'd done it before — twice in our marriage. During Cassia's brief affair with that charismatic woman in her master's program, when we could barely speak to each other but didn't want the kids to be hurt in the way kids can be hurt by the tensions of an unspoken chasm and abyss in their parents' relationship. And later, when my father was dying and in incredible pain despite the medications, and I was feeling helpless, dying inside, but, like him, living on and on, and isn't that the real horror? That we keep breathing when those we love and who love us must die even if it takes years of knowing that we will, in the end, lose them?

I should have done more both times. Instead, I watched nature footage with my wife and kids.

"Yes," Cassia said. "Let's."

I spoke quickly to the house. It spoke back in the chipper voice Cassia had chosen for it, one not unlike her own, asking which channel from a list of ten we wanted to watch. Cassia chose—it didn't matter which—and I said, "The ocean—the wonderful ocean," and in an instant we were all watching seas we'd never been to and probably never would.

ৰ

When the kids had fallen asleep on the sofa, and I couldn't avoid Cassia's gaze anymore, I said, "I'm sorry. I couldn't get away."

"You could have called."

"You're right. I could have and should have, Cassia. You know how I get when Marc wants a report 'yesterday.' I get lost in it...."

"What's on your sleeve?" she asked.

I stopped breathing but kept smiling. There was plaster on my right sleeve, where I'd rubbed against drywall as I'd slipped into the aquarium past the guards. I stared at it for a moment.

"That should tell you what it's like there. Marc is having the offices remodeled. There's drywall and dust everywhere. Been like this for days."

"You didn't mention the remodeling before."

"I didn't?"

But it made sense, what I was saying, so she smiled and simply said, "Next time, please?"

"I promise. You married a void cadet, a numbers pilot. You deserve better, Cassia."

ॐ

I didn't go to the aquarium the next night. The voice had stopped whispering, and I was grateful for that. It knew I would come back, but that I needed to rest for a while. Hearing the voice, sneaking past the guards, heart hammering, hands shaking, wondering whether I'd be shot by a guard I'd missed seeing or, insanity taking me, I'd end admitted to a mental institution that same night—all of it had been tiring for a desk guy like me.

I will return, I promised.

I know, the voice answered, *and because you will, you will be free at last, Jude.*

It knows everything, this creature we have made.

So I got back at a reasonable time from work that day, felt a deep sigh move through me as I stepped through the door, and Cassia and the kids were chatting happily with the house. As soon as I came in, the kids ran up to me, jumping up and down. "Let's do it again!" August insisted. "Let's go to sleep watching *nature.*" He said the word as if it were very very special, as if it had a capital "n."

"Of course," I answered. Cassia was smiling, too, and Birdie was chanting "*Nature! Nature!*"

It was as if the previous night hadn't happened, or if it had, it had been as banal as my reason for lateness, and as banal as Cassia wanted it to be. If I were having an affair, which I'd never had, Cassia would feel it was her fault, something karmic she'd created for herself, and *that* she did not want to think about. Plaster on my sleeve didn't fit an affair anyway. Teenagers made out in unfinished houses; adults just didn't do that.

"Maybe *we* can fall asleep on the couch, too, Jude—from all that nature," Cassia said kindly.

We watched the porpoises, chimpanzees, elephants, and tigers, all that footage from decades ago—long before the extinctions and the cloning of mega-species for reintroductions that rarely worked, and certainly before the bio-engineering by

DreamPet and other mass and custom-engineered-pet companies. Kittens that never grew up, purple poodles whose color didn't wash out, custom-made songbirds with the initials of their owners genetically stitched into their breasts, singing their owners' favorite songs. And certainly before these companies began engineering brand new bio-products for zoos, aquariums, and private owners. A condor-sized "dragon," using bird and reptile stock, for a billionaire in Asia; all colors of unicorns for a children's zoo in Holland; and three controversial, wide-eyed "angels" (bird and simian stock) for a megachurch in Nebraska.

"Can we go to the aquarium?" August asked, and a generic aquarium appeared instantly, by triggered algorithm, on the walls around us. Just flat screens. We weren't a very "immersive" family.

"*Our* aquarium," August added, speaking to the house.

"*Our aquarium,*" the house echoed, adding, "Aquarium of the West, San Pedro, California."

I nodded for the benefit of the house, its cameras, but it already had the aquarium on the screens. The original Early Millennial architecture. What it would look like after the remodel. How it looked now, the closure, all of those shadows, tarps, tents, guards.

"Yes! Yes! Yes!" Birdie was saying, and Cassia was bouncing on the sofa with her, like a child, innocent.

"There's going to be a merman exhibit," Cassia said suddenly.

"Really...?" I answered. I stopped breathing but smiled.

"*Merman!*" Birdie echoed.

"I really want to see it, Dad — that merman," August was saying, eyes fixed on the screen, hoping the word "merman" would trigger at least an artist's rendering of the exhibit, but it didn't. Instead, the screens — as if the house didn't know what else to give us — were showing awful mermaid and merman art and then more extinct mammals — this time "spinner" porpoises turning like slow bullets above the waves just for the fun of it, and harbor porpoises or *vaquitas*, I couldn't tell which, splashing in the waves like children. Mammals as smart as we were. That had been proven. And telepathic. Research had shown that, too, by the end. Scientists hadn't been able to explain completely the communication-dependent behavior of cetaceans by the traditional models of acoustic or other-sense communication, and experiments controlling for the five senses, and for "cuing," had proved it: They knew things they shouldn't have known. They were using a kind of telepathy. And then the animals went extinct. Their DNA could be used for cloning, though there were laws restricting that, and for new, engineered creatures. But that was another matter.

ॐ

The second time I went, the voice woke me in the morning with the same request, and I prepared Cassia with lies: I'd be late again because in the re-modeling certain Financial computers — parts of the system, with the backups offline for the day too — had to be down, and I wouldn't be able to get the work done earlier. It was a favor to my boss, and he'd return it somehow, he promised. He'd always made good on his word, Cassia knew.

I'd return with plaster on my sleeve again, the other one this time. It would help.

ॐ

The voice was quiet this time. I stood in front of the dark aquarium, looking for fish and stingrays and other animal life living with the thing that hung before me, but there was nothing. It had to eat, I knew, but clearly it didn't, or couldn't, catch its own food.

Those jaws....

I could see particles of something drifting from them in the green, cloudy light of the tank. Was this food, remnants of it?

I stepped closer. The voice didn't stop me.

What do you want? I heard myself ask.

The outstretched arms didn't move. The hole of the jaws

142

didn't move. It didn't need to. The kelp just beyond it — a strange kind, not one I knew from California waters — swayed a little this time, the body with it.

The dim light was behind it. I couldn't see its features because of the backlighting, and it did want me to see them. I could feel it did.

But I didn't want to see. I wanted to go home. I'd left work two hours ago.

The voice didn't argue. It didn't say *Please stay*. It didn't say *Leave and I will destroy you as your guilt will in the end* — which is what I sometimes felt when it spoke, that it could, somehow, beyond the acrylic, even miles away, destroy me if it wanted to; that it could make me take my own life if it wanted to, knowing me so well.

I wanted to leave and yet I didn't, and it knew this, too.

I stepped closer, and, as I did, the creature turned its face so that the dim green light behind caught one side of it and I could see what I hadn't seen before.

Its eye was a great, browed hole, a green glint within it. The skin of its face was ragged, imperfect, not the sandy sleekness of a shark or what, like most of the body and some of the brain, it probably was — cetacean, porpoise. Patches of cheesy white — a fungus — grew on the skin, and the face twitched, as if the thing wanted to pull its arm in, the hand with it, and scratch, but could not. *I cannot scratch the imperfection I have been given* —

Was the voice talking to me, or was I just imagining how it felt? It wasn't words. It was something else, darker than the light I knew with my family, but whose darkness was it really?

I squinted. The face didn't move. The skin was sloughing off slowly in the water, from the whiteness, the necrotic tissue.

I looked away from the face, toward anything but the face. To the outstretched arms, but they were a lie as well:

One arm was shorter than the other, and the hand was like a claw, useless, the fingernails curved impossibly into the palm, growing into it like the teeth of rabbits unchecked. There was no blood. The nails had grown too slowly for that, but the hand, I could see, was shaking.

Do you understand? the voice asked suddenly — it was no whisper — and I jerked, stepped back, looked at its face again, which was backlit once more, and felt the pain.

༉

Was it from the nails or the jaws or the white fungus, or much much more? I wondered as I drove home. Because the jaws couldn't close? Couldn't chew? Was that why it was fed what it was fed, whatever had become particles of green light drifting from those jaws in the still water? Was it the dying tissue under the fungus, sloughing off and clouding the water, eating its way to the bone?

It was much more than all of that, I knew. It was its entire body, its being. *It wasn't supposed to be in this world.*

I had not looked at the legs, the tails. I couldn't bring myself to do it.

That night I dreamt of jaws big enough to swallow me, though they did not. They wanted me to do something.

༉

The third time I went I brought a flashlight with me. I was shaking, but now I did want to see it. Was this my own feeling or what the thing wanted? Both, perhaps. Every time, it was both, I think.

I stood before it in the silent, darkened wing, the guards elsewhere as always.

I waited for permission.

It raised its arm a little, as if to give it, and I looked at its legs at last. The two tails, patches of white sloughing off on them, too, stirred the water just enough to keep it upright. The voice said nothing.

I clicked the flashlight on, but kept the beam on the floor. I looked up and now the voice said clearly:

What are we if we cannot see, Jude?

א

I stayed a long time. I didn't want to use the flashlight, and yet I also did. I stopped breathing more than once as I stared.

Against the dim light that filled the great tank behind it, the dark blue creature hung in the water like — yes — a cross. Its eyes were white and blind — mistakes of DNA sequencing — upturned, without any need to look when thoughts could tell it who stood before it.

The dark gills, like tiny eels on its neck, moved as gills should move. Was it fish stock? Amphibian? Something engineered just for it? There were lungs, too. The chest was too big not to have them, and they would start working when the thing was in air, if it was ever allowed to be in air, and the gills would stop then.

Hair like the finest thread floated up from the head, too sparse on the skull to be decorative. A relic of the primate stock, not a desired design. The jaws — yes, the jaws — when I found the courage to shine the light there — were broken, or born that way, and unable to close completely. Savage teeth, sharper than any seal's, were scattered across gums as thick as hoses in a careless design, or an accident of birth, or of transportation. Did it matter in the end?

The claw-like hand, webbed, fingernails embedded in the palm, tried to unfurl and failed, tried again, and still failed. The immense chest at first seemed okay, but then I saw scales flaking from its pectoral muscles. Not just porpoise, but that fish stock again? There was no whiteness, no fungus, and yet scales were drifting one by one into water cloudy from algae, lack of oxygen, something.

Where were the feeders, the veterinarians, their assistants? Where were the tank's fish?

Had it cost so little, this creature, that you didn't want to spend staff salaries on it, but you also didn't want to dispose of it? Maybe its health would improve and you could show it to the public. Maybe it wouldn't, but why act prematurely?

There was no waist. The hips weren't even, one higher than

the other, one swollen, and below them, between the legs was no organ (you couldn't show such a thing to children, and it had no mate, so why bother?). There were wastes, and they had to leave the body somehow....

On its inner thighs, pale-blue and muscular—exactly what porpoise stock married to primate would provide—the whiteness of the fungus began again, and I could see the legs were trembling. The flesh was being eaten away in pain, and—

Neither arm could move, I saw then. Something had been done to them during or after its lab-gestation to this adult form that kept them outstretched. Why? Even if the jaws had worked, the hands couldn't have fed it. Why would you do that? Or was it, again, congenital?

What is it that you want me to do? I asked it at last, trembling too.

You know, Jude. You knew that day in Chino Hills, it said to me.

ঽ

My father died in a nursing home in Chino Hills, in and out of hospice, taking a long time to do it, and miserable every day. I told myself that love was keeping him alive. How could I not want this to be the truth? Everyone else in the family said the same, didn't they?

When he'd been hanging on month after month and beyond what any human body should have to manage, when the morphine no longer worked because sometimes you just can't stop pain when it's cycling, fueling itself, and the medication was making him scream at night anyway, he said to me:

"Kill me, Jude. Please. If you love me."

I was visiting him every day then, and every day he said it.

When I couldn't stand it any longer—when I knew I couldn't do what he was asking and couldn't stand to hear him ask it anymore—I stopped visiting.

It felt terrible to do this, but I had to. My visits (I told myself) took him to the place where he felt he could; if I didn't visit, he wouldn't go and would be happier. I'd told him again and again that I couldn't do what he was asking me to do, but he didn't stop. Sometimes it was all he said, and he'd say it five or six times before I left, shaking.

After I stopped going, Cassia took the kids twice, but stopped too. It was scary to the kids, she said, to see the pain and how he'd ask anyone in the room — even the kids — *to kill him*. She couldn't visit anymore, she informed me.

His best friend from Reseda, where they'd both worked for the utility until retirement, visited him three times and stopped as well, apologizing, making excuses, too.

I was ready to see him again, I decided — I had to do it or he would die before I could and I would feel like shit — but I didn't. Another month passed. Cassia would ask gently whether I was going to see him, and I always found a way not to answer.

When he died, I knew it had been cowardice on my part, not love.

ॐ

My uncle had given me a sidearm, a Makarov, a PN, with an 8-round clip, when I was twenty-one, something he'd brought back from Syria when he was in the Marines, where he'd gotten a Purple Heart. My father hated guns because he'd seen a boy blinded by a pistol when he was little, but his brother thought I needed to know about them, for The Big One, for "home defense." My father relented. My father respected Miles, and I think he wanted me to be more of a man, too. My uncle took me to a shooting range twice.

The Makarov was in a lockbox in the attic, away from the kids and anyone who might steal it. I'd kept it, yes, because it might be useful in The Big One, which was by now nearly two hundred years overdue.

ॐ

I'm standing before the tank now, gun in hand, eight rounds in the clip. I don't know how many it will take, even if bullets can

147

do it, but it's the only plan I could imagine. I've considered others — spear gun and mask, explosive (but what kind and from where?), a high-powered rifle (from where?) — but they were complicated and might fail.

The figure doesn't move, though I can see, with the maglight in my other hand, that at the center of the whiteness in some places is a pink, ropey flesh. The legs are trembling, as always. The eyes stare at me but do not see.

I'm sorry I did not come before, I say.

You're here, it answers. *That is what matters, Jude*.

I fire into the acrylic wall.

I fire four times before it cracks open and the sea swallows me.

ॐ

When I wake, coughing water, barely able to see, the tank water is in pools on the floor. The water reflects dim light from somewhere. I am on my back, holding something in my left hand. Not the maglight. The thing moves, makes a wet, ragged sound. It is hair, like fine thread, that I'm holding. It moans again.

Is it saying, *Please*, or am I imagining this?

I grab the body to pull it closer (it's still alive, it should not be, I can't let it be), flesh comes off in my hand, salt water burns my nose, and the gun is somehow still in my other hand.

When, in the dim light, I am touching the head, the broken jaw, the sharp teeth, I move the gun's barrel to it, shaking so hard I can barely grip it. The stench of the body is beyond imagining. I close my eyes, choking on water and something else.

Do not leave me like this, Jude. If you love me —

I fire twice because I do not want the voice to have to ask again, as it did every day in Chino Hills all those months.

ॐ

I see exactly how it will go from this moment on. Because, as it lay dying beside me only moments ago, the creature told me how it will go:

The guards will not come, despite the gunshots, the cracking of the wall, and the roar of water. They are elsewhere, and they are elsewhere because the creature made it so. I will limp to my car in the parking lot across the street. I will drive home, keeping the Makarov with me. I will tell Cassia about "sprinklers," why I was wet, about the remodeling. I will, before I go in the house, wash the salt water and whiteness and scales from me so that it is pure, clean water I smell of. I will take whatever time I need to calm my shaking.

I will return the gun to the lockbox.

You will not be caught, the voice told me.

Did it know about the files? Did it choose me because of them? Did it direct everything?

I will never know, but I don't need to. I will use the evidence I have, and I will certainly be punished for it. I will be the whistleblower no one wants. The copies I send to the right company board member, or, if there's complicity at the highest level, to the USDA or other federal agency, may destroy the company, or they may not. I will do what I need to do.

I will get a job in another field. It will not be enough for us to keep the house, the life we've had, but I will do it. We will survive; the kids will grow up in an engineered world and not be unhappy with their lives, and Cassia will be happy because of their happiness. I will always smell like the brine, the white sloughing-off of skin, of jaws that will not close, and that is all right. It is better than the lie of what we make in darkness.

I know you will do what needs to be done, Jude, the voice is saying to me even now, and I know whose it is. I have known for a long time.

STAMPS

It is well known now the role the Arcturians[1] played during the Cuban Missile Crisis in averting global nuclear disaster — specifically, by whispering telepathically and remotely simple phrases like "Trust!" and "This can be fixed!" and "This is definitely worth fixing!" in the sleeping ears of both John Fitzgerald Kennedy and Nikita Sergeyevich Khrushchev. What is less well known, because it does not concern the averting of global nuclear disaster, is what one Arcturian did during the Cold War that ninety-one years later would play a role in a Terran crisis of another kind, namely, The Singularity of 2053.

The Arcturian in question, T'Phu^Bleem^, a nondescript male of bureaucratic personality but also devout conscience and unusual curiosity, was one of ten Arcturians sent clandestinely to Earth for the Galactic Commission's monitoring of the planet's drift toward possible nuclear annihilation (see "Galactic Commission — Monitoring" and "Galactic Commission — Member Responsibilities"). With a little cosmetic and laryngeal surgery, T'Phu^Bleem^ was able, like his nine Arcturian *confreres* and *consoeurs*, to pose as Terran. The last thing the Earth needed at the moment was the destabilizing revelation of other sentient life in the universe — specifically, benign, well-meaning

---

1 As we now know, the orange giant Arcturus, type K1.5 IIIpe — "star of stormy weather" and "star of joy" in Terran myth — carries not only one substellar companion, but three: two larger than our own Jupiter and equally inhospitable to carbon-based life, but one smaller and quite hospitable. Why Terran astronomers of the period in question failed to perceive these companions is unclear, unless (as our Arcturian brothers and sisters have so compassionately suggested) they were blinded by the phenomenon of "plasma masking."

life that had both an interest in Terran affairs and the skills and resources, both biological and technological, to help solve Terran problems. "Who will the aliens side with?" both sides would ask (given how the human psyche worked), with one or both rushing to pre-emptive strike so that only one side remained for the aliens' favor.

As the nearest Commission members to Sol, Arcturians would, if they could, need to conduct their monitoring and, if necessary, their intervention in secret for the sake of Commission Principles and Terran self-respect. If that turned out to be impossible, Plan B or C or both — "Sentient Aliens as Policing Force" or "Sentient Aliens as Planetary Threat Toward Bilateral Cooperation," as Terran media would later call the two postures — would be pursued.

T'Phu^Bleem^ was posing as an American stationed in France, at a NATO air base, and as a clerk. Because he was a civilian rather than a soldier, he lived in a flat in a small village nearby, with the privacy he needed. Since he was not part of the six-member sub-team that would actually solve the Crisis when the time came, all he could do was watch and wait as events moved inexorably forward. Receptive telepathy — almost always worthless with another sentient species — was proving of little worth to him in his daily life in understanding human beings. ("Trust!" and "This can be fixed!" were targeted projections and another matter entirely.) And he did want to understand them and not just monitor the "news." How else could the Commission know when or whether to intervene for the good of any species in ways consistent with the Principles?

T'Phu^Bleem^ was an Arcturian of typical Arcturian patience, and, as has been noted, of bureaucratic persuasion, but with a greater preference for "color" in life and (driven by a hobbyist's passion) a greater desire to collect "curiosities" than most Arcturians demonstrated — especially those in Galactic Service. In his secret life as a human clerk, he opened physical correspondence and filed the wood-pulp communications in metal cabinets five days out of seven for eight hours each working day. Through this work he had become fascinated with the colorful postage used to transmit the machine-imprinted or human-hand-inscribed letters from one human being to another. His own race had, he supposed, once upon a time used something comparable — either a "pre-paid stamp" applied with some adhesive or printed into the physical material of the transmittal container itself — but this was not something Arcturian children learned about in school. That period of Arcturian history was so far in the past that one's education in history had to choose other details to address.

"Stamps" were used on Earth by two main groups, T'Phu^Bleem^ observed: (l) Individual humans sending communications (personal or professional) to members of family units and social communities of whatever size; professional colleagues (vertically or horizontally); absolute strangers; and agencies, corporations, organizations, and institutions in the private, public, and non-profit sectors...not to mention nations and coalitions of nations. (2) Representatives of agencies, corporations, organizations, institutions, nations, and coalitions of nations sending communications to *other* agencies, corporations, organizations, institutions, nations, and coalitions of nations. What truly caught his attention, however, was how *colorful* the stamps were, when they might have been simple and drab and served the same purpose — namely, the prepaying of transportation delivery costs. Instead, each had a face of a historical or otherwise culturally important human being (real or imagined), or a famous edifice, or technological achievement, or grand landscape, or aesthetically pleasing animal worthy of collective pride. How different they all were! — as if created not by states — those entities that charged for the delivery costs — but by individual human beings, or at the very least individual visual designers assigned to capture and communicate the unique "image" a Terran state wished to convey to its fellow states, their inhabitants, and its own, so that it might be seen as both celebrantly different but also universally human.

The tiniest states often had the biggest, most colorful stamps, and the largest (and most militarily and economically powerful) states the smallest and least colorful. Some states seemed afraid of color, trusting instead small stamps with detailed, engraved human faces and barely any color at all to convey their cultural personalities; while others seemed uncomfortable unless proclaiming themselves to the universe with flamboyant designs and stamps as long as a human finger. It was difficult to reconcile all of these expressions as the products of a single species. The more T'Phu^Bleem^ tried, the less he was able. Were the differences misleading? Were the stamps not as important as he perceived them to be? How else to explain it? And yet they *had* to be important. Otherwise, the states and their inhabitants would not have gone to such pains to proclaim those differences to their own species.

One Friday, T'Phu^Bleem^ took the transmittal containers—the envelopes—he had opened and saved during his work hours, unwilling to throw away their mysterious postage, and added them to envelopes he had surreptitiously removed from refuse containers in his building. Tearing off the corners that contained the postage, he reduced dramatically the bulk of what he would take to his flat. These corners he placed in a large manila envelope, which in turn he placed in his satchel as he prepared to leave work. Security would check his satchel and find the envelope because he would tell them about it even before they opened the satchel. They would open the envelope and see the corners with stamps on them; but the stamps clearly had no military value, and they would assume he was simply a hobbyist—especially if he announced that he was one. He would help this impression by using authentic terms like "stamp collector" and "hinges" and "the Scott book," terms he had learned from the French edition of *Stamp Collecting for Beginners*, a book he had purchased the previous week in his village—a village which, like so much of Europe in that period, boasted an astonishing number of stamp collectors of all ages.

If they had reason to suspect him as a spy, or wished simply to be thorough, they would detain him and check the stamps for the presence of steganographic "microdots," a crude but nevertheless ingenious approach to intelligence transmission for the historical period in question. They would then let him leave with the stamps.

Let him leave they did. What spy for the other side would have an envelope full of stamps — and announce it so proudly and ingenuously — if he were carrying microdots on one or more of them? He would carry his microdots in some other fashion, and security would have no idea where.

Following the instructions in *Stamp Collecting for Beginners*, T'Phu^Bleem^ placed the envelope corners in a bowl of water on the kitchen table at his flat. By the end of two hours, the stamps had loosened, and he could follow Step 5 in the book: "Place the wet stamps on a paper towel and let them dry."

When the stamps were dry, he took the other book — the one the first book had directed him to purchase, and one he had found of course at the same philatelia shop in Varles — and began to append the dry stamps to the pages with "hinges." These he wet with a little sponge in a bowl of water (Steps 7 and 8) rather than using his tongue — an act which, though physically as possible for Arcturians as it was for humans, the book advised against for sanitary reasons.

Some of the stamps he had collected were pictured in the book, so that he would know where to put them by nation, but most had to be hinged to blank pages, where he placed them by geographical area or another logical grouping he had devised.

When he was finished with the hinging, he sat rigidly upright on his chair — the best way, he had discovered as a child, to think clearly and for long periods of time — and went through the pages slowly and carefully.

The more he studied them, the more he saw, but the more he saw, the less he understood. There was more in these stamps than he had imagined. More than Arcturians and even the Commission knew, and perhaps more than even humans knew. The stamps were like a puzzle, one that could explain how human beings actually thought and felt (when their own scientists of the human mind — not to mention Arcturian mind-scholars — were not really very good at explaining it). If he didn't try to figure that puzzle out for the sake of the human race and the Ten Galactic Principles, who would? There were only ten Arcturians on Earth, and he would be ("eccentric" as he knew he was by Arcturian standards) the only one of them so inclined. If it came to nothing — if he were wrong that the answers to so much about the human predicament were in this puzzle — he would relinquish the matter to more important Arcturian activities. If the puzzle, however, indeed held what he continued to feel it did, how could he not pursue it as an Arcturian in Galactic service, with a family back home, a familial reputation, tribal face, honor, conscience, and the Ten Principles whispering to him...just as the Arcturian telepath team would soon be whispering to John Fitzgerald Kennedy and Nikita Sergeyevich Khrushchev as they slept?

As events leading up to the Cuban Missile Crisis — events watched carefully by the Galactic Commission at a distance and by the ten Arcturians on the planet much more intimately — unfolded, and the Crisis itself began, T'Phu^Bleem^ collected what stamps he could, realizing that this was not necessarily the best method. How could he make sure he had as many pieces as possible of the puzzle if he did not have stamps from every single state, and samples of its most current stamps? How could he have what he needed to understand *Homo sapiens* on the eve of its possible selfdestruction if he were not more methodical and comprehensive, as any agent of Galactic Service should be?

He composed the following letter, for transmission by paper, envelope, and postage stamp, to the heads of all 226 states on Earth at that moment, a list of which he found in the little library in Varles.

Dear Prime Minister:
My name is Frederick A. Moffet. I am a citizen of the United States of America. I currently work for NATO in southern France. I believe in the harmony of all nations on Earth. Toward this I have begun to

collect stamps from every nation. I realize this is what children —

He started to write "human children," but struck the modifier.

— often do, but what I wish to accomplish through my collection is an understanding not only of the differences among people that are so worth celebrating —

He started to write "human beings," but changed it to "people" — a term human beings used in their daily discourse because of their centricism (which of course all species shared to one degree or another and certainly early in their developments).

— but also the universals of human nature and human society which, if acknowledged, can afford a bridge between and among nations. Toward this goal I am requesting, should you have any free and available, canceled postage stamps from your country. Should you be able to provide any, I will be profoundly and eternally grateful.

Since the planet was not as aware of the developments leading up to the Cuban Missile Crisis as it would be later, life went on as T'Phu^Bleem^ composed by hand and typing machine the 226 letters (efforts which, understandably enough, consumed all of his evenings and weekends for a month); posted his letters from Varles, rather than the air base; and waited to receive responses. He expected security to visit him either at his flat or at the base offices, but they did not. Perhaps they were not yet aware of his letters, mailed as they were from Varles. Perhaps they were indeed aware, but believed them to be merely the acquisitive tactics of what he claimed to be — a "stamp collector," one who simply wanted his collection to grow larger.

When the responses began to arrive, they did not speak in a single rhetoric or tone, and even their basic message varied. The two patterns he first noted made little sense: Some countries, those the West called "communist," were the friendliest and most forthcoming, while those who were not "communist" — who sided with NATO and the United States of America in Terran geopolitical matters — were often the least friendly. These cited internal policies which forbade them from sending canceled stamps to those who requested them. He would need to be patient. A stamp was complicated enough; a letter from a human being, even or especially one representing a state or a department within it, would be complicated, too. Even official policies could, he knew from experience, become personalized by individual bureaucrats.

Government House
Suche-Bator Square I
Ulan-Bator
Mongolia

Mr. Frederick Moffet
45 rue d'Ulm
Varles
France

Dear Sir,

I have the honour to send you a number of Mongolian Post-Stamps for which you appealed in your letter to H.E. Yu. Tsedenbal, Chairman of the Council of Ministers of the Mongolian People's Republic.

With best regards and
good wishes

Remain
Yours truly

Personal Secretary

D. Yondong

ঽ

Office of the Prime Minister of France
Paris, August 20, 1962

Dear Sir:
Your letter has come to the attention of the Prime Minister, who was sympathetic to your undertaking.

He apologizes profoundly for not being able to comply with your request, but being faced with so many entreaties, Monsieur the Prime Minister had to establish a procedure in this type of matter that allows no exception and therefore no granting of a request such as yours.

Please accept, dear Sir, the expression of my distinguished sentiments.

On behalf of the Prime Minister and with authority,

The Cabinet Director

ॐ

September 15, 1962

Dear Sir,

You will find in this envelope several new and canceled stamps of our country and we thank you for the interest you have shown in our country.

With our greetings,

The Federation of Czechoslovack Philatelists
on behalf of the People's Republic of Czechoslovakia

ॐ

Stamps

Republic of the Ivory Coast
The Prime Minister

Dear Mr. Moffet:
On behalf of the President Houphouet-Boigny with his finest feelings and his wishes of prosperity for your beautiful country, we submit gladly a selection of canceled stamps of our nation.

ॐ

August 26, 1962

Committee for Friendship and Cultural Relations with Foreign Countries People's Republic of Bulgaria

Dearest Sir:
We are responding to your letter in which you express the desire to have some Bulgarian stamps. To your address we are sending one hundred (100) examples from different series.
Zv. Gheorghiev (Assistant Section Head)

ॐ

Provincia de Angola
Direccao dos Servicos Dos Correios, Telegrafos E Telefones

Exmo. Snr. Frederick Moffet
Luanda, the 31st August, 1962

Dear Sir,
On reference to your letter of the 22nd August 1962, please you will find here enclosed some unused Angola stamps.
Please remit $30.

Yours very truly,
The Eng POSTMASTER GENERAL — Antonio Jacino Magro

ॐ

Ministere des Communications et Des Postes
de la Republique Populaire Hongroise
Department des Postes

Sir,
Referring to your letter addressed to the Chief of the
Hungarian Government, I am to send you enclosed our stamps
representing Joseph Garibaldi, Istvan Turr, and Lajos Tukory.

Yours truly,
I. Bujaki/Assistant Director general

ॐ

Direction Generale des Postes
Telegraphes et Telephones

Subject: Gift of Postage Stamps

In reply to your letter addressed to the President of the Swiss
Confederation, we would inform you as follows.

The PTT-Administration is not authorized to give away
unused postage stamps free of charge. Its canceled stamps,
detached from envelopes, waste forms, etc., are sold every year
for the benefit of charity. Requests for free postage stamps
cannot be considered, for in complying with individual requests
we would swell their numbers beyond control, which would
cause serious difficulties.

We regret being unable to give you a more favorable answer
but hope that you will like the philatellically stamped envelopes
of this letter.

Yours faithfully,
Postage Stamp Section : I.S. Hagnauer

Stamps

ॐ

Governatorato
Stato della Citta del Vaticano

Preg.mo Signor Frederick Moffet

Numerous inquiries, all of the same nature as yours
expressed by your letter, keep on being received at all levels by
this Administration, and even by the Pope.

You may realize that a general policy does not allow us, as
we would like, to please all who request the Holy City's stamps,
canceled or otherwise. However, to please you, we are sending
the present registered mail letter affixing multiple stamps to
offer a variety of postage of particular interest.

Representative of the Office of External Communications

ॐ

The United Arab Republic
September 27, 1962

(a generous number of stamps and an embossed card
reading:)

With the compliments of

Gamal Abdel Nasser
President of the United Arab Republic

The last responses arrived a few weeks after the resolution
of the Crisis. At that point, for reasons determined by the
Galactic Commission and therefore beyond T'Phu^Bleem^'s
understanding at the time, the Commission decided to reveal

161

the presence of Arcturians on Earth and their role in the resolution. This was not aimed to take away from human beings — from valuable, charismatic leaders like Kennedy and Khrushchev — what was legitimately to their credit and worthy of Terran pride. In fact, the communication from the Commission put it this way: "We could not have whispered meaningfully into your psychic ears if you did not have the heart, conscience, and good will to hear those whispers...and act upon them." This was not only true, it made human beings feel better, as was appropriate by the Ten Principles.

Plan A had succeeded, which made everyone at the Commission, as well as the ten Arcturians on Earth, happy. Plans B and C had proven messy in the past and considerably less worthy of celebration.

ৱ

Three weeks after the resolution of the Crisis, T'Phu^Bleem^, though no longer working for NATO, having quit his job, still lived in France. As far as those around him were concerned, he was still a human being. He had postponed his return to Arcturus III as long as he could so that he might study his Terran stamps and, just as importantly, write thank-you notes, as any civilized being would, to the heads of state (or the agencies and organizations to which his letters had been referred) who had sent him stamps and even to individuals who on behalf of their states or organizations had demurred for whatever reason.

In his thank-you notes he revealed only indirectly who he was and did not recant his reasons for asking for stamps. Those reasons had not changed. He wrote simply: "Thank you for the stamps you generously sent me when I wrote to you under the appellation 'Frederick Moffet.' Though I was not honest with you about my identity, my goal in requesting the stamps remains the same: an understanding of humanity and a desire for harmony among its states. Sincerely, T'Phu^Bleem^." Or:

"Although the policy of your office could not allow you to send me stamps, new or canceled, I thank you for the courtesy, both professional and personal, of your reply, which ensured that one or more canceled stamps would reach me. Both the spirit of that courtesy and the stamp in question will be remembered by my own office 36.7 light years from Earth in years to come. Sincerely, T'Phu^Bleem^."

Human beings—especially those well-positioned in governments or educated by news media—knew by now what the ^'s meant, namely, that T'Phu^Bleem^ was one of the ten Arcturians who had been present on Earth during the Crisis. Mention of "light years" simply corroborated.

ঽ

One human, an assistant postmaster in Asia, wrote him back immediately, asking what life was like on Arcturus, and whether he had a family waiting for him; and another—a prime minister of an African nation, in fact—wrote back just as quickly to ask for his autograph ("with your name written in Arcturian for my daughter, if this is not an imposition") on a photograph of the Terran night sky with Arcturus shining brightly, "star of joy" that it was. Delighted, T'Phu^Bleem^ complied. Others who answered *toute de suite* simply thanked him—on behalf of their people—for the Arcturian role in the Crisis. He did not know what these various responses meant exactly in human terms—which could not possibly be exactly the same as Arcturian terms—but he would add their mysteries to the stamps and original responses for later study.

So that he would not be in Varles when Terran media or security agents sought him out, T'Phu^Bleem^ left Earth shortly after the first thank-you-note responses arrived, requesting that the local postmaster forward any further responses to the U.N.—for further forwarding.

ঽ

T'Phu^Bleem^ kept the human stamps for ninety-one Terran years. Although Commission members must have heard about the stamps and letters through Terran circles, no member asked to see them, nor did T'Phu^Bleem^'s division within Galactic Service request that he surrender them as prohibited relics of service on another world. No one, in fact, seemed interested in them at all; but this, T'Phu^Bleem^ felt, was understandable. Wood-pulp documents generated at high levels of Terran governments — letters, memos, cables, and other communications produced before, during, and just after the Crisis — that would be another matter, something worthy of the commissions' or historians' interest. But stamps? Those tiny works of Terran cognitive and affective expression adhered to wood-pulp envelopes for transportation by air, land, sea, and human organism from one human to another? Why would anyone care — especially those with more important matters to attend to between the stars?

T'Phu^Bleem^ worked for ninety-one years with his stamps, trying to see patterns. He indeed saw them, but one pattern folded into another, like fractals, like chaos and ^Loome^ (the Arcturian notion of "productive entropy"), and the folding became endless. It reminded him in the end of the famous Arcturian riddle: "How, in a sub-atomic particle, can there be both infinite variation and infinite repetition?" The answer, of course, provided by the fifteen riddles that followed it in the Litany of Universal Exclamations, was that there couldn't be... *unless* one believed it so and held it in mind until, by that very holding, the two became one.

ৰ

In 2053, as we know, the Earth found itself facing "The Singularity," that is, the prospect of the conversion, by collective human choice, of biologically discrete individuals into a machine consciousness — that humanity might be free of its biology (and therefore its suffering) and experience true harmony at last. T'Phu^Bleem^ had by now — through the very curiosity, bureaucratic diligence, and insistence on insight over glibness that had brought him considerable attention in his profession—become one of the Galactic Commission's members. The Commission had had little contact with Terra in the ninety-one intervening years. When word reached the Commission that *Homo sapiens* was about to relinquish its individual organisms for a cybernetic existence, T'Phu^Bleem^ found himself listening for days to his fellow Commissioners' confusion, to their inability to perceive a solution for what might not have been a crisis at all, but a natural evolution of human beings into cells within a single electronic mind. Might "human culture" itself, he found himself wondering, now simply become an electronic one where the ideation of individuality worked no differently really (if individual identity is indeed simply the product of culture) than individuality had always worked for human beings with discrete biological loci? He had no idea. Arcturians and the other Galactic races had never faced such a decision. He was not sure, in any case, whether this Singularity was really a crisis, that is, something for a Commission to meddle in with good intentions, or something to be left alone even if the evolution of a species through its own technology, by its *becoming* that technology, left other more biologically intact species feeling uneasy.

He did, however, have one thing he needed to do. He needed to do it because of the time he had spent on Terra, with human beings, and because of the stamps he had spent, without fully understanding them, so much of his life studying.

The Commission agreed to his plan for the simple reason that the plan did not *impose* a solution on humankind. The plan simply asked humankind to determine whether there was indeed a crisis...and, if so, to resolve it itself in whatever manner it could.

So T'Phu^Bleem^ sent his collection (by prepaid delivery) of human stamps through jumpspace mail—through the system of concentric toroidal tokomaks that comprise the "spacelocks" we know so well today—to the Terran body that oversaw Earth and would make the decision of cybernetic connection for all human beings. In his correspondence to that body, speaking on behalf of the Galactic Commission, T'Phu^Bleem^ said: "We, a commission of eight sentient species, ask only that you and the artificial intelligences you are considering welding to human minds evaluate carefully the postage stamps in this modest collection before you proceed with your plans. We believe it is important to know—and only you can tell us—what these stamps reveal about human beings, patterns within them, patterns joining patterns, and details that do not appear to fit patterns but that of course do in the infinite variety and repetition that all matter and life are. When you have explained to us what these stamps reveal about humanity at its most profound, we will be able to understand and respect your race's decision to abandon or transcend (and is that the real question— what the Singularity is?) its own biology, even if we will indeed miss your biological presence not only as a comforting mirror of what we ourselves are and have always been, but as actual, physical brothers and sisters in this carbon-based plane we share."

Was there a veiled threat in these words? Were they the words of a Galactic Commission whose technology could punish a decision it did not approve of? Is this how the Terran body would receive them? The other Commission members were not sure. When asked, T'Phu^Bleem^ said only, "There is no threat. There is only a promise."

The other members had no idea what this meant. T'Phu^Bleem^ seemed to know what he was doing, however. He was, after all, the Commission's *de facto* president now that the old leader, an Antarean, was reaching the end of his physical and mental functioning; and he was also (it was whispered both by words and thought in the Commission chambers, hallways, and shuttlecraft) the Commission member who best understood, paradoxical though the notion was (or perhaps because it was so paradoxical) the very difficulty of understanding human beings—a difficulty that human beings obviously knew well.

Stamps

T'Phu^Bleem^'s message, the Commission learned later, spread rapidly from the Terran governing body — which felt, in its amusement, no tredipation at sharing with its constituencies such an absurd request. The Arcturians — and the Galactic Commission they represented — had saved the planet decades before, but how dare they? And what a silly assignment!

The message spread to hundreds, thousands, then millions, and finally, through the wireless "cranial-interface" planetary communications system that Terrans had achieved (one that had of course inspired, in the poignant dream it tended to foster, the very notion of Singularity), to a billion human beings — beings who still retained their discrete physical forms and who, prompted by T'Phu^Bleem^'s words, began to collect Terran stamps and to study them. The sudden pressure on nations to manufacture new stamps was staggering; the pressure to find used stamps in "the basements and attics of the world," as Terran media put it, was even greater. The fashion became, as Terran scholars would articulate it, "a charmingly seductive virus." (Whether this meant a carbon-based microbe or a cyberpest did not matter.)

For the Terran governing body, which had been assuming (and with no little justification) an overwhelming approval of its Singularity proposal, the degree to which human beings now amused themselves with stamps was indeed an epidemic — and a disturbing one. When the Singularity Council finally asked its constituency — ten billion planetary citizens strong with most, according to Terran media, connected wirelessly and "in virtual clouds of virtual words" — to vote, the outcome was far from approval. The Council asked for another vote, and the response was the same: "The Singularity can wait. We are doing our homework!"

Terran villages and vast metropolitan cities started philatelic groups — physical and digital communities of varying sizes whose members soon forgot that they were collecting stamps, sharing them, celebrating their differences and with passion voicing their respective opinions about them because of a cryptic epistle from an Arcturian light years away. Ninety per cent of all Terran nations established state-sponsored philatelic organizations. Even the Terran governing body had created a Council on Philatelic Considerations, with a dozen sub-committees for each "consideration." These groups (as more than one boisterous Terran media personality would point out) could not have existed without bodies, that is, were there only One Mind instead of individual physical beings with hands and opposable thumbs. How, after all, could One Mind possibly follow the steps in *Stamp Collecting for Beginners* without fingers?

The council asked for another vote, and then another.

It continues to ask.

It is 2153 on Earth. The Galactic Commission has not yet received an answer.

We are all—humans and Arcturians alike—happy to wait.

STEALING GOD

I still don't know why my mother made me steal the little Apache dolls and crosses and let loose what whispered in them. It was the last thing I'd have imagined she would ever do — since she was part Native American herself. You could see it in her eyes, the way the lid seemed to fold down at the outer edge, and in the color of her skin. It wouldn't have been much — maybe a fourth — but her father, who'd had more, had been so dark and his eyes so "Indian" that people in the oilfields of Long Beach, California, where he could fix anything and everything, had called him "Chief." She certainly had enough in her that she'd gone to college and then to graduate school to become an anthropologist, one specializing in Native American cultures. The culture her father, who'd been born in Oklahoma Territory, world of the Chickasaw, had in his blood, and so she did too. As do I. A little anyway.

She'd already taken ten years on her dissertation, and her advisor, who wanted her studying "diffusion of cultural traits through the familial complex," not an Apache religious leader, wasn't happy. That may have been part of it — a frustration with the world, sure, but also with herself. My father (they'd met in college, at a noisy party) had died when I was two from a heart attack that always took men young in his family, and I was ten now. She was a single mother in a time when there weren't many single mothers — the '50s — and she was doing her best, I tell myself. She taught high school in Southern California, where we'd lived when my father, who'd worked as an aerospace engineer for Rohr, died. She hated teaching high school students. She wanted to be an anthropologist and, if she were going to teach, to do it at a big university. But in those days her professors in graduate school said things like, "Women should be home with their children" — maybe with a smile, as if it were a joke, though it wasn't — not completely.

We lived in an apartment in Chula Vista, in San Diego, which was a tough neighborhood even then. We didn't have many things. We took trips to the Blackwater Apache reservation — which was actually two reservations, one in the hot desert, one in the pine trees — in Arizona. Those were our vacations. She needed to get her dissertation done. Even at ten I understood that. She would probably, one of her fellow graduate students told her — a guy, but not one with romantic interests — get a college or university job if she finished her PhD, and it would pay better than high school social studies did. We both wanted that.

For her dissertation she was studying a charismatic Apache shaman by the name of Edward John Thompson. Why? Because she wanted to understand his power, she told me once. "No woman could have had it," she said. He had an incredible following, or had had one in the '20s, before someone — Apache or White, it was never clear — framed him for the murder of his wife, and he had to go to prison. A lawyer who would, years later, become a famous novelist — with a famous TV series based on his novels — heard about his case later on and got him out, but only after two decades of incarceration.

Edward John with his broad, kind face was back on the reservation now, both at Blackwater and San Marcos, combining as he always had the Christianity carried by the early missionaries with his own people's Eagle Medicine, and in simple English saying dangerous, heretical things like "We have always known Jesus, we Apache," and "Jesus is inside us all." Looking back, I can see exactly what he was saying — anyone could if they looked beyond the words — that love of others can save you, that selfishness can destroy your life — but back then, in the '20s and '30s, it was the kind of thing that got you in trouble with the missionaries and the White reservation barons who charged a buck for a Coke on the rez and might even frame you for your wife's murder if a fellow shaman, full of jealousy, didn't. Rule of life: Don't get too popular if you're singing a song that scares the powerful.

The little dolls were nailed to willow crosses about the size of my hand. They were ones that Edward John used in his sacred dances, healing ceremonies, and the White Shell Woman rite for teenage girls he presided over (for the families that chose him over other Blackwater shamans), and they were strange. They made me feel empty — like a glass with nothing in it — until I'd handled them enough; and then I didn't know what I felt.

They didn't really look like dolls. I knew dolls — girls I'd known had played with them — and these weren't those dolls. One might have a head, but no face. One might have two lines, like little cuts, for eyes, but nothing else. You kept wanting to see their faces, to know them by their features; you wanted to paint faces on them, but that you couldn't do. If you put faces on them, you knew, the power would disappear. They were made faceless for a reason. You knew that, too. Maybe so that their power could go to *anyone*, affect *anyone's* life, health, happiness. Maybe because the dolls were gods and the gods had no faces. Or maybe some other reason. I was a kid. How would I know?

The dolls weren't wearing clothes — except for one. It was wearing what my mother called a "missionary dress," a flower pattern, red and brown. Their cloth bodies had been sewn roughly, but it was real hair on their heads. You knew that. It was the color of Apache hair, some of it gray-streaked, some of it pitch-black, too much for the head, jutting in all directions.

The dolls were bigger than the crosses they were nailed to. Their arms went past the wood. The arms weren't nailed to the crosses. The feet weren't crossed like Jesus' or nailed to the cross either. The dolls had a single thick nail in each of them, and it went through the chest, to the thickest part of the wood, where the two pieces crossed, as if they might struggle to get away if they weren't nailed tight.

171

Each had a little feather, dusty from what the winds blew in, tied to its neck with a rawhide cord. The wood was painted yellow, just like the pollen used on the teenage girl in the White Shell Woman ritual, when she danced for three days without stopping, in a trance, covered with the yellow pollen of the Sun. The Sun had made White Shell Woman pregnant with the First Man. The girl became White Shell Woman, with her god-like power, for three days after that, and could heal you if you deserved to be healed, or, instead, abandon you to darkness, to a hell where no one cared about you for eternity. That's how my mother put it. It didn't sound very Apache, and it didn't sound like Edward John Thompson's Christianity, its message of love. But it's what she said, and she should know, right? She'd interviewed many of his disciples, and he had dozens. She'd had an Apache interpreter translate their answers when they couldn't explain it in English. Hell was full of demons, she said. Hell was where you were alone if you betrayed someone who trusted you. Hell was where everything you deserved lasted forever.

The paint was the same corn yellow, too, as the color Edward John Thompson used in his sand paintings, the ones he made (my mother also said) to show his people their destiny and to help them follow it...or break it if it too led to darkness...if he could...if they believed in his medicine enough to give him the power to do this — which they did, of course.

The dolls and crosses had been dipped in something and were streaked red. The red looked wet, as if it would never dry. When I said it looked like blood, my mother said:

"It's iron. The resin that makes it glisten." She sounded angry, and I didn't know why. "It represents blood, but also the earth, where First Man walked, and a dozen other things...."

We were sitting off to the side, where my mother was taking notes with legal-size yellow paper on a clipboard and her favorite pen. Edward John was dancing on the other side of two fences. A wind was blowing, sand and dust with it, and we had to squint. My mother had to fight the paper to keep it flat.

"Go get three of the crosses," my mother said.

She couldn't have said that. I looked at her. "What?"

"Get three of those crosses, Keith!" She was definitely angry now. Sometimes I think she was feeling sorry for herself — that she had a kid, a boy, one who liked animals and books and not much else, and there was no one else to help her. That she was dying inside without that help. That she could love something as much as anthropology and Native Americans — which she had in her — and not be able to reach it because of her situation, her son, a dead husband, the need for money, the need to be here on the hard earth and not dancing free to become a goddess for three days like the fourteen-year-old Blackwater girls every summer. That the universe was unfair. That she deserved better because doesn't love — a love of something, of anything — deserve better than a life of struggle, frustration and the weight of duty? Shouldn't love be rewarded by God? Shouldn't God want us to feel His love? Haven't we always had God in our hearts even if we didn't know it?

Whether these were her exact thoughts, I didn't know, but I thought them because she was my mother and I wanted to love her. I thought them because I knew there was something behind her anger, something that was there all the time. When you're the only son of a moody woman who probably doesn't want to be a mother, wants to pursue what she loves, you tend to know — to sense — what's there even if it's not spoken. Sometimes you feel it so clearly and intensely that your body hurts, and you can't sleep at night, and the only way to feel better is to imagine what she's thinking and feeling, to try to understand, and feel love if you can.

"Why?"

"Get the damn crosses, Keith."

I'd never heard her talk like this, or if I had, I'd forgotten it.

I crawled over to the pile of little dolls and their crosses — which were on the other side of the wikiup where Edward John kept his things — and took three. I'd gotten there on all fours, and was not sure how I'd get back with only one hand free. I hesitated. They were strange, and their dangling feathers touched my wrists like little wings. They were small and shouldn't have scared me, but they made my hands tingle. I didn't know how to take them without shaking — whether it was fear or guilt, it didn't matter — so I did something silly. I'd done it before with things I knew were wrong, or that might have been, though I had to do them. I looked at their faceless faces and said, "Forgive me...."

These dolls and crosses, my mother said, gave you power to heal, to be a better person, to make good things happen in your life. That had to be why she wanted them. She wanted to have good things happen. But it had to be the right person holding them, using them, didn't it? It had to be someone like Edward John Thompson. It couldn't be just me or her, could it?

I put them in my jean's pockets, one per pocket. Then I crawled back to her on all fours.

When I sat up and took the crosses out of my pockets to give them to her, she didn't say a thing. I thought she might act embarrassed, but it was anger — that's what I saw — only that.

Two days later we went home. She had tried to get photographs of the Apaches who were there for Edward John's dance, but they wouldn't let her take their pictures. It would steal their spirits, they said.

This made her angry, too.

Sometimes I believe in past lives, in reincarnation — and for a moment I see my mother as a Chickasaw or Chocktaw, captured by another tribe — maybe even Apaches — two hundred years ago, angry because only anger would keep her from despair — trapped as she was in their world, someone's *shi'aad*, their slave-wife — when she wanted to be free, to sing songs, to explore God's world and be happy — which no wife like that could be. This was how it had been for some women back then, I knew. Just awful.

႙

A month later, in our apartment in Chula Vista, I came home from school to find her in the living room, colored sand on the carpet, yellow pollen on the furniture, my mother dancing around making chanting sounds, the three dolls and crosses in her hand, their faces smeared, like her fingers, with lipstick.

She'd been dancing for a long time in her nightgown and was sweating. She barely noticed me, and finally she stopped dancing. The dance wasn't making anything happen; it wasn't making her happy.

ॐ

The dolls didn't work. Didn't matter how many times she tried. The dancing, the sand, the pollen, the chanting and the dolls, regardless of what she did to them — what she made them wear or how she colored them — didn't change our lives. I don't know why she thought they would. Six months passed and we were still where we were, the same apartment. It didn't bother me — when you're a child you accept what life gives you, what adults make for you — but it bothered her.

ॐ

The first time she was arrested, it was downtown, at a department store, J.C. Penney's, and she had shoplifted a diamond necklace — the kind a man might give a woman out of love.

Her friend — that same guy in graduate school — bailed her out, and she didn't have to go to jail if she promised not to do it again. "Do you?" he asked, standing in our doorway, a tall man with a cowboy's weathered face. She wouldn't look at him. "Of course!" she said, angry that he would ask.

ॐ

The next time she did it, she made me come with her. She drove and made me stand by a display case in Jessup's jewelry store downtown, so the owners would watch me and not her. I went to school with their daughter, Kathy. "Fuss with the glass," she told me. "Just keep your hands moving." We didn't get caught.

She had diamond earrings now, but they didn't make her happy.

The next time she made me go with her, she drove to a cemetery, Holy Cross — the closest to us. It was a Friday. Not many people were there. She told me to dig up a body. She wanted the bones. She wanted the jewelry on them. She was trying to give me a shovel from the trunk. "They take it off before they bury them," I said and I walked away. I wasn't going to dig up a body or even try. She started digging herself, and when she found no bones she started crying. I came back and patted her head, her sweaty hair. I didn't want to see her unhappy, but she'd brought this on herself, hadn't she? She wanted life to be different, and she was making it different, but not the right way.

ॐ

One Saturday I woke to find her gone from the apartment. I knew she was out looking for something to steal. I waited. I was eleven. Sometimes you're pretty smart by the time you're eleven.

When the police called, they asked whether my mother had mental health problems, whether she was on medication and had a doctor for it. I gave them the name of our doctor. She had broken into a gift store to steal some Native American objects. She'd done it in broad daylight, as if wanting to be caught, but I knew it wasn't that. I knew it was just that she wanted those objects so much she couldn't help herself. I knew, too, that it wasn't just her inside, a mental problem, making her that way, but what we'd done in San Marcos in the wind. What we'd stolen.

The doctor, Dr. Wallace, who'd been a family friend for years, bailed her out, promising to be responsible for her, and — hoping it would help — lied: "I'm afraid she has, yes, been developing problems...of a mental nature."

We didn't go back to the Blackwater reservations. She stopped working on her dissertation, and she'd taken so many leaves from her teaching job that the principal was telling her he'd have to fire her.

Stealing God

ঽ

It was a school day, and we were supposed to ride together — first to my school, so she could drop me off, and then she'd go to hers. She was gone again when I woke, as she often was, and I knew I wasn't going to go to school that day. That was fine. I'd wait for the police or someone to call about her. Someone always found our phone number in her purse.

I went to the living room where the dolls and crosses were gathering dust on the coffee table. I often held them when she wasn't there. I told them again that I was sorry, and without words they said: *You did what any child would do, any son for his* shi ma. *First Man would have done it for his* shi ma. *You stole because she told you to.*

Usually they didn't say this much. But there was something I needed to ask.

But stealing them, I said, *isn't making her happy.*

Sometimes the medicine does something else....

I didn't want to ask, but I did:

It punishes....

Yes....

The person who stole can punish the one who made him do it?

Yes, cye....

I'm the one making her steal now?

Yes....

Why...?

You know why, cye....

I knew. Because I was angry. Because she had betrayed me — a mother asking her son to steal when it might mean he would spend eternity in darkness. Because she didn't ask me to do it out of love, but out of her own anger and selfishness. That's how it felt, even if I didn't have the words to say it.

And because the power — since I was the one who took them — is mine, not hers?

Yes, the voice whispered. *That is how it works, and always has, and always will...world without end,* cye....

And also, I said, seeing it suddenly, *because she is in me.*

Of course, they answered. *You are her son.*

I didn't want her to be in me. I didn't want to be making her steal. I waited all day, trying not to cry, but she didn't come home.

ॐ

I can see it as if I were there. Sometimes I think I was. She died at midnight, they said, on the El Camino Real highway in Leucadia, stealing a pretty car—a two-toned convertible blue as a Blackwater sky and white as snow on Blackwater pines—because she'd always wanted a nice car. She was drunk. She'd started drinking that week, but that was her, not me. She hit one of the big, thick eucalyptuses, and it was over.

Three of her fellow students at graduate school, my mother's sister from New York (who hadn't had any contact with us since my dad died,) and a few teachers and students from the high school attended the funeral. Her mother and father didn't. They'd divorced when she was fifteen, her mother moving to Florida and her father passing away not long after that. Some of the people at the funeral cried. I did too. She was my mother.

Throughout the service I kept thinking how, if her ghost ever came to me and asked me to dig up her bones, to take them away, to free her from the earth, I'd say "No, it is time the stealing stopped. I will not do it again, *Shi ma*."

I lived with my aunt and her family in Syracuse, New York, after that. I assume the dolls and crosses were thrown away with so many other things that belonged to my mother. I didn't want to hold them. If they gave me a power, I no longer have it. Sometimes I have a dream about a doll, one with her face, her features, stained with something dark—mineral or blood—a nail through her chest to a cross that's too little for her. Sometimes it's me, *my* face, not hers, and I feel nothing. But mostly I live the way everyone else lives, feeling what I'm sure others must feel.

DON'T ASK
(with W.S. Adams)

So what is love? I don't know. I do what I do. You do too.

They tell me where she is in the big portamorgue. Corporations need morgues too — big ones — when they're doing the military's work where the military can't afford to be. Mercs die as easily as mils.

The rooms of the dead glow blue in the light of the screens — the corporate version of the Pentagon's Ob Force Warrior system.

I pull her out by the shoulders and it's not easy. The bag's cemented to her. All that blood.

Black hair thick with it. Like someone else's hair — like a wig. It covers the eyes and I'm grateful. I pull harder, get more of her out. In the mess I see damage that makes me think *Femur snapped and shot up through the abdominal wall into her bowels,* and *Did the shock kill her before anything else could?*

It's the brain trying. It needs to know exactly what took her, even if it can't. It chatters: Shaver mines. VIVA mines. EMP mines. Jumping mines. Mobile claymores that will stalk you for a klick. I knew a merc who died from a mine over seventy years old.

High velocity projectiles make cavitation in soft tissue. It opens like a stone hitting water, the tissue ripples out from it, and then it all comes back in a mess. When it hits the bone, the bone frags out into flesh. I can see the pieces as I lift what was once her pelvis.

Maxil-facial, below the brain, but brain destruction.

I always wondered what her bones were like, under her skin, in the darkness when we were at last in darkness and could touch each other, or in the light, once or twice in down-time bungalows, when we could look at each other and touch too, but see our bodies bright as day.

I've pulled her from an OD green body bag with coolant lining. The coolant's important, for preservation of the tissue. The operation was JSOC, Free Uganda, so it was chameleon recyc gear she had on. I was south, with Red Flare, when they let me know. Kamuda heard and risked an intel violation. He's always had my back. I had to finish the action. I heard her voice in my headset—the words weren't clear—though I couldn't possibly have. She was gone. Was it a carryover? Not possible, Kamuda says. *You heard her because you wanted to.*

The right hand is gone and so are ribs, along with the right leg. I remember the soft skin of her thigh, both of them, and now one's gone. I remember how strong that leg was. Her right one. She kicked me so hard the second time we made love I had blurred vision for a week and had to fall out of the operation we were in. That leg.

I don't understand it. Exsens mines don't usually do that to a leg. Then I see the pelvis and it makes sense. Not a laser flash, but an old IED hitting her low. A kill takes out one soldier. A WIA takes out three—two to carry the injured, especially when there aren't any bots because an EMP has hit and scrambled the impulses or a virus has transed past the blocks.

No, that's wrong.

Her leg is in the bag. I didn't see it when I pulled her out. I see it now. It doesn't look like hers. It never does. It only matters when it belongs to someone.

Her jaw's gone and the top of her skull, but enough is left that I can, if I work hard, wipe dried blood off the forehead and see it—that scar, the one I teased her about the first time we hooked up. "Got it as a kid," she said, letting me know she was more than the shit we do. "Outside Atlanta, where we lived—fell off my favorite fucking bike. I was ten. My baby sister just died of encephalitis. My father was shooting slick again...." I nodded to say I knew—I knew about losing people you don't have money to bring back, and how you save and save thinking you will but never do. Then I bragged—told her I had a better scar on me somewhere, one I'd gotten in the Stans. She snorted and said, "And I'm going to have to find yours, right?" "Sure," I said. She laughed and gave me that look with her eyes and said, "Maybe I'll get another one first." I didn't see her again for three months, until R&R at the Corp's Rimini compound, that beautiful sea. And she did—she got another one—down her left arm, like a pink snake—singing shrapnel in the Congo. That night she found mine, too, but we'd been stupid to wait. We liked each other. That's enough. When did we know? The first time we heard each other's voices through the throat mics. That's what she'd say. All I could see—actually *see*, in the battlefield light, helmet hiding the rest—was that scar on her forehead, a little one, and a shadowy grin. What did *she* see in that light? Did she see anything at all? Did she need to?

I'll never figure out exactly what made such a mess of her. You never do, but I said that already, didn't I? It's just a game— so you won't cry or fire a big FPR on auto where you shouldn't or smash your team leader's teeth in over nothing.

I remember a simtrainer, this old guy who once said to us *It's not your buddy's brains on your shoulder. It's not a week later, another guy's brains on your shoulder, and another after that. That's not the horrible thing. The horrible thing is when you stop feeling it.*

That's not true. Sometimes it's when you don't stop.

ॐ

"She was with Blue Flare, point assault outside Gulu," Kamuda tells me later, when we connect at the mess on the Corp ship off Kenya and he wants to know what I've got in the wallet-sized cool-pack I'm carrying. I don't tell him and he's not sure.

"I know where she was, Snake-Eyes," I say.

"She got stupid," he says.

I wait. She'd agree, I'm sure.

"She kneels down to look at these two kids on the road," he's saying. "Brother and sister, infants—maybe twins. Torn to pieces. Automat fire—rebels or NPs—doesn't matter which. She's seen it before, but she stops. Why?"

"I don't know," I say. I don't.

"Her TL is shouting at her to get the fuck back to the squad and she gets up slow, like a dream—that's what the helmet cams show—and she's staring at the babies, that's what it looks like on the video—"

"I get it, Kamuda," I say.

"—and because she's not looking she steps—she steps into it. I guess it was a fence, a gate, something the villagers had avoided for years—like she was trying to go to their hut, where they lived, and she forgot what she was doing there. She's looking back at the infants—that's what the cams show—I said that, I know—and she walks into it. An old IED from Peacekeeper days. Makes no sense."

"No," I say.

"There are pieces of her all over the babies," Kamuda is saying. "The guys don't know what to do. They need to get as much of her as possible—no 'usable tissue,' that's the reg—but there's a lot of her on them and the squad doesn't have time to scrape it off. So they take the babies. They're little. They don't weigh a thing...."

"I know," I tell him, but I don't tell him how. I don't tell him they were the last thing I found in the Dupont bag at the back, past the leg that once belonged to someone.

ॐ

I take a slice out of her thigh with my K-blade. In the portamorgue, I mean, before I leave. Not a big one. Just enough. "Usable tissue." The morgue tech is watching but doesn't say a thing. You take souvenirs like this in war all the time and no one asks why. *Don't ask, don't tell.*

ॐ

It'll take a lot of money, but they can do it — they do it all the time — these companies — if you've got the money. *Identical copies of the ones who matter most.* I've got money from my biggest ops — Azerbaijan, Kashmir, Mali and Juarez. They'll take the tissue and get the DNA, and then try fifty denuked ova before one takes. Because of the law, they'll need a pro — a "Dolly woman" — and they're expensive, too, more than you think. The Dolly will be gone the day after she's born. Will I hold her that day, little and crying, eyes familiar because I want them to be? I don't know. Will I watch her grow up, pay a woman or a series of them to live with us, be there for her when I'm not, when I'm away making money for us both? I don't know how. I don't know how much I'll be there, but I'll write her letters even if she's too little to read them. Someone will read them to her. If I die, I'll leave her a lot of money. Policies, bonuses, property. If I'm still alive when she's ten or eleven — whenever kids start to ask those things — she'll ask and I'll be there, I'll make sure I am. I'll look at her forehead for a scar — anything at all — and I'll take her in my arms and I'll say, "*What is love?* I don't know, sweetie. No one does. You stay in the world. You do what you do."

MY FATHER'S CRAB

*"We're not alone in the universe. Even crabs
know that. Watch them sometime...."*
> —Jasper Cummings, marine biologist,
> Scripps Institute of Oceanography, 1962

I don't know where it was—that miniature golf course in the
sand—but it had to be the Gulf of Mexico somewhere. We were
driving from one coast to the other, like always. "The Great
Southern Route," my dad called it. It had to be Florida, Mississippi,
Louisiana, or Texas—one of them.

I was seven, and my dad had driven us across the U.S. and
back half a dozen times by then. Looking back, I don't know
why a young officer doing "top secret" work for the Navy was
making that many cross-continental trips by car, but maybe it
was what his constant reassignments demanded. Or maybe he
just liked to be on the road, see relatives, get away from his desk
whichever coast it was on. That changed as he moved up the
ranks and was given more responsibility, but I remember what
he was like back then, in the '50s, the Cold War, when he and I
would play miniature golf wherever we could on the way to the
other coast. My mother and her mother—my grandmother, who
lived with us—would watch TV in the motel rooms or go
shopping for souvenirs in the beach towns. We were happy on
those trips. My dad was the boy who'd left the Blue Ridge
Mountains of Virginia to "see the world." I'd never see him
quite that happy and alive until the end of his life, when he
wasn't in the same world as the rest of us.

It was evening. That was half the fun. The golf course had a hundred lights strung on wires, and all were shining brightly so people could play as late as possible. You could hear the ocean somewhere, but the sand was close. You'd step in it if you didn't watch yourself. It was fun, the sand still warm from the day's sun on your bare feet while you'd tried to get the ball into the miniature castle or windmill. When you did, you got to listen to it spin around — inside the little structure and make its way to the next hole — this one a loop-de-loop or tiny mansion or an alligator with an open mouth.

"Great job, Brad!" my father would shout, even if it weren't a great job (four attempts to get the ball into a candy-cane house?). He said it the same way he'd say "Rise and shine!" or "Up and at 'em!" in the morning to wake me up. Corny lines, but I loved them. These trips were the only time I got to do much with him, and they mattered to him, too. I could tell.

When we were at home — and home changed every year or two — he'd leave for work in San Diego or San Francisco or Washington D.C. or Key West so early I'd have to get up at five if I wanted to have breakfast with him (Cheerios, of course) and listen to the radio together before he headed out. He'd return at 6:30 in his uniform, change into civilian clothes, and after dinner fall asleep in front of the television set watching Edward R. Murrow or *Perry Mason*. Watching him sleep, I'd get sleepy, too.

ॐ

That evening, as we reached the farthest hole — where the ocean waves were loudest — he looked down at the sand and laughed.

"Well, would you look at that!"

I did and jumped. There were crabs everywhere, gray-green and walking sideways, and about as interested in the little buildings on the holes as they were in us. Where were they heading?

I had no idea.

"Where are they going, Dad?"

"Who knows?" He was staring at them the same way I was — I remember that — as if they were the most remarkable things in the world. Which they were, the ocean breeze ruffling our hair and freezing time forever.

"Sometimes," he said, "crabs migrate. Sometimes they've got some place they're going, and they'll cross roads and fields and swamps to get there."

"Do you think that's why they're doing that?"

"No. I think they're here to play miniature golf."

At that, he grabbed me and swung me around laughing, and my club flew into the twilight.

When we'd retrieved it, I said, "Can we hit them like golf balls?"

"What?"

"Can we hit them like balls?"

He looked at me, then at the nearest sidestepping crabs, then at my golf club.

"I guess so."

I thought it would be cool. I wanted to see them fly through the air — crabs that could fly.

We hit a dozen. They didn't fly very well. They came apart, claws going one direction and carapace going another, and I could tell my dad's heart wasn't in it. He liked living things. I did, too, but I was a kid. I liked to experiment.

When we stopped swinging, he picked up one of the crabs we hadn't hit, holding it behind the shell where the claws couldn't get him. Then he carried it to a light and looked at it, watching the legs and claws flail trying to pinch him.

That was cool, too, I remember thinking — how you could hold them that way, and they couldn't get you. I was glad we hadn't killed any more than we did.

"Look at this thing, Brad. This is a different species than the ones in Key West."

I looked closely. He was right. It was the same color as some of the crabs in Key West. What made this one so strange was its shell. It looked like plastic. All crab shells look like they've been made in molds, but they don't look like toys. This one did.

"Maybe it's not a crab," I said.

"Of course it's a crab, Brad. An *arthropod*, a crustacean. It's just a kind we haven't seen before. When we get to San Francisco, we'll see new kinds there, too."

My dad loved sea life. He didn't just want to float in ships on the seven seas, be a sailor sailing the world. He wanted to know what was living in those seas, miles and miles down, and what kinds of ships you could build to explore them. If he could have taken a bathyscaphe—which he almost got to do a few years later—to the bottom of the Marianas Trench, he would have. He was an engineer, an inventor, and a naturalist at heart, not a battleship captain or a warrior. I didn't know it, but the work he was doing then was about "special warfare": sonar for finding Russian submarines, jammers to stop them from firing missiles, microwave communications before anyone really knew what "microwave" was, and the beginning of GPS. As a lieutenant in Undersea Research, he was interested in what would help our country defend itself, sure, but he was also interested in how marvelous it all was—the sea, everything in it, creatures and the human beings visiting it.

I loved my father if for no other reason than that he loved living things. I know that now. "You're a living thing, too, Brad," he told me one day. "Don't you ever forget that. A wonderful living thing." So I knew he loved me, too.

ॐ

"But it looks like plastic," I said.

"Yes, it does. But it's moving, so it must be alive, right? Did you know there's a crab where your mom was born, on the Big Island—a kind called *Carpilius*—that has spots on it like a cow; and another one—Big Island, too—that has pom-poms on its claws like a cheerleader? And dozens of kinds, big and small, that can pull their claws in to make boxes of themselves—so no one can get into them."

"Really?"

"Yes!" His eyes were bright and wide, and my heart skipped

a beat. What wonderful things to know.

"Does this one make a box?" I asked.

"I don't think so. It's long and thin, like a runner."

The crab was still flailing, trying to pinch, but all I could do was stare at its shell. The surface was bumpy in a too-perfect way, and that made it look like a toy, too. And the color patterns, green on gray, weren't very natural-looking either. They looked like a commando's camouflage.

Before I could ask him about that, he jerked and nearly dropped the thing.

One of its claws had pinched him.

"That was stupid of me!"

He put the crab down on the sand, let go, and shook his hand—the one the claw had gotten.

"Now *that* hurts."

He was looking at his hand. I was, too. There was a mark near his wrist, and for a moment I thought the skin was wiggling there, that something was in it and moving around. But then it wasn't moving, and I looked up at my dad. He looked a little white, as if he might be feeling dizzy.

"You okay?"

"Sure. It just surprised me."

He was lying, I could tell. He didn't feel good, but what could I do? I was a kid.

ॐ

Back at the motel, where I had my sleeping bag on the floor, and my grandmother had her own room next to ours, Dad lay down on the bed.

"Shouldn't you go to an emergency room?" my mother asked, her long hair beautiful as always. She was Hawaiian. A lot of Navy men had Hawaiian wives after the war. He'd met her in Pearl Harbor when his ship—his first cruise after the Academy—almost sank that famous day.

"It's feeling better. If it's worse tomorrow morning, I'll go.

Crabs don't carry rabies and aren't poisonous, so I'm sure I'm okay...."

He was falling asleep, tired for some reason. As he lay there on his back, I walked quietly over to him and looked at his hand. The pinch mark, which looked more like a big spider bite, hadn't gotten any worse. Again I thought I could see something wiggling under the skin near his wrist, but Dad didn't seem to feel it, so I had to be wrong. Besides, skin didn't wiggle like that. The rest of the way to San Francisco, Dad scratched his hand but didn't look white or dizzy anymore.

We stayed in a motel in Palo Alto for a week, looking for a house a lieutenant could afford, and finally moved in when the van arrived from Florida.

He was still itching. "You need to go see a doctor," my mother insisted, her brown eyes flashing. "It could be infected."

"Yes, infected," my grandmother added. She would have wrapped his hand in herbs she'd dug up herself with an *o'o*—she'd been born in 1898 near Pahoa and knew traditional Hawaiian cures—but he wasn't going to let her do that.

I wasn't there for the meeting. School had started. But I heard them talking about it:

"The doctor thought I might have a splinter of crab shell in me, but he couldn't find one even when he opened it up."

"Does he want you to take medication for it?

"Yes. Just in case."

"Be sure to do that, John."

"I will, Beatrice."

ॐ

My dad got better. He stayed better, and before long, we all forgot about the crab pinch. In three years he was a commander. We were living in San Diego, and he was executive officer of a Navy research laboratory—more anti-submarine warfare research. It was a beautiful bay, San Diego, and I knew I wanted to be a marine biologist. It's what my father would have been if he hadn't joined the Navy, I told myself. We lived near the bay on the base, had a beach we could use, two little boats, and a tiny base grocery store—even a barbershop. Life was easy, and I could collect all of the ocean creatures I wanted.

One day after school, I came home and found my father lying in bed in their bedroom.

He looked white.

"What's wrong, Dad?" I asked. Mom wasn't back from the high school where she taught, and Grandma never came up to the second floor since her bedroom was downstairs.

"Sometimes, Brad," he answered, scratching his wrist, "I think I got a bug of some kind that day. Do you remember?"

"Yes."

"You can get a bug, and it'll last for years, coming and going and coming and going."

"Do you feel sick?"

"Just a little. Once every couple of months."

"I'm sorry."

"Nothing to worry about."

Why, a voice whispered to me, *did it choose him?*

Back then I didn't even know what the question meant. It was a whisper, an idea I could barely see.

ॐ

He went to see a Navy doctor. My mom was pushing for an answer, and the doctor did blood tests, probed more, took more x-rays.

Some things don't show up on x-rays, I remembered thinking. I was in middle school now.

Again, they found nothing. He felt better in a couple of days, and we went back to living our lives.

ॐ

One Sunday, when he was napping, I went to their bedroom

190

and watched him for a long time. I don't know why. I watched him breathe, worried about him even though he hadn't said he felt sick. I was afraid he was going to stop breathing. That was silly, and I knew it. I wasn't five or six anymore, with fears like that. I was thirteen and knew better.

He twitched once or twice. I moved in closer, putting my face down next to his arm, and for the first time in years could see it. I could see the skin move again.

I jerked back in surprise, my chair moved, and my dad woke up.

"What's going on, Brad?" he asked.

"Nothing. Just wanted to see how you were doing."

He looked at me strangely, we talked for a while, and then I let him get back to his nap. If he didn't catch up on his sleep on the weekends, he couldn't do his "top secret" work well for the Navy, could he? He might get sick, too. Sleep was important, I knew.

ॐ

Three years later he was the executive officer of a NATO antisubmarine warfare research center in Italy (a big step up from San Diego), and we were all living in a fishing village not far from that center. We'd be there for two years, the Navy said. My mother and grandmother loved it, the green hills and the beautiful Ligurian Sea, but I didn't know what to think. I'd left my friends behind and didn't know if I'd make new ones.

I'd forgotten about Dad's "illness" because he never talked about it, it didn't show, and I thought it had disappeared a long time ago. I'd asked him once, back in San Diego, and he'd said, "Think of it like malaria. It won't kill you, but you feel lousy sometimes."

I could've gone to a base school in the Navy port of Livorno to the south, but Dad wanted me to learn the language and stay closer. With a tutor helping the first summer we were there, I pulled it off, and the more Italian I learned, and the more days I attended school, the more friends I made. Even two girls—one part German, with braids; the other dark with the biggest eyes I'd ever seen.

Dad liked to take me on Saturdays to fish in the village's little cove. The fish were tiny, but very colorful, and the place was like a pretty postcard. We could swim with masks, check out the fish and other creatures, talk about them all, and get back late with no complaints from Mom. She knew it made us both happy.

We didn't have TV — or at least didn't watch it much — but I knew from the adults and the American kids who went to school in Livorno, where we bought our groceries, that the Russians were about to do something. It was in the news. Everyone was scared. My dad and I hadn't really talked about it, but I knew it was on his mind. It would have to be. Besides, he had a newspaper with him that day in the little boat and kept looking at it while our lines sat in the water, bobbers not bobbing.

He was reading an article and then suddenly stopped. He stared at the page — no, past it — and cocked his head, as if hearing someone talking. He wasn't blinking. Then he was blinking again, as if he'd come awake.

"Jesus!" he cried and sat bolt upright. The little boat rocked. Fear raced through my chest, but it wasn't about capsizing. I didn't know what it was about. "Why didn't NAVSIC tell us?" Dad was saying.

I had no idea what he meant — it was a Navy acronym, but I'd never heard it before. His eyes were wide open.

And then he stared into space again, was quiet for a long time — long enough that I got scared again — and suddenly began talking. But it wasn't to me.

I didn't understand what he was saying. It was English, sure, not another language, but every other word was technical. He was talking as if someone who could understand it were there in the boat with us, wanting to know, and it was time for him to report.

He was white as a sheet, but he didn't sound scared. He was just white.

He had a short-sleeve shirt on. Something moved in his arm

near the wrist. I could see it. Anyone could have. It was moving to the words he was speaking. He talked, and whatever was in his skin listened. That's how it felt, though I had no idea what this meant.

I was scared, sure. The world was a scary enough place — with the Russians putting down a revolution in Hungary, launching a satellite, and frightening everyone with the kind of submarine my dad was trying to defend us against — and now this. This wasn't a "bug" you got from a crab, I told myself. This was something else. I wasn't dumb, and I wasn't a kid anymore. I thought of the movies people were seeing — *Invasion of the Body Snatchers*, *It Came from Outer Space*, and all the others. Movies my mother hated but my dad loved to see with me. I wondered again whether a crab could be something other than a crab, whether there were things in the Universe that could think and watch us even if they weren't like us.

And then it was over. My dad relaxed, color returned to his cheeks, and he said, "Let's go in. I need to contact a couple of people at the center. There's something they need to know."

Without explaining why, I let my mom know Dad needed to have his arm checked again. She pressed, but I that's all I would say: "He needs to have it checked, Mom." The doctors — even a team on the base at Livorno — still couldn't find a thing. They didn't know you could make incredible things out of plastic. And the thing the crab had put in my dad when I was seven moved in his skin only when it was told to, when something in our world was important enough — scary enough — to have it wake and listen and transmit...so that those who'd made it could do what they needed to do.

I didn't think these things all at once. They came in fragments, whispers, and it wasn't until I was a man myself that I saw them all in a single picture — a lifetime to make a picture.

Someone had been watching and listening and wanted to make sure we didn't destroy the seas. Not the land. The seas.

When my dad was eighty, he got dementia. Alzheimer's. It ran in his family. Dementia is common enough in the world, especially after a certain age, but his was different.

With each passing year of dementia he lived more and more in the sea, with the creatures that lived there, with the wonders of it—both in our seas and others. His doctors had never seen anything like it. He was so happy, they said. Alzheimer's so often has its darkness. His didn't. Sometimes he was a whale, sometimes a seal, sometimes something he just couldn't describe. Sometimes he lived for weeks in a submersible at the darkest, deepest depths of the sea where fish had their light and worms that were usually a few inches long in our world were the size of ships. His eyes were always wide when he described these things, as if he were already in heaven and could spend his days reporting how beautiful it all was and always would be even if he weren't there yet.

Sometimes, he said, he was an immense crab-like thing in a purple sea, happy to be there but knowing that creatures in distant seas by distant stars needed to be cared for, too; that machines—ships that didn't travel on water—needed to be built to reach them, so that what needed to be done could be done.

Sometimes (he said) he was a mechanical thing, tiny, one of thousands crawling across the sands of another world, or flying through its skies, or scampering across its fields, waiting for an alien creature to pick him up, to present skin and flesh so that the device could be delivered, so that it could begin to tell what it needed to tell to keep that world from dying in the terrible fires the creature and its brothers were about to make.

Sometimes, he once told my mother and me, he was the purple sea itself, alive and aware, wanting only the joy and wonder of living things to last.

Were they grateful to him? I'm sure they were. All of this— these dreams, his heaven and happiness, not fear and worry—is what you give someone when he's worked for you his whole life even if he never knew it.

I did become one—a marine biologist—and as the years pass I'm still waiting for my crab.

FROG HAPPY

New research challenges the notion that
invasive species can't coexist with native
animals.
           — *ScienceDaily*, 2015

When I was in the third grade and living outside Washington
DC, in the middle of still-undeveloped forests and creeks and
even a marsh or two, turtles were still turtles, and frogs frogs.
The crayfish and minnows the turtles ate were still crayfish and
minnows. The insects the frogs ate were still insects. The world
hadn't yet changed.

Every day, as school was ending, I would get so excited I'd
start to shake. Kids would notice it and say, "What's wrong with
you, Marcus? You're *shaking*." Even the teacher noticed, but my
parents told her I was fine, it wasn't seizures — "He's just 'frog
happy.'"

I knew where my bucket was — just inside the tree line of the
forest, behind a gnarly old maple, and under a pile of leaves —
and I couldn't wait to grab it and find the frogs and turtles I
knew wanted me to find them in the woods. The closer the clock
got to two-thirty, the more I shook. Only when I was running
from the schoolyard into the trees and, seconds later, had my
bucket in hand did my shaking calm down at all.

In the shadows of the trees were ponds with water so black
from rotting leaves — "blackwater," my dad called it — they
looked like things you'd dream about, holes in the Universe, the
gaping mouths of monsters. But there were wonderful creatures
living in, around, and above them — dragonflies swooping down

for the little insects that swarmed over the water, minnows that hid in the leaves at the edge of the pond, turtles basking on half-submerged branches, and the frogs, little ones and big ones ready to leap from pond's edge to the safety of the pitch-black water.

The bucket was one my father, who worked as a carpenter for the city, had made for me. It was wooden, hexagonal, and had a thick wire handle. On my own, I'd made a cover for it—because frogs jump even if turtles don't—and I'd go home and put the creatures I'd caught in old aquariums my father and I had found at the unfenced dump outside the city.

If I was greedy and brought too many frogs and turtles home, I didn't feel bad about it. I just put the extra ones in big mason jars with holes in the lids or in turtle bowls we'd found at a thrift shop. Then I took them in my red wagon door-to-door in the neighborhood looking for kids and grownups who might want to buy them for a nickel or a dime each. I thought everyone loved living things as much as I did, and I was right. They bought them, and that made me happy.

When the world began to change, with reports here and there, it was newspapers, magazines, radio, and television that carried the news, but not in a loud, end-of-the-world way. Besides, news was what grownups paid attention to, not kids. At first even the grownups paid little attention, because it was just statistics, observations, insect-like animals and rodent-like animals and unclassifiable small creatures that hadn't been there before and suddenly were, and no one knew why. It was odd, sure, but not like the giant ants or blobs—"mutants" from radiation—that appeared in science fiction movies to threaten humanity like an atomic war.

The first one I saw was a katydid—you know, that delicate, green grasshopper-like insect that looks like a ballet dancer or a man on stilts with a green vest. It was on the brick wall, the forest side, of our apartment building, and it was a Saturday. Because the woods were calling, I took only a quick look. It had to be a katydid, I told myself—I knew insects too—but it was pink, and its legs were twice as long as they should have been. I stopped just long enough to see — or think I saw — not just tiny little wings, three sets rather than one, but also tiny claws that looked like little hands. But this wasn't possible — my eyes had to be playing tricks on me — so I ran on toward the trees and my bucket and the ponds I needed to visit that day.

ৡ

The next one I saw was in a jar another kid brought to school. It looked like a mouse, but its head had no skin, like a naked skull, and its fur, which was a purplish-blue, grew in little tufts. It made a chattering sound in the jar the way cats sometimes do seeing a bird through a window, and then, looking at us — at each of us (at least that's what it felt like) — it opened its pointy jaws and gave a rusty squeal. Then the teacher came and took the jar away. For a long time I told people I didn't remember what it looked like, but I did. When you see something you've never seen before — something that shouldn't exist — you doubt what you see.

There were also three strange new fish — a minnow with a big fin on its back, a bright orange miniature perch, and a long, skinny gobylike fish — in the creek behind our apartment building. But it wasn't until my dad took us out one night in the car to look at the cottontails at the end of our street, on the grass by the woods, that I saw something bigger. We did this, these "bunny trips," at least once a week because my parents knew I loved it, seeing the rabbits completely still in the headlights, then leaping away, but also because my dad liked it too. He loved living things as much as I did.

That night, as the car turned in the cul-de-sac and its headlights moved to what was always there in the grass, dozens of nibbling rabbits, I saw something else. We all did.

It was bigger than the bunnies or maybe just looked like it was because it was standing on its hind legs, walking that way until it dropped back down to four. The rabbits didn't mind.

They were grazing. It was grazing, too. It wasn't a threat. It had a nose just like theirs, twitching in the headlights' glare, and big whiskers like theirs.

"Is that a kangaroo?" my mother asked. My dad had stopped the car, headlights not moving. The rabbits were staring back at us, blinking, blinded. The other creature was staring at us, too, up on its haunches, jaw no longer chewing.

The creature's ears were rabbit-like, but the nubs of horns — that's what they looked like — baby horns — were not. Neither was the size of the eyes, which were huge, as if the night they needed to see in was darker than ours.

Why, I don't know — the car hadn't moved, nothing had made a loud sound, and no predator had appeared — but the creature leaped. It leaped straight up, and, when it landed, it leaped again, like a pogo stick, this time toward the tree line. Because it was big and making such a fuss, the rabbits startled and ran too, their tails lit like little moons by the beams.

We sat there for a while. No one said a thing. The green grass between us and the woods was still. The animals were gone, the strange creature with them. It didn't *fit*, I remember thinking; but somehow it also did, I remember thinking, too. The rabbits had accepted it as they would a — well, just a bigger rabbit.

"I don't know what that was," my dad said at last, starting up the car and taking us home. We talked about it a couple of times after that, and then didn't. Only when the news articles got more frequent — and the discussions of the "new animals" louder — did we talk about it again, how we'd seen one of them together much earlier than many people had.

ৰ

A couple of months after that night, as the end of summer arrived, and I knew I had only a couple of days before school started again, I went to the painted-turtle pond, which was deeper in the forest and took longer to get to. A painted turtle looks like it's on fire. *Painted* with fire. Yellow and red flames. It was my favorite pond, and because I wanted the turtles always to be there, I never caught them. Besides, they were fast and slid into the blackwater quickly. I'd have needed a net on a long pole to catch them, and even then, they might have been too quick for me. Some animals — the old, smart ones especially — always were.

It was late in the day. The sunlight was slanting down through the oak, beech, and maple trees, blocked by their branches and leaves. At first I thought the turtles were gone. My heart started pounding, and it wasn't from "frog happiness." I was afraid something had happened to them. Dogs or big raccoons or older boys, like the ones that had chased me in the woods once.

The pond was as black as ever from the rotting leaves that fell every winter, covered the ground like a crackling blanket, but turned black in the pond.

No, I was wrong. The turtles were there. I could see their red and yellow fire in the darkness. If I got closer, I told myself, I'd see their shells, legs, and heads.

I blinked and squinted to see better. The fire was even brighter now as I stepped closer, walking as quietly as I could.

Something was wrong.

I couldn't see any turtle shells, legs and heads.

Something had to be wearing that fire — that red and yellow — but what?

Closer now, I could see that whatever the creatures wearing it were, they didn't have turtle bodies. How was that possible? No other animals had coloring like that.

These animals were too long for turtles, with four legs, sure, but with what looked like two elbows on each leg. And the heads were huge.

I had no idea what they were. I remember thinking that with all the new animals appearing in the world, and grownups not particularly upset about it, just puzzled, these — like the katydid and the mouse-creature and the little kangaroo that wasn't a kangaroo — must be okay too.

I wanted to catch one, but did they bite? Had they eaten the painted turtles or just scared them away? Were they the new painted turtles of this pond, and I would come to love them too?

I stood there like an idiot. The creatures — about fifteen of them — made a circle around the pond just as the turtles had, at the very edge of it. If I took a step toward them, to see them better, would they slide into the water too?

It was getting darker. The leaves were blocking the sun even more. I needed to get closer.

The one nearest to me — I could see the crinkly black shine of its skin now, just like a turtle's — was chewing on a crayfish, the shell of the thing falling in pieces to the leaves. I couldn't tell whether I was of interest to the creature or not. It didn't turn to look at me.

And then it happened.

I had a *thought* that wasn't my mine. I don't know any other way of saying it. That's how it felt. The thought was in my head, but I hadn't put it there. It was coming from somewhere else, and as I looked at the creature nearest me — which had turned its head to look at me and no longer looked sleepy — the thought came again.

A voice that wasn't mine.

You may, it said.

I could pick it up, it was saying. It was okay for me to pick it up.

Was I imagining this, and, by trusting, I'd get bitten?

I thought maybe I was sick. Sometimes you hear things likes voices when you're really sick. But I didn't feel sick, and the creature kept looking at me, as if waiting.

I put my bucket down and walked toward it slowly. It watched me. I watched it.

When I reached down and saw the spines on the back of its head and at its elbows, I was sure it would bite me, but wouldn't it be worth it? To hold a creature like this, one of the new ones, and one with gorgeous "painted fire" on its sides.

But it didn't bite me. Its body felt cold, the way any amphibian or reptile does, and it turned its head away from me, resting it on my hand. I'd had a chameleon in a store do that once, and even a snake. It wasn't a kitteny thing, what it did —

no purring, no rubbing — but it was trusting me.

It *knew*.

Then the voice came again, and what it said made me shake — not out of fear, but out of the wonder I always felt in the woods, with living things. What it said made me dizzy, barely able to stand, barely able to set it back down by the water, barely able to walk through the darkening trees to the apartment where I lived. What it said that day, somehow knowing me better than I knew myself, would change my life.

When I put the creature down, and it moved away from me, I also saw I'd been wrong. There *were* turtles there. Three or four of them sat at the edge of the pond, too, as if they'd always known the strange creatures sitting beside them.

ॐ

We all know now why the animals appeared gradually in our world, where they came from, and why it was our world they chose. Many things changed after that day at the painted-turtle pond. I don't catch the creatures of pond and forest and creek anymore, except to study them and treat them kindly. I certainly don't sell them in bowls and big jars from a red wagon for a dime.

I became a zoologist, and then, through more study, what today they call a "comparative xenozoologist." I study the animals of our world that have always been here, and I study the animals that are here that came later, and I compare them. The differences in anatomy and physiology are wonderfully there, of course, but they pale beside what both share in eco-context — what made it possible for us to have both as we do today. "Convergent evolution" on two worlds can produce very similar morphologies when the worlds are similar enough. "Niche balance dynamics" and "biodiversity resilience" explain tolerance and even cooperation among species from two worlds and, in turn, the prevention of a biosystem's overstress. "Reclamation ecology," "the invasive species paradox," "mutual assimilation"—these and other theories that evolved with what faced us explain it, too, I learned. The old "symbiosis" model and romantic fallacy of "pristine environments" certainly couldn't describe it, nor should they. Science must grow up, just as boys and whole civilizations must, and what might seem like impossibility, or a miracle, is, we now know, simply how life anywhere prevails if it is to *be* life.

Ten years after that visit to the pond, I returned to it. The woods were still there, though big streets were nearer—you could hear them in the distance—and more apartment buildings and their shopping centers had reached the forest's edge. The pond was still there, too, but the creatures were gone, as I knew they'd be, leaving just the painted turtles. The creatures had become something else, something the world was slowly coming to understand.

The turtle-like things had taken another form—a bird-like creature that could eat the rodents of the woods—and the bird-like creatures had become something else, something that lived in the earth like vast networks of fungus and its spores, communicating with us from there, within the earth, thought to thought. Their message was the same as the one I'd received that day by the pond when I held that gentle, spiny larva, the child of what would soon be living under our feet.

It was a simple thing, what the creature in my hand had said, and yet it changed everything—my life and the lives of those I've touched in my life.

Thank you, it said.

I didn't know what to say—I mean, to *think*.

Why? I answered.

For letting us come, the voice said.

There had been another world, we learned—a beautiful, dying world light-years away that the science of a remarkable civilization couldn't save; and an immense ship, an "ark," containing many of the species of that world. The ship had traveled for twenty thousand years looking for the right world, one with a biosphere and ecosystem so close to the one they'd lost that the species they carried could, with just a little tweaking of things—all managed at a distance by the ship's great machines—fit in without real harm to those who were already there.

Thank you for letting us come.

We never saw the captains or the crew, the beings able to build such a ship and keep the species in its vast belly alive. They sailed on because they needed to—because one planet is never enough if you want the living things you love to be really safe—and that's all right. We know what they were like by what they did, and I'm sure they shook as they did it.

THE COURTSHIP OF THE QUEEN

When he was a child, he was stranger than many children, but
not as strange as some. What he lacked in normalcy he more
than made up for in passion, sense of wonder and
acquisitiveness — the virtues that make any collector (or hunter)
great. By the age of ten he had collected more than two thousand
seashells, providing each, as any good scientist would, with its
own neatly labeled card that listed its Latin and common names,
where it had been collected and when and by whom, and the
temperature that day. If he or his parents had purchased the
seashell or it had been given to him by someone who did not
have such information, that was all right; the card would at least
bear its names. What mattered most was the beauty of the
bivalve or univalve, the clam or snail, its personality, its
character, and its role in the larger scheme of things, which the
boy saw clearly.

He kept his seashells in the drawers of two nice oak dressers
in his room and, as well, in the drawers of the ten junkier
dressers his father had with affection purchased for him at yard
sales and Salvation Army outlets and made room for in every
garage or basement or attic they had, moving them carefully
with their other furniture each time the family relocated from
one coast or country to another.

How the boy's collection had come into being was not as
strange as the boy himself, even if the size of it was: his father,
a Navy enlisted officer, moved his family often because the
Navy ordered him to, and often, because it was the Navy he
served, they lived on or near military bases by the sea; and the
boy, when he was old enough to crawl, had discovered that the

one thing he could truly make his own and take with him from one place to the next was the seashells of that place — whether they lay dead and clean on the sand of nearby beaches, lived on the mud below in shallow water, hid under seaweed at tide pools, were gifts from kind people, or were purchased by the boy, when he or his parents had the money, in local shops.

He could not take the people with him, friends he made at school, or the old women who walked the beaches in palm-frond hats, or the fishermen from the jetties. He could not take the houses his family lived in with him. He could not always even take the pets, which were sometimes lost in the moves and which, like all pets, sometimes died because pets rarely lived as long as their keepers.

He even felt that he could not take *himself* because what he was at each of his father's "stations" was different. But he could always — with his parents' encouragement because they knew he needed to take something with him or he would forget who he was — take the seashells of each place. They understood what moving meant, and they understood what could be lost. His father had fled a small town in Virginia to join the Navy and make a life for himself, and his mother was one-quarter Chickasaw Indian and, though quite educated, knew what it felt like not to know who you were.

Though it seemed odd when it began, his parents encouraged his *playing* with his seashells, too — the way other boys played with soldiers and toy boats and cars. His wanting to play with them as all children play with something did not, in fact, seem as strange to them as the cards with their scientific names and other information, which felt so adult and made them worry, lost in books as he often was, that he would never be a child. It made him — this playing — seem more normal to them; and so they watched and smiled when their ten-year-old son took the large, pink-lipped Queen Conch (*Strombus gigas*) which a shrimp fisherman in Key West, Florida, had given the boy (one his mother, without complaint, had boiled and cleaned so that it would not smell, as seashells sometimes tended to do), put it for the thousandth time on the rug in his bedroom, placed around it the fifteen tiny but feisty *Strombus alatus* — Fighting Conchs (shells he had also collected in Florida at his father's previous station) — and, as he liked to put it, played "Kingdom of the Ancient Sea" with them. After all, the Queen needed protection, he explained, looking up, and the Fighting Conchs, loyal as they were, would protect her. In actuality, Fighting Conchs could drill through the armor of other seashells and kill them, so why not here, in his fantasy, in the boy's very own kingdom, make them "the Queen's guards"?

ॐ

The big, elegant Horse Conch (*Pleuroploca gigantea*) — whose knobby shell was covered with a *periostracum* as dark as his heart — was even then approaching the Queen, whose reign (the boy explained at dinner that night) the Horse Conch wished to overthrow with his own forces, his own battalions of Fighting Conchs and his company of poisonous Cone shells, *Conus gloriamaris* (two specimens of which his parents had bought for him in Australia when he was six).

Because of the *Conus gloriamaris*, the Horse Conch would certainly have been able to defeat the Queen, who was much older and vulnerable to flattery from handsome suitors and a little tired from her centuries of reign over the Kingdom of the Ancient Sea, had it not been (the boy explained four nights later) for the ingenuity of the Queen's Carrier Shells. These shells, disguised by the broken shells and coral they had glued to themselves (as Carrier Shells do) with a calcium paste, were able after only two attempts, and in the darkest of ocean's night, to penetrate the Horse Conch's perimeter of Fighting Conchs and by their gifts of persuasion (namely, the promise of more Venus clams than any Cone shell could dream of) turn one of the dreaded Cones against the Horse Conch itself. The Horse Conch, not suspecting treachery in its own ranks, had left its naked body exposed the following night as it slept and, pierced by the

Cone's radula, had succumbed to the poison. The Fighting-Conch guards, upon discovering the horror the next morning, had, fast and nimble as they were, dispatched the traitorous *Conus gloriamaris* with ease, but the Horse Conch was dead and even the spectacle of a hundred species of the most refined and colorful Murexes in the funereal procession that followed could not restore him to this world.

Upon hearing all of this, the boy's parents did not know which was stranger — that a ten-year-old boy might daydream such political intrigue or that the actors carrying out its mortal drama might be the very seashells favored by girls, old-fashioned eccentrics or proper European ladies who had combed the beaches of the world for centuries. Their son was a marvel to them and always would be, and one strangeness would simply be replaced by another in his life, they suspected, so what was left except to love him?

As he grew older and played for even longer periods of time with his collection, he sometimes reported at dinnertime the transactions of the Kingdom and sometimes did not. Sometimes, in fact, he would say nothing for a week, even a month, and in one or two instances, even a few months. If he seemed melancholic at times, what children were not? If his hands shook on occasion — from excitement and exertion — and he scratched his arms as if he had been swimming, the salt of the sea irritating his skin — this was normal, was it not?

Once, he had been silent about the Kingdom for six months before, in passing at dinnertime, he finally revealed that the late Horse Conch had been replaced long ago as ruler of the Greater Reefs by his eldest son; and even this was ancient history because the eldest son's younger brother, a particularly fine specimen of his species, had replaced that brother at his brother's untimely death of natural causes; and that this younger brother — who had been killed by a Thersite Conch in the employ of a certain Knobbed Triton (*Charonia lampas*) out to expand his own territory with cocksure prematurity — had in turn been replaced by a cousin from the New World, the stately

Pleuroploca princeps Horse Conch, whose intentions for the Queen's territory and usurpation of her rule would soon embroil him in an intrigue that would put the first Horse Conch's machinations to shame.

The boy had seventy-five Horse Conchs of various sizes and seven species, and these did not include the *Strombus* family, of which he had three hundred specimens, among these at least four companies of Fighting Conchs of three species. The companies of Murex, Auger, Volute and Cowry were another matter entirely, numbering in the dozens as well. History and politics could not stress the boy's resources, which grew each month as he acquired more specimens, and so, his parents knew, the Kingdom of the Ancient Sea would only grow.

The new Horse Conch's intentions, naïve and inexperienced as the Princeps was, were foiled daily and in Byzantine course by the unflagging efforts of the Queen's special agents, namely, the Juno's Volute (*Scaphella junonia*), seductive in its whiteness and beauty marks, which had posed as a courtesan to obtain intelligence on the Horse Conch's western and more vulnerable reefs; five spiny Mediterranean Murexes sent as moneylenders which had, with their squidlike dye, blinded a platoon of key Fighting Conchs in the Battle of the Gorgonaceans; and the great and bilious Tun Shell, sent as an emissary, whose fragile bulk (offering no threat to His Majesty, according to the Horse Conch's key advisor, the Cameo Helmet), had actually hidden a small army of Flamingo Tongues (*Cyphoma gibbosum*), which overwhelmed and killed the Horse Conch's second youngest son.

The Queen had calculated perfectly, of course. She was not without a heart, not without compassion, and yet for her people—the fifty thousand species and countless individuals who had lived in the Kingdom of the Ancient Sea forever and only wanted peace, a peace which Princeps and five generations of Horse Conchs had threatened—she would do what was necessary. Princeps loved his second son more than he loved himself and could not bear the boy's death, and so within days he took his own life in the great Sea Fan Forest of the Eastern Reefs.

The Courtship of the Queen

When the Princeps' reign ended, and the weakest of the *Filementosa* line took his place, the Queen Conch ruled uneventfully for a time. The boy was twelve now, his arms and legs covered with the scrapes he had apparently received in the tide pools he so loved. If his scrapes — red and puckered though they were — did not bother him, why should they, his parents, make a fuss?

One day the King Helmet Shell, from the Indian Ocean, came to court the Queen despite her advanced age. His arrival and intentions were announced by twenty young and quite pristine specimens of *Charonia tritonis*, the Trumpets, and the King Helmet seemed flattered by the attention of the spectacle. The King Helmet had any number of assets of which the Queen was keenly aware: the finest corps of thirty dancing Venus Comb murexes, their spines flawless; the finest orchestra of fifty red and orange Lion's Paw scallops, *Lyropecten nodosa*; and a castle-bastion of living *Tridacnae*, not only the great giant clams called *gigas* but the smaller, more colorful *squamosa* and *hippopus*, with seven immense Pen Shells, *Pinnis nobilis*, towering over it all. Yet these assets were but entertainment, and what mattered much more, and would to any Queen, were the battalions of lethal Spider Conchs and tall, imposing Augers, which, though no match for the Queen's Fighting Conchs, represented nevertheless a threat to the stability of the Ancient Sea. A marriage of their two kingdoms might, both parties knew, bring a far-reaching and lasting peace to the Kingdom.

And yet (the boy explained, gesturing with bruised hands as his parents listened, their forks and spoons raised) the goal of lasting peace for the greater Kingdom, practical and enlightened though it might be, was not enough for the King Helmet. He could not, he had decided privately — out of vanity if not sheer jealousy — humiliate himself by marriage to an aging conch long past her years of beauty, especially one whose stature and legendary imperiousness would in the end, he knew, reduce him to mere figurehead. To be remembered in the history of the Kingdom of the Ancient Sea (for that is what vanity demanded), he would need to be more than her husband; and to be more he would, yes, need to gain command however he could of the Queen's own forces—not only the Fighting Conchs, the companies of the Cyclopean *Hexaplex fulvens* (the Giant Murexes), and the even more numerous complements of Neptune Whelks—but also her spiritual advisors, the revered and powerful Miters.

But how to accomplish this?

ॐ

At first (the boy explained a few nights later, arms folded in front of him, long shirt sleeves hiding them as if the scrapes now embarrassed him) the King Helmet was not sure. He had grown his own armies by the simple conquest of coral reefs where those who would become his soldiers farmed and hunted. He had acquired them by the sheer size of the soldiers in his first mercenary platoons, namely, other Helmets like him; and after that, by sheer numbers; and later still, by his growing stature and mystique in the Indian Ocean, Red Sea and China Sea. How to seduce forces already aligned with another?

And how, as he pursued this—the seduction of her army, its generals and her priests by whatever stratagems were needed—to distract the Queen so that she was unaware and would not interfere?

One night, as the moon ("my flashlight," the boy explained), illuminated the sea around him ("my rug under the bed, Dad"), the King Helmet saw it at last:

The Queen had mentioned more than once, and wistfully, to her attendants and others, how much she wished she had had a child—whether boy or girl, it did not matter—a child to whom she could pass her kingdom; and how this was impossible now because, even though she occasionally received male visitors who were of her species and stature, her body had lost the ability to conceive.

The King Helmet was of enough stature to be acceptable as

the father of her child, but he was not of her species. The latter was simple fact. And yet the King Helmet, as he pondered his dilemma in his guest quarters that morning, remembered a certain seashell he had once encountered, a beautiful and possibly useful one. She too was a conch, like the Queen, and one of the rarest and prettiest; but most importantly, she possessed the Queen's great pink lip. She was a gorgeous creature — her lip crenulated, her body decorated with a red embroidery — and the Queen would, he felt certain, find in the smaller conch's visage a mirror of what she herself wished to be. Rare...and beautiful...and young. If he used her carefully, she could be what he needed.

He would find this seashell, this *Sinuatus* conch. He would set his minions to the task, and when they had found her he would take her to the Queen and say, "As I have confessed more than once these past months of our courtship, Your Majesty, I too cannot bear children, whether the cause be age or the wounds of battle, of my sacrifices for my people; and this flaw within me haunts me, for what is a life if it does not leave to this world a legacy of beauty and bloodline? But what I have not told you, Your Majesty, is that once, years ago, in another life, another kingdom, I bore a child, and I bore her by a conch like you, a princess whom, because Neptune's plan is greater and wiser than mortal love, my love could not save from death in childbirth. Forgive my forwardness, but I wish I had sired her by you, my Queen; and yet she is all that I might offer you to relieve what haunts us both in our old age. I have found her again, this daughter I assumed I had lost, whose great pink lip shines in the sunlight or moonlight like your own, and whose channel twists like yours, even if she also bears a shield not unlike my own."

How would the Queen react? Would she find in this lie the answer to her most profound sadness?

As the boy posed these questions to the air at dinner that night, his parents truly felt them. The story — the boy was thirteen now — was as real as anything else in their lives, and of course they wondered how it would go, this subterfuge, this manipulation of an old queen's heart by the vanity of a king unable to love.

But when they pressed him a few nights later, the boy did not answer. He seemed withdrawn, more upset than usual about the Kingdom, and he made strange, slow gestures in the air as if defending himself from something they could not see.

When they pressed him again that weekend, he said only, "It isn't right, what is happening now. I tried to help him, but suffered wounds in my attempt."

"Wounds?" his father asked, not knowing what his son meant, and wanting very much to know. He stepped toward the boy, to check his body for injury, but his son moved away.

"They are minor," the boy said to him. "They will heal on their own, Dad."

His mother and father looked at each other and, without a word, knew the truth: The boy was referring merely to his tide pool scrapes — which in the Kingdom of the Ancient Sea would of course be "wounds."

When they had given up hope of finding out what had happened in the story — when the story had faded enough from their own lives, from his father's work at the base and his mother's teaching at the local high school, that the Queen's fate no longer held them in the morning when they woke and at night when they fell asleep — the boy did tell them. It was many months later, and at dinner, as always, that he said:

"The Queen was too cynical to fall for his lie. She had never sensed in the King Helmet's heart the capacity for love that would have allowed him to sire a child with a conch, with a woman of another species. And in this she was right. He was too vain, too proud, to be sullied by such mixing, and the Queen knew this. But this was not all that protected her from his ruse. It was her own cynicism, her own insistence on the profound sadness (the idea of her barrenness) with which she had lived so long that she could not live without it, that protected her most from his lie."

His parents stared, waiting. "Yes?" they both said.

"Nevertheless, the Queen agreed to marriage—though in name only, with separate quarters, their lives sharing not even breakfast—that their kingdoms might be joined for the sake of the people of the Ancient Sea." The boy paused, as if sad, though perhaps (they told themselves) he was only feeling thoughtful. His mother had seen a mark on his face the week before, a little puncture wound, like a spider bite, one that made a hole, but it had healed. He'd had a fever then, too, but there was no reason, the boy insisted, to think the two matters were related. "She was a queen, after all," he was saying to them now, "and did in her heart, despite the sadness that told her who she was, truly care about her people. Is this not what a queen must do, even if she despises the partner of the union that may achieve it?"

The boy's parents nodded. Of course that is what a good queen must do; and it made them proud that their son, whose whole life was reading and seashells and had so little in common with the world other people lived in, could be so wise, could in fact understand that world perhaps even better than they, who had lived in it for so long.

೭

"It is the story of the Queen's Minister of Coral Reefs that matters now," the boy said, obviously upset, "because he is the one who may actually destroy the Kingdom in the end, though that is the last thing he imagines he could ever do. He falls in love with the Queen. That is how it happens. I have tried to help him see the truth, but it is impossible...."

There was indeed, his parents saw, a sadness in their son's eyes (which were still red, as if a trace of the fever were still in him). He was fourteen now, and had been asking about girls recently—what they were like in their hearts and minds, in the way they thought and felt, how they were different from boys, if they were, and the same, if they were—and, given his words now, it was difficult for them not to imagine that the two were somehow, in a way only he understood, related.

"Love doesn't always—" his father began, stammering, then tried again: "Love doesn't always need to end in tragedy." As soon as he said it, he felt embarrassed; but his son, who was looking at him now, smiled. "I know, Dad, but thanks for reminding me. I'm just speaking about the Minister, who is not experienced in love and so can be taken advantage of. Those who do not walk the corridors of power can afford to engage in the playfulness of love without tragic consequence, but I'm afraid the Minister is not one of these."

His parents did not know how to respond. What could they say? The boy understood it better than they possibly could. But shouldn't something be said?

"Is there no way," his father went on, "to warn the Minister, to help him understand?"

The boy's mother stared at her husband as if he had lost his mind; but then she too looked at the boy, nodding, wanting an answer. There were no marks on her son's face, no marks on his arms (which were bare), so she did not have to worry and could listen.

The boy sighed. "I wish it were so, but those who live as the Minister lives are too isolated to be warned, or to listen even if they are."

Again, his parents thought they saw in their son's eyes something more personal than the story he was telling, but what words could they give him? His father was not going to say, though he wanted to: "Could the Minister not listen more carefully to his heart, to find wisdom there that might protect him from foolishness?" Or: "Could he not stop for a moment and see that love might not really be a trap, but a way to live— to really live—even if the corridors of power make it so difficult?" His mother was not about to say, "Whatever happens to your Minister, Brian, that is not what *your* life needs to be." Certainly not that, though that was what was in her heart, both as a mother and as a woman who loved a man, and whose life was good, even if they both worried sometimes about their son.

When the boy entered high school, his body—which often did not feel like his own—changed, and with it his mind and what that mind saw in the world; and though the seashells were still with him, so were girls and other boys and teachers. Without planning it—without seeing at first the dynamic of mind and heart that might allow and ensure it—the people he came to know at school and after school, those willing to speak to him despite his manner of speech and the rash he often had, suddenly seemed real to him; and he began to write about them in the diary where he now recorded the Kingdom's story as he knew it; the diary he had been keeping for the past year and, like the marks he brought back from the Kingdom each night, had not confessed to his parents.

One day at school, in the corridors of the main building, he spoke to a girl, one he had two classes with and noticed frequently outside of class. They spoke on the Ninth Grade patio. How it had occurred, he could not be sure when he looked back at it that evening in his bedroom. She had been standing there, talking to other girls, and had turned to look at him as he passed. She did not stare at the rash on his neck, which itched from the sea, but simply looked at him, eyes open to what she might see. He had stopped because she had looked at him this way; and when she said, "Hi, Brian," he stood there looking back at her until he heard himself say, "Hi," too. The other girls left, and he and she remained, sometimes finding words (she found them more easily than he) and sometimes just standing there, looking around at the other students, not saying a thing, but also not leaving, as if being together mattered to both of them somehow. What all of this meant, he could not be sure.

They spoke again two days later, impulsively and spontaneously and more thoroughly, as if they both knew, without needing to think about it, what to say. She had long dark hair and pale, but not unhealthy, skin. He liked looking at her, though it made him shy, too; and, as he looked, he felt not only an excitement—the racing of his heart—but something else; a tenderness, a kindness, toward her. He had said something that morning in English class that the other students had laughed at and that the teacher, a conscientious woman, had praised, but with a look on her face that suggested she hadn't perhaps understood it. The girl had *not* laughed, which told him that she was not afraid to be alone in the world or pursue in her life what she believed was right.

Standing there on the Ninth Grade patio again, she asked about his own life, where he lived, what his parents did, and what he enjoyed doing most—what made him "happiest." He answered the first questions easily—the way other boys and girls would answer them (something he was learning to do)—but the last question left him silent until she said, "If it's against the law—if you like to shoplift and that's what makes you happiest—you don't have to tell me." It was a joke, he saw. There was a light dancing in her eyes, which meant she was being playful. He said, "I love the sea." It was not an answer to her question; but he did not know how else to phrase it.

"I do too," she answered quickly, and he could tell she meant it. She had touched his hand, a hand whose raw skin would have frightened many. Should he ask her to come to his house after school? She lived only a few blocks from the military base, from the beach were he spent so much of his life, the one that was always empty because even the sailors never used it, and that always displayed on its sands the seashells of the bay, the *Chiones* and *Tellinas* and *Turitellas*. His father could get her a pass so she could visit, so the guards at the gate would let her through; but he didn't know what she would think of his seashells, or the Kingdom, or whether she had a place in it, or even wanted one.

ॐ

That night, as he lay in bed, a voice said: B*e careful, my soldier. Remember, you are in my service. In her beauty this Volute of yours may be a subterfuge. The King Helmet will, I am certain—and this haunts my sleep—never relinquish his plans of empire.*

Two nights later, however, as he began to fall sleep, the same voice spoke, with a sigh: *I advised you poorly, Soldier. An innocent and a commoner, she may not be a spy....*

I believe this, too, Your Majesty, the boy answered, *but is she the one? Is she the one that I, simple servant that I am in your service, have been waiting for all these years, stationed with the other Fighting Conchs on Your Majesty's northernmost Barrier Reef, here to repulse what may threaten you, our bodies wounded and yet prevailing for your sake? Is she, pretty and pale as she is, the one I will fight and perhaps die for if I do not die for you – for love is worth nothing, is it not, unless the lover is willing to risk everything for love?*

The boy waited, very awake. He would go to the Kingdom this night, as he did every night, and fight for his Queen. He would go as soon as she ordered. But the voice did not speak, and its silence made him shake. The next morning he still did not have his answer. Not knowing what else to do, he wrote about the girl in his diary. In his story, where the boys and girls he knew were all seashells, each with a role in the story of the Ancient Sea, she was indeed a young, impulsive Juno's Volute, pale, with beauty marks, though she might as well have been the Black Cowry, *Cypraea nocturnis,* in its enigmatic, starry beauty. He could not make up his mind, and he could not be certain of her role. He wrote about her five mornings in a row, posing again and again to himself and to his silent Queen the questions of who this girl might be in the great tale the Kingdom was and would always be, and whether his body would ever be truly his; but on the sixth morning he stopped, put down his pen, and stared at the page, which no longer made sense. She – Carey – her name was Carey – was a *girl.* Was there anything more important than this?

At school that day, near his locker on the bottom floor of the main building, he asked her if she would like to come over sometime, after school or on a Saturday, to do homework together, if she wanted, and also, if she wanted, to see his seashells.

She cocked her head. Then she laughed, though not

217

unkindly, touched his hand again, making it tingle and burn as any touch did; and, with the light dancing in her eyes again, said, "Sure!"

As she did, he saw suddenly that all was well at last in the Kingdom, that a peace not easily ruined — one that might prevail for years — had at last been achieved by the most willing of hearts; and that, because it had, his Queen might no longer need him and might soon (if he listened carefully enough for her voice) let him go. Only then would he stop bleeding from the battles he engaged each night in another body, returning with countless small wounds to his own. Only then would he stop having to clean spots of blood from his sheets after his parents left for work in the morning; stop worrying about the venomous bites of the Cones and Augers (which made his body burn); stop hiding his wounds with every trick he knew; and let his body heal at last, his once more.

She was looking at him still, and she had, he could tell from her eyes, which were darker than any sea, no intention of looking away.

SIDHA

I wasn't present in the Comm Nexus on Work Level 73 when the ancient starship arrived in the Lock — or should I say "tried to arrive and somehow succeeded"? — but I felt it. Everyone did. The entire Station, two hundred levels of it, shook. Why? Because the starship shouldn't have gotten in, I was told later. It registered, by its proton profile, as a Highland Class A, one of the first designs — which it was, or had been once, though it was bigger now, bigger than the newest classes. When our starlock and its concentric tokomaks accepted the ship's jump, the stress of it cracked viewing plates throughout the Station and the Lock itself spit out rivets trying to hold the thing that had appeared suddenly in its embrace.

When you are a ship that has been traveling the galaxy for a thousand years, and the nanomechs have been repairing your outer skin for those thousand years, you have a lot of scar tissue. Your outer hull is twice as thick. The starship-class identifier just doesn't know it and you get a go light. It thinks you're the same size you once were and realizes too late you're not.

Had the ship collapsed, its pilot would have died in the implosion. Had the Lock ruptured, the Station and its five thousand citizens would have died. Somehow neither gave. It was like a strange homecoming, one that both pilot and Station community wanted even if they didn't know it, and so the Lock took the ship in.

"Sidha!" the starship pilot called out on a hundred frequencies, a cry. He called out the name the instant his ship materialized in the Lock, and he kept calling it, like a beacon, as the ship sat there. Or should I say the ship called it out, since the

219

pilot had, over that millennium, become the ship. They had been a single thing for a long time.

"*Sidha! Sidha! Sidha!*"

It was a forename, not a surname, and one the Station knew. It was a common first name. Hundreds of women had it, and I was one of them.

That he — that *it* — the pilot and the ship — was calling for *me* and not any of the other Sidhas, became clear only when the scanners bio-scanned the starship, found a tiny sample of genetic material on a slide in an empty, lonely lab, saw that it was tagged to the name being called, and realized which Station Sidha it most closely matched.

He — it — had once known a Sidha who'd had many of my genes, including those associated with personality, minor emotional pathologies, and the likelihood of certain behavior. He'd known her well, the Station administrators concluded. "He loved her in the way human beings loved then," they told me when Protocol on Work Level 127 called me in. "The way we cannot afford to love if the Station is to survive...if it is to prevail."

"He knew a matrilineal ancestor of yours," they said. "Someone who used the same forename and shares to a remarkable degree your gen-profile. Someone who was important to him, one of the initial workers on the Station. He is insane — because any millennial cyborg, after all that radiation and interface bleeding must be insane — and he has come back to find her."

"Why?" I asked.

"As I said, he 'loved' her."

"'Cyborgs don't experience love,'" I heard myself quoting.

"This was from before. His first assignment as captain was to take the ship out into the galaxy from this very Station, this very Lock, when it had only five hundred citizens. Its brief maiden voyage, one without other human occupants. He was here, Memory says, for two weeks before he did that and must have met and spent emotionally and physically intimate time

220

with her then.... He was human, a trained pilot, and still a discreet human body. He must have gotten lost, the ship malfunctioned, communications failed, and the ship kept him alive by taking that discreet body and making it something else...a part of it."

I tried to imagine what it must have been like, and could not. No one on the Station could. No one would ever be able to, I knew.

"Did you tell him she isn't here?" I asked quietly.

"Yes, but he insists that she is."

"Why?"

"Because he has scanned us, too. He has scanned the Station, and he has found here a genetic profile he believes is hers. You must have realized by now — by our calling you for this meeting — whose profile that is."

"I do not wish to do this," I said quickly.

"You are afraid," the Protocol deputy answered, her broad face so much like mine.

"Yes," I said.

"We cannot indulge your fear. You must do this for others. For the Station."

When I saw that I did not have a choice — that we never really had a choice on the Station — I felt something different. Something *new*.

An *excitement*.

ঽ

What is love? It is, scientists tell us, what it needs to be to serve human beings in whatever circumstances they find themselves in. To serve them by providing connection to others in the formation and function of a "tribe," and to nurture emotionally — because millions of years of evolution on a distant home planet cannot be overridden in mere millennia — the individual who must operate within that "tribe."

"Romantic love" as it was once experienced in other

"circumstances" occurs occasionally on a Station like ours, but it does not serve the operations and survival of the Station as it may have once served small, planet-based communities or a societal economy based on consumption of cultural "stories" and values. On this Station, if we feel a "romantic" love, we are told, it should be for the Station itself, the greater cause and purpose of it, and not for another individual with a forename and surname and number. "Romantic love is selfish," they tell us, "unless it is for a higher purpose."

Have I ever "loved" another discreet human on this Station? No. I have never needed to. Why would anyone here have that need? In my units on the Domicile levels (I have lived in four) I have had sex in order to nurture body and psyche, those relics of evolution, but that is not the same. I may have felt affection for my sexual partner, whose face was attractive, but that is not what I mean by "love" as the Protocol staff used the term in our meeting a few hours ago. I have had more than one long-term, shared-cell partner in my life of thirty-three standard years. I am of course attracted to the human body, but that isn't "love." Though partnering may generate comforting emotions simply by a routine of a psychologically safe intimacy that may or may not involve sex, partnering isn't "love" either.

I have often wondered whether human beings, still the children of that evolution, need love of a more ancient kind in the circumstances we have made for ourselves so far from our planet of origin. I do not have the answer for this, and the scientists on this Station seem unable to provide the answers, though I have asked many times. I have, in fact, recently been told by my work supervisor in Health Services to stop asking. "Constant questioning may reveal a dissatisfaction with your identity and service to the Station's operations," she informed me. "I do not want to have to send you for testing. That would reflect badly on us all."

I understood what she was saying. It had happened before, and I'd been warned. I was *unhappy*, and all the scientists could say was that it was "genetic," a "coded proclivity," perhaps

Station inbreeding, and not "situationally determined." It could not be fixed, they were saying, and I could not argue. They had prescribed medications — the psychotropics many of us take on the Station — but these had made me feel *nothing*, as if I were not alive, and I had stopped them without confessing it. Some do not mind that feeling. It may help them. But I did not want to feel that way.

I can remember being unhappy when I was little, when my caregivers would use the word "discontent," and even the toys — the miniature plastic Station and miniature Lock and the little figures of a medical assistant (what I would become someday, they insisted) and her professional colleagues and sexual partners (all in a plastic clinic you could carry in your arms) — did not bring me joy, and later I would argue with the assignation, to no avail. When I was eight, I had a friend, a girl, who made me laugh, and that made me happy. But we were separated when the relationship analysts determined that I'd become "too attached," and my assigned parents agreed.

২

Why the Station is willing to oblige the cyborg pilot, who has asked to see me, I do not know. They could refuse him, citing the same reasoning my supervisor cited for my endless questions: it would be "destabilizing to Station operations." Perhaps it is because of an old law. Or simple courtesy. Perhaps it is at the request of the Station's behavioral scientists. Perhaps only the "curiosity" of someone at a supervisory level, though why resources would be spent satisfying that emotion I do not know, especially if the cyber-consciousness running the ship is, as they claim, "insane."

I spend time on the Station's computers as I wait to be called again. I spend it wisely, but what I find myself looking for surprises me, though perhaps it shouldn't: What is "insanity"? Can it be fixed, and even should it be? And this too: What is it that really lies beyond the Station and Lock? What is "the universe," "the galaxy"? How can something that is dark and endless, so blind, also be full of light and wonder and *seeing*? How could one be unhappy *out there*?

This is *curiosity*, I know, and it creates problems, the behavior analysts say. I have been reprimanded before.

ॡ

When the time comes later in the day, the Protocol staff escorts me through three quarantine-styled mini-locks (they have tested for microbial contamination and there is none) onto the starship. We walk for an hour from one deck to another, our bootsteps echoing, a strange energy everywhere, and finally reach the bridge, which is smaller than I imagined it would be for such a vessel. I have never been on a ship before. Few of the Station's citizens have, though a dozen ships pass through the Lock every standard day.

Standing on the bridge, they show me a hand-held hologram of what they imagined he would have looked like as a discreet body. Pale skin, pale hair, brown eyes without an epicanthic fold, short but big-boned. A uniform of the kind the interstellar fleet officers once wore. The hologram is small and doesn't move. It tells me less than what I need to know. Than what *curiosity* would want me to know.

"Where is he now?" I ask.

"On the other side of that wall," a staff member answers. "It was once sleeping quarters, but was long ago refitted to contain, oxygenate, feed and rejuvenate a human body to whatever degree the ship's resources were able. You could say he is sleeping, but he is quite awake, and waiting for you. If you speak, he'll know it is you. We've synched your voiceprint to the gen-profile."

"Hello," I say to the air, not knowing what else to do.

We are not wearing suits. The ship makes its own oxygen, stale though it smells, and the Station's own vast system is ready to supplement if necessary. I can hear the breathing of the six

Protocol staff members near me, and I can hear my own.

"Hello, Sidha!" a voice booms suddenly. The software is old and the voice like an ancient transmission from space, from another corner of another galaxy. It is strangely androgynous, neither man nor woman, or both, but for some reason it makes me happy.

"Hello, Captain Salceda." I have been given his surname and told to use it. It was a name from three of Earth's continents, from a strange world where the people often spoke more than one human language and traveled from continent to continent when they were able.

"Let me look at you, Sidha," the voice booms. I let it.

"Don't move," a staff member has whispered beside me. "Let him see you."

"You do not look the same, Sidha," the voice says at last. Is it disappointment I hear, or do I imagine it?

I want to ask him what she looked like, and why I look different to him. Is it my height (I am short, too, by the Station's average)? My skin? We are all the same color basically on the Station, with only occasional regressions. My face, its features? The shape of my head? It is round, and perhaps was not.

I don't ask him because he is saying:

"You are older. But you are still my Sidha."

What does he see with his ship's sensors that I cannot see in the mirrors of my unit?

A sharp look from a staff member is meant to remind me how insane the captain is.

"We were together for only two Station weeks, Sidha," the ship is telling me. "Not long enough for two people in love. Would you like to join me on my next mission? We will be going to 'The Goblin,' to 2015 TG387, which should have been visited long ago. I'm not sure why it wasn't, but your Station's records show it unexplored, and what an insult that is, wouldn't you say? There is a berth near mine. You can sleep there, my Sidha."

Did I expect to feel at least something from his words? *Do* I feel something? Is it simply curiosity, that ancient impulse, or something else—something that can make you spend hours in Station Memory?

Is insanity contagious? Is there something in the conditioned air of this ship that is making me feel what I would not, were I sane, feel?

"Tell him 'no,'" the staff member whispers at my side. "We must end the meeting but keep you available to him so that the scientists and technicians can continue to study the anomaly."

Would the pilot and the ship he has become allow me to leave?

The staff member guesses my thought:

"The Station will override any objection from him."

I'm quiet for a while, and then, instead of a "no," I say:

"*Yes. I will go with you, Captain.*" That is what the first Sidha, the one he knew, would say—the woman I am to him.

The staff member nearest me, in his clean smock, steps back, shocked. The other members stiffen, looking at each other, trying to decide what to do. It has taken them completely by surprise, but they are not Security. They are not trained in physical restraint.

"They are trying to override your self-protections, Captain," I announce loudly, not knowing the right words to say it.

A Protocol member has grabbed me by the arm, and I do not struggle at first.

"I know what they are trying to do, Sidha," the captain's voice booms. "They will fail."

"I will go to your L-15-2002," I hear myself say quickly, and the member who has my arm lets go in disbelief.

As I waited for this meeting, I found the Highland Class A blueprints. They were easy enough to locate in an information system stretching back thirteen hundred years, one of the Station's prides. I knew, because it was logical, that, despite the changes to its hull made by assaults of objects in space and the repair work done by the nanomechs, the ship's interior structure would probably be unchanged.

"They cannot stop us this time, Sidha," the voice booms.

"You wanted to come with me. You fought to come with me. But they beat us. They drugged you and locked me in my ship. They made me go. I pray that you have forgiven me for not fighting harder. They made me leave you, Sidha, to a life on this Station, and I have not forgotten. I will *never* forget."

I found nothing about any of this in the system. Why would I? It was personal, a discrete body's life and feelings. That is not what the Station's computers hold.

I jerk away from the Protocol member, who, despite lack of training, has grabbed me again, and I avoid the hands of others as I run from the bridge into a passageway, then into another, and another, bootsteps behind me.

"Take the next one," the ship's voice whispers, and I do. The bootsteps begin to fade. I am breathing again.

The ship has started to shake. It is, I know, getting ready to jump. Will the Lock let it?

"Yes," the voice whispers, as if we are together already, our bodies the ship, my thoughts his, and his mine.

The starlock must let him leave, I realize. It must help him jump. If he were to destroy the ship in the Lock, the Station would be destroyed with it, and everyone would die. How can one Station citizen, a useless ancient ship, an insane captain and a single burst of energy from the tokomaks compare to such losses?

I run, falling twice, getting up, the voice telling me where to go even as the engines grow louder, the shaking steadies, and the ship begins ever so slightly to grind against the Lock, to loosen itself.

When I stop running because the voice tells me to, I am at a small room whose four sealed doors the captain opens for me one by one, and then closes again behind me. I am safe.

The ship is about to launch into Lockspace. I feel it. It is positioned where it needs to be. I remember this from the research, too. Our Lock is almost ready to send us to another Lock among distant stars. That is what the research says.

I know how it will go. What will happen to me. I can hear

the captain whispering again, telling me.

It will go like this, my Sidha, he says:

When we have jumped a thousand light years to the next Lock and its Station, we will exit that Lock and come to rest in Real Space. He will guide me to the bridge again, and I will walk there, my breathing calm. At the bridge, I will stop by the bulkhead, the one on the other side of which he sleeps and yet is awake, speaking to me whenever he wishes from a dream that is not a dream.

He will tell me what I must do to join him. He will tell me what berth to go to, and all the things I can do on this ship as we travel the stars, talking like people who've known each other for years.

Will I *feel* it? Will I feel anything like what he feels for me, or felt once, his body still flesh and blood, for the woman whose name I bear?

I do not know, and I do not need to. I will feel *something*.

Something *new*.

I will feel *alive*, and isn't that what love should always make us feel?

THE WITCH MOTH

The Black Witch moth can grow up to 16 cm.
and is known as "La Mariposa de la Muerte."
— *Encyclopedia Americana*

The Black Witch moth should be seen at night when it cannot
be seen because it is so black. In the daylight it is a hole in the
universe, one that leads to a world where there is no light.

The first Black Witch moth I ever saw was in the sunlight of
Balboa Park, when I went there for a dahlia show to keep my
grandmother company — which I did often when I was ten
because my grandmother's love kept me from darkness in my
family, where my mother's spells could reach us all.

The moth flew from a hydrangea bush I had rustled with my
hand, hoping something might burst from it — a lizard or
butterfly perhaps. At first I didn't understand what the darkness
was. A small rubber bat on the end of a child's string? A
black handkerchief given life by a spell? Or was it just my eyes
playing tricks on me, blinded by the sunlight that made the
flowers so bright?

It limped through the air and disappeared into the hole it
had made in the universe. My grandmother had stopped
because I had. "Are you all right?" she asked.

"I don't know," I answered. I often said such things to her,
but she didn't mind. She knew that all light carried shadow and
that there were things in the world — and in every family — you
couldn't see even if you had the entire sun to see them by.

"You saw something," she said, as if she knew exactly what
it was and where everything was going to end.

"Yes."

"I'm sure you did, but if it's important you will see it again; and if not like this, then later, when you need it even more. Let's go look at the dahlias now. We can come back here later if you want, if you haven't seen it somewhere else in the park by then."

I nodded. She was right. I would find it again if I needed to, and if not today, then sometime, in some way.

Some people who love see only the light. My grandmother saw the darkness, too, and still loved. That made me feel safe in a world where, she'd once told me, "There are more witches than even the witches know...."

২

Because we lived on a Navy base, one that hugged the bayside of the peninsula, I took my little brother, who was six, with me when I went to the tallest piers, to their oily pilings and oily planks, which you could smell. He felt safer when we went to the floating docks, because the water was close to you. You didn't have far to fall. But the boats there were small—patrol boats, skiffs, and a sailboat or two for the personal use of officers. We both liked the great steel ships—which could only dock at the tallest piers—and if I promised we would stay in the middle when we walked on them, Tommy could come with me. I held his hand so tight it hurt him sometimes, but I did it because I was scared for him. I didn't want him running to the edge of the pier and falling to the water far below, which sometimes happened when I dreamed. I wouldn't be holding his hand tight enough in the dream. He'd pull away and, screaming, run to the edge and not stop running. He'd go over, and the screaming would stop only when he hit the water. It was as if this was what someone wanted (and I knew who). To drown him. To make him go away. To make *us all* go away.

Even when we walked down the very middle of the pier, he could look down and see the green, oily water far below through the narrow cracks between the planks. I'd tell him not to look, but sometimes he would, and it would stop him. He'd sit down on the planks, oily as they were, and he wouldn't move no matter how hard I pulled. He'd start crying. "She's going to get me, Jimmy!" he'd say. "She's going to put me in the trash cans, or drown me." He meant our mother, and he was right — spells can pull you through cracks — but what could we do? She was our grandmother's daughter, and (so our grandmother said) *a witch who didn't know she was one — or didn't* want *to know...because it was easier that way.*

I thought he might start screaming, like the dreams, but he didn't. He would instead cry in hopelessness, in the most terrible sadness I had ever heard. I'd have to pick him up and carry him a ways to get him to forget the water.

When I told our grandmother, who lived with us, how Tommy behaved on the pier, she stopped her ironing and said to me: "My little brother did the same thing. His name was Ralph. He had curly hair and died when he was six, taken away by a stranger. He was adorable, and I loved him very much. I don't think I've ever told you about him, have I?"

"No, Grandma. He must have been special."

"He was. He would get scared of falling through the cracks. He would carry on and on, sitting there on the pier and looking down through them."

"It's so silly, isn't it, Grandma. To be scared like that."

She looked at me. "No, it isn't. Your little brother has reason to be scared. I do what I am able, but she never stops. She does it in her sleep, too. She's just too strong."

"I hold Tommy's hand so hard it hurts him."

"I know, Jimmy. You love him, but sometimes that's not enough. Sometimes they die anyway, even if you don't want them to. Sometimes people take them away, if not in a stranger's car then in a dream that is no dream — one you don't know is coming...."

འ

We would go out to the end of the biggest pier, Tommy and me, because there we could look out at the whole bay and to our right and left the steel ships tied with immense ropes to metal cleats taller than I was. Sometimes a sailor would be there, one we got to know. He would be at the end of the pier looking out at the bay, too, but he would be waiting for something.

He had a rope tied to a cleat that no one used for anything. He wanted something to take what was on the end of it. The first time we met him he said: "Know what's at the end of this rope?"

"No," I answered.

"They shouldn't be this huge this far into the bay, but surfers down on the Strand disappear every once in a while. You never know what's in the sea — even in a bay."

"I guess not," I said.

Tommy seemed scared of the sailor, but I held his hand tight and finally he stopped pulling.

"You live in one of the quarters by the banyan tree?" the sailor asked.

"Yes."

"Must be nice."

It was — except for the smells at night, and how our father cried. But I didn't say this. I wanted him to tell us more about the rope and what was down there in the water.

He kept looking out at the bay. His hands were slick with something I'd seen on my own hands before. Fish scales and fish slime. You couldn't fish without getting it on you, but where was his catch?

"I've got a tuna hook on that rope, and I put a whole mackerel on it, case you're interested. You boys fish?"

I nodded.

"Thought so. I've pulled in a lot of leopards and blues out here. Eight-footers and ten-footers. Even a twelve-foot mako. There's a four-foot steel leader. They can't get through it — even the big ones."

I nodded again. I didn't know what else to do. I loved to catch things. I loved fishing, even if it smelled. It was a different

232

odor from the one that filled the streets around our quarters at night, under the biggest banyan tree anyone had ever seen.

ॐ

The next time we went, the sailor wasn't there. It was as if he'd never been there — never existed — but I knew that wasn't true. I knew what was real and what she could take away. I'd always known. That was why (Grandma said) she hated me so.

Tommy was frightened of how empty the end of the pier was, so we came home.

The time after that, the sailor was putting a live mackerel on a hook that was wider than our father's hand. He let Tommy touch the hook. Tommy touched it without getting scared. He just stared at it, eyes wide, and touched it more than once.

I knew she would have put Tommy on that hook if she could, but I was watching Tommy, and my grandmother was watching me even when she wasn't around.

ॐ

The next time, the sailor was leaning over and making a sound. When we got up to him, we almost left. He was throwing up.

He looked at us and straightened up, embarrassed. His eyes were red, like he'd been crying.

The rope was gone.

He looked so sick.

"You all right?" I asked. My parents and grandmother had raised me to be courteous.

He didn't answer that. Instead he said:

"I found a dog, a pretty big one, over by the barracks. He was starving to death." He stopped talking and bent over again, but didn't throw up. "That's what I used. He didn't fight me. He was weak. I don't know why I did it. I knew something was out there, something bigger than twelve feet, and I wanted it...."

233

He pointed to the cleat where the rope had been.

"It took the whole thing. What would it have to be to take the rope, the whole thing, like that?"

I didn't know what to say.

"I keep seeing that dog. I had a dog once when I was little...."

I saw Tommy on the hook—because that was what she wanted. But she'd have to find another hook. This one I was watching.

ॐ

The next time we went out, and the four times after that, the man was gone. When I asked another sailor—one that worked in the metal shops by our quarters—he said he didn't know any sailor like that.

"He was out at the end of the first pier a lot," I said.

"A swabbie catching sharks?"

"It was after work," I said. "On weekends, too. I think his name was Curt."

"He'd have been with the shops. No one by that name here. You sure he was a sailor?"

"He wore blues," I said.

"You must have been imagining things," he said suddenly, and for a moment he sounded just like our mother. He *was* our mother. Her voice, her body just below his skin. Not in our heads, but completely *real*—because that is what witches do. She could do things like this, I knew, and she knew I knew.

I looked away. I didn't want to see his eyes, which weren't his. I took Tommy home. I led him down the street between the machine-shop Quonset huts to the dirt path, past the goldfish pond and the greenhouses, into our house with all its rooms, holding his hand tightly because he was my brother.

ॐ

I missed talking to the sailor, the one with the rope and the hook, even though Tommy had nightmares about the dog. The nightmares stopped. I had bad dreams, too, but they helped me remember that I had a dog—a little one, a fox terrier named Walter. How I'd forgotten him, I didn't know, or I did, but didn't want to think about it—that she'd taken him away without my knowing.

I asked her—I was feeling brave—but, busy as she was with her schoolwork, she just looked at me with those black eyes of hers, the ones that wanted to kill someone or something, and I finally went away—which is what she wanted.

I didn't tell anyone I missed the sailor, but my grandmother knew.

"You missed him because he was a piece of you, Jimmy. You'd made him one. You both loved fishing. But he wasn't scared enough. You've got to be scared sometimes."

I asked her about our dog. She didn't know either. It bothered her. "Sometimes things die and you just don't know they have," she said, looking up at the ceiling as she folded our clothes, trying to remember our dog, not able to, upset. "She's getting worse, Jimmy. She's my daughter. I don't know what to do...."

※

My father would cry when he got home from the submarine warfare laboratory he directed—the one high on the peninsula, looking down on the bay.

He hadn't always cried like this. He'd started crying a month before, the day our mother started screaming about how she had a right to be happy but how could she with all of us?

He'd take off his uniform, which smelled like him (I loved that smell), and he'd go upstairs to his bedroom, shut the door, and start crying. Sometimes he wouldn't come down for dinner. I thought my mother would take him his meal, but she said no, he could come down if he wanted it. When I tried to take it to him once, she knocked the plate out of my hand and started shouting about how she was going to leave us one way or another.

I tried to do it another time, too, and she slapped my face. She wanted to do more than that, but Grandma's voice—she was at her card group in town, but she was in the room somehow—said: "No, Martha. *Do not*...."

Later, when she couldn't see me, I stood by his door and listened to the crying. I wanted to think it was headaches— "migraines" could make a grown man cry—but it wasn't. He was just very sad. Grandma said he'd never gotten over his mother's death when he was little, in that epidemic that killed so many in the world, but we knew it wasn't that really. It sounded, the way he cried, like someone who was dying— because she wanted him to, I knew—and he was remembering what it was like before, and he missed it, so he cried.

ॐ

We had the quarters we had—a tennis court, a little beach, a sailboat tied to the floating docks, a big front lawn—because my father's boss didn't want them. He was an admiral and, like all admirals, liked to give parties. He wanted to live up by the laboratory, in a modern house, looking down on the lights of the bay and the long island in the middle of it where Navy jets landed and took off day and night. He could have parties on the patio there, looking down at everything, he said.

There were other quarters like ours, though not quite as nice, on the other side of the old banyan tree. Another captain and his family lived there. He had a wife and a daughter who was "slow."

The terrible smells at night, after taps played and night covered the base—and the sailors were in their barracks— didn't come from the buildings or the banyan tree or the streets that wound among the metal-shop buildings, the two quarters and the great tree. They came from the gray dumpsters and trash cans everywhere.

I thought at first it was dead fish. It might have been at first, but not later. The other captain's wife—in the other quarters—

liked to fish, but she hated to clean the creatures she caught. Even when they were twenty- or thirty-pound Black Sea Bass, she would dump them in whatever garbage cans she came across that weren't near her quarters.

This was when the bay was still young and the peninsula was still pretty wild. You could see coyotes at night moving like ghosts in packs up by the laboratory. You could catch big fish in the bay, as if no one had ever fished for them before, and so they trusted and bit and you pulled them in. But to catch something as beautiful as a thirty-pound Black Sea Bass and throw it away was a terrible thing.

When I told my grandmother about it, she said, "You play with her daughter—the girl who is slow but is also so happy when she makes a basket, the way you've taught her to make one, laughing like a baby even though she is fourteen and becoming a young woman and doesn't know she bleeds. That brings you happiness, too—to help her like that. But what is it like for the captain's wife, who didn't expect a child like Diane, who thought life would bring something else. Why clean a wonderful fish when your daughter will never grow up the way you want her to, never tell by her own life the story you, her mother, want so much to have told in yours? It would make you scream and shout, wouldn't it? It would make you catch and let die and then throw the most beautiful creatures away, wouldn't it? Does this sound familiar, Jimmy? Do you know someone else like this? A mother and a special boy—one who sees what he shouldn't see, knows what his mother is doing and gets in her way, and she can't stand it?"

I didn't understand what she was saying, but I could tell from her eyes—which were blue and bright and crinkled when she smiled—that it didn't matter. It didn't matter because I would when I was grown up, a man, understand.

ॐ

When taps sounded at sunset through the loudspeakers all over the base, I had to stop playing on our front lawn. I had to put my hand over my heart and wait. Standing there as the world got dark, I could smell the odors even worse. When the bugle stopped, I could move again, and I went looking for them. I looked for them every night for a week.

I started in the dumpsters by the machine shops because they were closest. One had the smell, and one didn't. It wasn't fish, but it was definitely something dead *because she wanted it to be*. If it was a dog or a cat or a rat, one dumpster or trash can made sense, but it wasn't just one. I walked on under the electric lights on wires strung over the street and found another dumpster that reeked even worse.

The third one was just a garbage can. It smelled too, and of the same thing. I knew what was in it, but I also didn't know. I was afraid to think of it—of what it was—even though I knew. It was a *person*. A boy whose hand I held every day. I did not want to remember his name...*because she does not want you to*.

How could it be *someone*? How could a smell in a garbage can or dumpster be *someone* and someone I knew?

The next one—a tiny gray dumpster—smelled the same, and I knew who it was even though I wasn't supposed to. It burned my nose, but that wasn't why I was crying. I was very sad, sad as he was, knowing that he was dying and crying because of it.

Something stirred in the eighth dumpster and called my name. I knew the voice—it wanted to help me. It wanted to stop the witch, but how? How does a mother stop a daughter she has to love?

When I stepped up to it, the voice stopped. Only the smell, the rotting, stayed.

I was crying now just like my father, and I was scared that someone would find me like that. MPs patrolled in their cars at night—not many, but sometimes. They would take me back to our quarters and say, "We found him crying by a dumpster. Why would your son be crying on a military base street at night, by a place where people put garbage?"

After they left, my mother would slap me. It wouldn't

matter. I would be waiting for my father to come downstairs, but he wouldn't be able to. He would be crying and so could not come down, and her slap would be about that as much as how I'd embarrassed her with the military police.

Later, with their door closed, she would tell my father, "They found him crying. Why can't you both go away?"

She wouldn't slap him because there would be no need to. He would already be crying.

ৎ

"They're all dead!" my mother was shouting. We were in an apartment—a dirty and tiny one—not our quarters on the base. Why were we here? I couldn't hear anyone else in the apartment.

"How can they all be dead?" I asked, but I knew. *She wanted them to be dead.* She wanted to be alone because only then, she believed, could she be happy. But she wasn't completely alone yet.

What to do about Jimmy? she was thinking, and it was like a scream that wouldn't stop.

I was shivering. I could barely breathe. The air smelled like fried fish, old and burnt. I'd said something to her about my grandmother, and she'd said, "Your grandmother died when you were two! What is wrong with you?" And then, though I hadn't mentioned him, she said, "You never had a little brother! You couldn't possibly have held his hand. And the piers—those are on the navy base. You've never even been there."

I hadn't mentioned the piers.

"And you couldn't possibly hear him crying."

"Who?"

"Your father. He's dead, too. He died three years ago, leaving me like this—with *you*—what was he thinking!"

How would my mother do it? I didn't know, but I could feel her gathering from the air around us, room by room, every shadow, every light, what she needed in order to do it. It would take her a little while, and then it would happen.

Would I just disappear? Would I become something else? Would it hurt?

꙯

That night she kept shouting to herself in the living room of the apartment, and I waited. There was nothing to do. Then, as I lay in my bed, in the dark, the Witch Moth appeared at my window. I couldn't see it, but I could hear it. I got up and let it in and felt its velvet hand against my face. It landed somewhere in the darkness. I knew who it was, and why she'd come. *One witch to stop another*, a voice had whispered — *one who doesn't know she's one...or doesn't want to know*.

The others came then, too, their wings whispering in the dark even if my mother had killed them and always would.

I opened my bedroom door because they wanted me to. They flew to her, and in a moment she stopped shouting. She didn't make a sound. I don't think she was there anymore.

Later, my grandmother, sitting on a chair in my bedroom under an old floor lamp she'd always liked, said, "Your mother — my only daughter — shouted a lot, and did even more terrible things than that, but you don't have to worry now. I shouldn't have waited. In this world — listen to me carefully, Jimmy — she went away three years ago, just ran away, leaving the four of us to enjoy these beautiful quarters. Everything is fine now...." She paused. She took a breath. "I love you. I've always loved you more than anything else, Jimmy, but you know that."

She was smiling. She was looking right at me under the lamp's light, more real than anything I'd ever known. Her eyes — which were like black velvet, not blue glass — were crinkling. The red spot on her nose was like a tiny flower. "Death is no more frightening than life," she said with a little laugh. "So why shouldn't we smile, Jimmy?"

I nodded, and I smiled — and, as I did, everyone who really mattered came back to me on black wings.

SUN AND STONE

The stocky young man from the north, whose German mother had given him his blond curls and his Milanese father his brown eyes, was at twenty-six the youngest professor of zoology at the University of Pisa. He was driving today to a destination none of his departmental colleagues would have been caught dead at, midweek or any other time — namely, the little pink and white stone city of Assisi, in Umbria, and the grotto in the sacred forest there where Saint Francis, lover of nature and nature's God, had prayed with his brothers eight centuries before. The same grotto, the young man remembered, where at the end of his life the saint had died in merciful peace, untouched by the secular compromises — some would say vicissitudes — of the holiest city, Rome. The same grotto where the hands of those who'd loved the saint but never met him had laid brick and mortar to turn the cave into a monastery both for Franciscan brothers not yet born and for the endless river of visitors who would over the centuries come to wonder at the tiny grotto — which, in the words of one Umbrian poet, was "so much like a pearl made of light and shadow."

"Family leave," the young man, whose name was Nardi, had told his chairman. "I need to take it this week. Two days, professor." The older man, though skeptical, couldn't say no. The new university regulations said so. "We'll have Ramarra cover it," the chairman said acidly. "Or another doctoral candidate."

"Thank you," Nardi answered, and he meant it. He needed two days off, even if they weren't for family reasons. He'd heard the strangest story from two students in his introductory zoology class—a story about how oddly the lizards of Assisi, of the grotto and monastery there, behaved, and how no animal behaviorist could possibly explain it. One of the boys who'd made the claim was, yes, a troublemaker in the intellectual sense—antiauthoritarian, with a "show me" attitude; but the other boy had a solid head on his shoulders, would make a good scientist one day, and was puzzled about what he'd seen the way any healthy scientific mind should be puzzled.

"You've seen these lizards yourself?" Nardi had asked them at lunch in the university cafeteria.

"Yes," the rebellious one answered. "Last summer."

"And they're green," the other boy added.

"You're certain they're not *Lacerta viridis*?"

"They're too small," the rebellious one said, contempt in his voice.

"Yes, professor," the good student put in quickly, embarrassed by his friend. "They're definitely *Podarcis*. Just greener than they usually are—right, Carlo?"

"I guess so," his friend conceded.

"Tell me again what they did," Nardi said. At first he'd thought they were pulling his leg, but now he wasn't so sure. In any case he was curious. Lizards were, after all, his specialty—his life's work, if one could be said to have a life's work at twenty-six. And his doctoral dissertation had been on this very lizard: "A Biometric Analysis of a Piedmontese Population of *Podarcis muralis*."

As a child, he had caught lizards whenever he could, and he knew well every species from Rome north. The greenest ones, big and gorgeous but not very common: *Lacerta viridis*. And the species that was everywhere: *Podarcis muralis*, the much smaller "wall lizard," green enough when sunlight fell upon them, but actually speckled with beads of black and green. This was the brave and haughty lizard of the walls and olive groves of this country—one that would chase you if you made it mad, one that would always do its territorial push-ups on the rocks and walls to tell you who was boss. He knew—had known it as a child but learned it even better as an undergraduate and better still as a doctoral candidate — where these wall lizards tended to live and how and why they acted as they did. A part of him — the child who'd grown up with them and therefore loved them — still felt possessive of them, of course. *Podarcis muralis* were *his* lizards, weren't they? It was a childish way to feel, he knew, but that is what happens when one's passion for science begins in childhood, isn't it? Why wouldn't he be curious about the lizards of Assisi?

The two boys told him again what they had seen, what was so odd about the lizards at the grotto, and as he sat there with them at the cafeteria table all he could do was blink, feeling like a *Podarcis* himself. It wasn't possible, of course, what they were claiming, and yet it didn't sound like a lie. They were obviously feeling wonder. Perhaps it was simply a matter of perception, a kind of magical thinking, as psychologists liked to put it: Raised on Catholic saints, the boys had wanted magical things to happen in Assisi, and so they'd perceived miracles there. He had done the same when he was little, hadn't he — finding magic where it wasn't, where a child's wishful thinking wished it, though an adult mind, with reason, with science as its tool, would know better?

But they were *his* lizards — that's how it felt and always would — and he needed to see for himself. He needed a family leave.

ॐ

There were no lizards on the wall along the path to the grotto, despite the patches of sunlight that should have brought them here. Just as the boys had said. It's the parking lot, he told himself. The cars. The noises there. The exhaust and sounds, but mainly the ground vibrations of the nearby parking lot. That's what was keeping the lizards away. But was it really? Fifty meters up the peopleless path, where the parking lot's sounds were distant, on a big patch of sunlit wall that was probably as old as the Etruscans, there still weren't any lizards sunning themselves.

As he walked on, one lizard appeared on the right-hand wall, which had more sun. That made sense. He walked ten meters, and another appeared on the left-hand wall, in sunlight under the still, lichen-encrusted oak trees. This was as it should be, too, he knew, so maybe he'd been right: They just didn't like the parking lot.

But around the bend, when the little monastery on the hillside came in sight, there were suddenly many lizards — dozens of them, maybe a hundred in all — and this made no sense whatsoever. There wasn't any more sunlight here on the stone. There wasn't a source of water that he could see. There weren't any more insects in the air or in the leaves. He checked quickly to see, and there just weren't. Nothing had changed in the environment, but the number of lizards had shot up. As he walked on, they only increased, and when he reached the end of the path, he could only stop and stare. There before him was what he'd never in his life, in all his childhood and teenage years and adulthood studying these lizards, seen — because it wasn't possible:

Hundreds of *Podarcis* were lying perfectly still, blinking in the sun, *swarming*, on the wall by the stone entryway to the monastery, where just inside, in the shadows, a Franciscan priest stood waiting to greet visitors, his smile like a crescent moon.

The lizards were like a blanket, a robe of green on the wall. It wasn't possible. Unlike Jamaican anoles and Papuan *Lygosomas*, this species did not swarm. And why swarm here anyway? There was no more sun on these walls than farther down the pathway, and there certainly was no privacy for breeding. So why here?

He found himself thinking then, and quite irrationally, of that unscientific notion, "fields of energy": Of the tranquility within the monastery, the quiet, the peace, and what an animal that simply wanted to eat what it ate and to live in peace might do if given the chance and the right place. *The "field" of a place.*

The "energy field" of it.

It was insane. Using energy fields to explain things was pseudoscience, the kind of thing — like the Triangle of Bermuda, the Lost City of Atlantis and the Tibetan *Australopithecus gigantus* — that if you pursued it would get you fired. You were supposed to label such things "inexplicable phenomena," leave it at that, and go home. Any herpetologist would look for a source of water or an increase in prey, check to see if the lizards were mating, try to identify any threats that might have driven them together on these walls by the monastery's entryway, and, finding absolutely none of these factors, would go home — because professional pursuit of such phenomena was not productive.

But how could he go home? The lizards — his lizards — were here by the hundreds, quiet and peaceful, and definitely *swarming*.

Were the other phenomena the two boys had reported true as well? As he wondered this, he found himself pulled toward the entryway, its shadows, toward the priest whose smile seemed, quite impossibly, to glow with its own light.

༄

The middle-aged couple from America had a new camera — a tiny little thing no bigger than a woman's compact mirror — and were playing with it like children. The man, a tall, lanky engineer at a big aerospace firm in Houston, kept hiding it in different pockets of his pants and jacket and surprising his wife with it when she least expected it. It was a silly thing to do, but it made her laugh and wasn't that what mattered? It was so small, the camera, that you could barely find the buttons, but there were only four you really needed, and it was a relief from the complicated Nikons he'd never been very good with and the terrible quality of disposables. He kept telling her to pose — first, in front of the dark entryway to the monastery, where the sunlight illuminated her, love of his life for thirty years, like a spotlight; then in front of the little marble birdbath in the courtyard just inside; then beside the Franciscan priest whose smile wouldn't stop and whose English was impeccable; then on the dappled, leaf-strewn path that led from the monastery to more sacred forest on the hill; and finally (he'd need the flash here) on the steps inside the monastery that led down to the grotto, which was just a little room now, after all the centuries of bricking-and-mortaring.

She kept saying, "Stop it, Jim — just stop it." She didn't want pictures of just her. She wanted pictures of the two of them, and there never seemed to be anyone around to ask — except the poor priest, whom they'd already asked twice and couldn't really ask again. If she couldn't, in her bright summer hat and matching yellow dress, have photographs of the two of them together — it was their anniversary, after all — then he should be taking pictures of this place, this incredibly peaceful place, and not just her. But he kept clicking away, checking the pictures he'd taken on the tiny screen, erasing some with a laugh, keeping others, and in any case taking more of *just her*. He couldn't help himself.

On the staircase that led to the roof of the monastery and a view of the Assisi valley, they saw a lone white wild pigeon — a pigeon, not a dove; it was too big to be a dove — land on an eave below them, and of course he snapped pictures of it too. "This is too much," he remarked. "Did they bring it from somewhere else — a pigeon-actor — Italy must have them, Catherine — pay it pigeon-wages to live here? After all, Saint Francis's grotto, this little monastery, needs a white bird."

"Maybe it just *knows*. It knows it's supposed to be here," she answered. He couldn't tell if she was serious or not, but he was thinking the same thing, though not about the bird, about the lizards instead, the ones he'd first seen on the wall near the entrance to the monastery and now noticed everywhere, the splashes of chartreuse they made on every sunny surface. They too looked trained, as if someone, a Hollywood animal handler, had coached them into posing, into scampering at the right moment to make visitors happy. It wasn't natural for so many to be here, was it? In places they were so thick they looked like moss. Even there, under the eave where the white pigeon lived, they made the wall sparkle green. He'd never seen anything like it.

His wife didn't like reptiles, snakes especially, but even lizards and turtles. It wasn't that she had a phobia about them; they just didn't speak to her in any way — "spirit to spirit," as she put it. They didn't speak to him either really, not spirit to spirit, but like many boys he'd had king snakes and gopher snakes as a kid, and how could you not notice the lizards here?

What caught his attention now, though, was how peaceful his wife looked sitting on the staircase's low wall (which, oddly enough, had no lizards on it), where he'd posed her, telling her to tip her head back just a little so that the camera could see her face. It was a face he knew well, and yet the peace of this place made its delicate lines disappear into softness, changing it.

"You sure look peaceful," he said.

"I am," she said.

"What I mean is —" He stopped, not wanting to ruin it, talk it to death, which was so easy to do in Houston. All he needed to do was take another picture of her, since that would make it real and impossible to lose. He would have it forever, and he'd pull it out when he wanted to, months from now, years, to remind himself of what they both could be when they had a chance — and the right place.

"I know, I know," he said. "I'm taking too many pictures of you. But this is a great shot, Catherine. Let me take a couple more."

Her face remained peaceful. The peace was not just the place, he saw, but something that had always been inside her. *It cannot be lost*, he found himself thinking, *for what we are — "a light in the shadows" — can never be lost, though we think it can and so become afraid it will be....*

Where had that come from?

As he took the last picture of his wife seated on that wall, her wonderful hat tipped up just right, her dress with its corn-colored flowers shining like little suns, the white pigeon flew up suddenly from below, from its eave in the courtyard, and, yes, he caught it, too.

As she stood up slowly, straightening her dress, he heard the voices of the priest and someone else, a man trying to speak Italian and doing it badly, in the courtyard below.

At that very moment a lizard scampered from a crevice in the wall and took his wife's place in the sun.

ॐ

Roberto and his best friend, Matteo, had driven up from Rome in Roberto's father's car, an old Fiat Topolino, one of the three or four kinds of cars you could drive in Rome without losing your mind. The boy and his friend had heard there wasn't a single *graffito* in Assisi. It didn't seem possible, but that's what they'd heard from two guests at his aunt's *pensione* in Roma Nord, and what better adventure for the summer than being the first to tag a famous town? Would they go to hell? Of course not. God had forgiven a lot worse. His cousin Paolo had mugged an old man at the Termini, and Father Lucerto had forgiven him. His uncle Marco had gotten a bad sex disease from a prostitute and wasn't going to hell for it either. Matteo had killed a cat once, when he was little, with a BB gun, and had confessed it finally, and been forgiven by Father Lucerto too.

If he, Roberto, was going to hell, it would be for the ten Euros he'd stolen from his father's wallet last month, bragged about to Matteo, and spent on condoms he would never use. All he had to do was confess it, but he couldn't. Father Lucerto and his father were friends. They'd even been in a gang together — *fratelli di sangue* — when they were in school. They had the same tattoo, a little hawk with a snake. He just couldn't. It was too embarrassing.

It wasn't God they were worried about anyway; it was the police — if Assisi had any. Their aunt's guest had said, "It's such a tranquil, peaceful little city, you don't really need police. Did we even see any police, Alain? No? I didn't think so."

To be the first—in a town of so many tourists. He and Matteo would be famous.

They parked down the hill—parking was expensive in Assisi and you couldn't park inside the little town itself—and walked up the main road. They saw one *carabiniere*, and he was killing time, talking to a *paisano*, some olive farmer from the hills.

His aunt's guests had been right. Though the boys walked from Porta San Pietro north to the Basilica of San Francesco, then west to Piazza Matteoti, then south to Piazza Santa Chiara, then north to the Rocca, there wasn't a single tag.

But it wasn't because of police.

There weren't any police.

"We're idiots," Matteo was saying beside him. He was skinny and nervous, and wanted to captain a cruise ship when he was grown, not work in the Fiat factory the way their fathers did.

"I know," Roberto answered with a sigh.

"There are too many tourists—*everywhere*."

"Yes."

"Do you want to stay until night?"

"No, my father will kill me if we're not back by nightfall."

"So what do we do?"

They had their two cans of spray-paint—black and red because they'd show up nicely on the marble of the town—hidden in a backpack so they'd look like students. Maybe they were down from Florence or Perugia. *College* students. That's what they'd tell anyone who asked.

They tried the southern edge of the town, and then the northern. There were still too many tourists. You couldn't get away from them. The problem with tourists was that they were interested in *everything*—even little alleys that went nowhere, even construction sites where no one was working. And they were probably wandering around all night, too, with the city's lights showing off the buildings. No wonder there were no *graffiti*.

In the northwest corner of city, near Piazza Matteoti, there were fewer tourists, yes, but still too many. There was also a sign to something called eremo delle carceri—1 kilometro, and they stopped. A retreat? What kind of retreat? They found a shopkeeper, one who sold cold cuts and souvenirs and had a stuffed wild pig in her window and asked her.

The woman looked at them suspiciously. Maybe they did not look like college students, after all.

"It's the grotto," she said.

"Yes?" Roberto said.

"The grotto of Saint Francis, and his monastery, and his sacred forest. You do not want to go there."

She was right. Why should he want to go there, where God might take more notice of a boy who had not confessed?

But Matteo was laughing at the woman, saying, "Maybe we do," grabbing him by the arm, and pulling him up the road to the *eremo*.

Roberto looked back once to see the woman staring at them even more suspiciously, and tried to pull free of Matteo's hand.

"Maybe not the grotto, Matteo."

"Don't be an idiot. It's just a bunch of rock. And a monastery? Who's going to stop us?"

Roberto stopped struggling. Matteo was right. They couldn't go home without doing something, even if it made him a little nervous to do it.

It was a long walk, that one kilometer, because it was uphill. Matteo, who hated exercise of any kind because (he said) it made his ears hot, was complaining after only a few minutes. Roberto called him "*Stronza!*" and that shut him up.

When they reached the end of the road, they found a little parking lot—one that charged money, too. The dirt path from the parking lot to the monastery was lit here and there by the sun, but the forest didn't look any holier than the parks in Rome. They reached the monastery quickly. Somewhere inside it was a grotto, they knew, but that didn't matter. They wanted a good clean wall and no one watching them—not some grotto.

At the end of the path, at the entrance to the monastery, a priest stepped from the shadows, startling them, but let them through without a fuss, even with a blessing. "*Laudato*" and "*mi signore*" and something else that made no sense.

Matteo, his big ears like handles, was grinning. The place was practically empty. An old married couple—English or American—were taking pictures in the courtyard. A younger man, a northerner, was alone and staring at the walls, at the lizards that covered it, as if he were stoned. Some old Chinese or Japanese guy in a robe had appeared, too, and was talking now to the priest, who'd left the entrance and was standing near a little chapel. These were the only people, and they were minding their own business, not at all interested in two boys.

They'd find a wall easily and tag it before anyone caught them, and then they'd be gone. If they were caught by a priest and a cry went up (were Franciscan priests allowed to shout?— he didn't know), he and Matteo would simply run down the hill through the forest and get to the main road and the car that way. *Easy.*

The wall they chose was a good one—no vines, no lizards, and no one in sight. It was under an eave where a white pigeon had just returned to its nest and was now looking down at them, head cocked.

But when Roberto pulled out the can of black and aimed it, there were suddenly lizards on the wall, exactly where he was aiming.

"*Idiota!*" Matteo teased him. "We're not here to spray lizards."

There were at least twenty of them. Where they'd come from, he had no idea. The lizards were there and in the way, and if he went ahead and sprayed, his tag—his own name, roberto m, with what was called a Sicilian flourish—would be ruined.

He moved his arm and aimed the can again, but the lizards moved, too. Again they were where he was aiming. How was this possible? Lizards ran away from your hand, not toward it.

Matteo was stifling a laugh. He was enjoying this too much.

It didn't even strike him as strange, the way these lizards were acting.

Roberto moved his arm a third time and watched the lizards move with it. There were even more of them now. They had come down from the eaves, moving like tiny pieces of his aunt's embroidered cloth—the one she'd been sewing on when they left—green and black and sparkling, down from the eaves but also down from the stairs that led up to the top of the monastery. There were so many now that wherever he moved his arm there'd still be lizards under it.

"*Funcu!*" he whispered.

"Spray the little fuckers!" Matteo said too loudly, but he was right. The only thing that would make the lizards run away now was paint in their eyes and mouths. He got ready to spray them—

And the first lizard jumped on his face.

It didn't just jump and hang there; it scampered all over his face. It made quick circles, as if doing a little dance, and he jumped back, dropping the can, which hit the pavement with a bang.

"*Merda!*" Roberto said. "*Merda! Merda! Merda!*"

Matteo couldn't hold it in any longer. He laughed out loud.

"*Zito!*" Roberto whispered. He was slapping at his own face, but the lizard was gone. He picked up the can, and now there were even more of them—like a big green blanket on the wall. It wasn't possible. How could Matteo not think it strange?

"Let's find another wall," Matteo was saying, barely able to stop laughing.

"No fucking way, *minchione!*"

He started to press the nozzle on the can—

And the wall seemed to jump at him. A dozen lizards had landed on his face, clinging to him, tickling him, blinding him with their bodies and tails, and then a dozen were on his neck and arms, running as quickly as they could toward his hand and the can.

Matteo's laugher had stopped suddenly, and Roberto turned

to see lizards crawling on his friend's face, too, and Matteo shouting, "Mary, Mother of God!" Now it wasn't so funny.

But it was when the lizards began to move across the wall — not to jump on him or Matteo, but to make a shape, ever so slowly, on the wall — a letter, the beginning of a word, that Roberto stepped back in horror, turned, dropped the can, and began to run, Matteo's footsteps loud behind him. *I know, I know! — I should have confessed it*, he found himself thinking as he struggled for breath. *I will confess it to Father Lucerto this very night if you will let us go, oh Lord — if you will let us go home.*

At the entryway to the monastery the priest stepped aside quickly to let them pass with a smile and even another blessing, and the forest was a dappled blur as they ran, as Roberto stumbled, fell, got up, and ran on toward the little car that would, if he was lucky — if God's lizards weren't waiting for him there, too — take him back to Rome without breaking down.

ॐ

Joten Roshi, former abbot of the Zen abbey of Sun on Stone in the Japanese Alps, in Nagano Province, was visiting the world's thirty-three most sacred places in the six months doctors in Tokyo had given him. Why his body should want to grow such a thing inside it was a mystery, but like all matters of the body, it meant nothing. It was time to leave that body, of course, and he wanted to find, by traveling one last time, what he had of course found before in his travels, and valued so profoundly. After all, his order did not espouse an intellectual or pious approach to spiritual matters, but instead "direct experience" — "epiphany as dharma," as a favorite student of his had remarked years ago.

The Taj Majal, Jerusalem's West Wall, the Alhambra, Angkor Watt, the Ganges River, the Vatican, Stonehenge, Westminster Abbey, Machu Pichu, Chartres, and of course the Great Buddha of Kyoto — not to mention relics of the Buddha and Saint Peter and countless temples, churches, mosques and shrines — these he already knew from the other travels of his life. But there had been twenty-six important others — a list prepared for him long ago by the fourteenth Dalai Lama of Tibet, with whom he had corresponded for years — and it had taken him four months of ships, planes, trains, buses, and automobiles to see them. He had wished to see the Great Buddha of Afghanistan, but fanatics had destroyed it with bombs before he could. Twenty-five was good enough. He was tired. He could feel the greed of the thing inside him. It was hungry, so it was indeed time. And any one of the twenty-five — even this one, the smallest and quietest of them all — could give him what he needed now, in whatever form it chose to give it.

As he walked up the path from the parking lot to the monastery — where the saint had prayed in his little grotto, in a room carved by time and water from ancient stone, and in the end had left his body there — Joten saw the lizards. Who wouldn't? Lively and cheerful, sunning themselves on walls, scampering about in the sunlight as if the world were theirs, they were everywhere. A stocky young man had stopped on the path and was staring at them, while a middle-aged couple — Americans or Canadians perhaps — walked by holding hands and laughing, the man playing with a tiny camera that obviously brought him joy. In the distance, back at the parking lot where he had left his rental car with a kind attendant, someone was revving an engine. A young person, no doubt. No one older would need such sound. He had needed sound, too, when he was young. After all, it is rare for youth to hear enough inside itself to be happy, or to find silence better than noise.

The stocky young man was so mesmerized by the lizards that he didn't turn when Joten stepped past him into the monastery's entryway. There, in the shadows, a Franciscan *padre* was waiting to greet everyone who came. Joten stopped in the shadows with him, marveled at how the man's smile caught the light from outside, and bowed.

"*Buon giorno, gentil signore*," the priest said with a nod, and a familiar understanding passed between them.

"*Laudato sie, mi signore*," Joten answered, doing his best to remember the words, "*cum tucte le tue creature....*"

The priest's smile grew, and he laughed—not at Joten's terrible pronunciation, but in happy surprise. It was medieval Umbrian Joten had attempted to speak—the Canticle of the Creatures of Saint Francis, of course. The priest had surely not heard it quoted by many tourists, though shouldn't it be quoted here, of all places?

"*Spetialmente messer lo frate sole, loquale iorni et allumini noi per lui*," the priest answered, finishing the stanza for him.

"*Grazie, padre*," Joten said, knowing the man would forgive him for his terrible *r*'s. He had mastered many languages in his life, but all eastern ones. His English was terrible and his Romance languages just as terrible, though many times—because laughter is a good way to turn fear into trust—that very terribleness had turned strangers into friends, and quite quickly.

ॐ

The grotto itself, Joten discovered, was simply a fracture in the marble of the hill, and could be reached only by the narrowing stairs of stone that turned and turned again. It had been walled in over time with brick and mortar so that there was only one room and an altar in it. It felt like a tomb, as perhaps it should, but he wished he could have seen more clearly than feeble imagination allowed what the grotto had been like in the beginning, when the saint had first discovered it and used it privately, before the centuries of building had begun. Human beings built in order to worship, of course, and here they had built to their hearts' content. The man who had first come here centuries ago, and his humble brothers, had done so for the simplicity of the rock, the darkness, a candle, silence, a prayer, that they might devote themselves to light and love. Others had followed them, and out of love, too, but also out of a longing and an illusion of lost innocence, and they had built this place to celebrate the saint, to bring him closer to their hearts, that they themselves might feel worthy of love. Which of course they already were, though like all human beings they insisted on doubting it.

But who was he to preach the faith of others? How silly. If he knew their faith at all, it was by knowing his own and through the truths he had discovered in his life by listening to the silence beyond the sound.

When he had toured the handful of rooms of the silent monastery and had peeked over a gate into the little chapel where the priests of this place met in prayer, he returned to the entryway. The Franciscan was gone now, though Joten thought he could hear him speaking to the middle-aged couple in the courtyard.

When he stepped through the shadows of the entryway and into the sun, the lizards were still there on the wall, just as he'd known they'd be. The sun was fading a little, but was still bright enough to keep them. They looked like big-headed children in green tights, happy as children are when they are happy.

One of the lizards scampered toward him, stopping close enough that he could reach out and touch it, and stared at him, as if inviting him to step even closer. It was not a lizardly thing to do, but he was not surprised.

He had known there would be a special one, and this lizard was obviously it.

"Thank you," Joten said in his own language. "Thank you for coming."

He sat down on the wall by the creature, which didn't move, and waited, watching the *eke*, the little lizard. The thing looked back at him, its skin like the tiniest black and green fish eggs, or more accurately, like the exquisite, colorful sand paper made by Tasaki, master paper-maker of Kyoto.

"*Now?*" the lizard asked suddenly, its voice scratchy, like a hinge needing oil, its jaw moving oddly so that it might make the words—the actual *sounds* of the words.

Joten laughed so hard he could not answer. The lizard's eyes were like teardrops, he saw, but tears without sadness. What would they have to be sad about in a place like this — number twenty-six on the Dalai Lama's list?

"*Nothing at all*," the lizard answered, hearing Joten's question because in the oneness of things all questions, like their answers, could be heard. "*Nothing at all*," the lizard repeated. "*But is there reason for sadness anywhere?*"

"Of course not," Joten answered, aware that he was grinning like a fool.

The lizard asked it again: "*Now?*"

Joten laughed quietly this time, as a deep peace settled into him.

"Yes," he answered. And then, because separateness is but an illusion, too, Joten's body shivered once, brightened for a moment, and then disappeared completely. There on the wall, in his place, was a second lizard, its body still for a moment as it woke and blinked and moved in that jittery way all lizards move because something might, at any moment, grab them, and then where would they be?

ৡ

As the sunset and darkness began to fill the world, the lizards on the walls on either side of the monastery's entryway began to move. They did not enter the cracks and holes in the walls or find rotten pieces of oak wood on the forest floor to hide under for the night. Instead, they gathered in twos and threes, then by the dozens, then the hundreds, and made their way toward a hole in the eastern wall, a hole no bigger than a man's hand, but one that wound down through the ancient stone upon which the monastery had been built and from which nature had long ago made the grotto itself, and toward a light that burned in the earth, in a cave no human had ever set foot in. The cave was oddly shaped, horizontal, no longer than a man and no wider, and there was no way that all of the lizards could fit into it even if they'd wanted to. Instead, they nestled against each other in the little tunnel and felt warm in the light of the sun that wasn't a sun, in the light that burned forever.

The new lizard, though it had trailed behind the others at first, getting used to its legs, making sure they worked properly, had no trouble following. It knew where the others were going. It knew that light. But who didn't?

BIOGRAPHIES

Bruce McAllister's short stories have appeared over the decades in many science fiction and fantasy magazines, literary quarterlies, college textbooks, and many "year's best" series. They have won or been shortlisted for the National Endowment for the Arts, Nebula, Hugo, Locus, and Shirley Jackson awards and many others. His Hugo-nominated short story 'Kin' was chosen by LeVar Burton to launch the podcast series *LeVar Burton Reads*, and his short story 'The Boy in Zaquitos' appeared in *Best American Short Stories*, edited by Stephen King. His first short story, which was written when he was sixteen, was chosen for Judith Merrill's "year's best" series that year and decades later appeared in the Isaac Asimov/Martin Greenberg series, *The Great SF Stories*. He has served on many awards juries and was for a number of years the associate editor of the Harry Harrison/Brian Aldiss "year's best science fiction" series. His novels include *Humanity Prime*, *Dream Baby*, and *The Village Sang to the Sea: A Memoir of Magic*. He lives in southern California.

Paul Di Filippo is an American science fiction writer and critic whose work has been nominated for the Hugo, Nebula, Philip K. Dick, World Fantasy, BSFA, and Wired awards among others. He is the author of several novels, including *Ciphers*, *Fuzzy Dice*, *Cosmocopia*, and most recently *The Summer Thieves*, and over two hundred short stories. He was an early champion and practitioner of both "cyberpunk" and "steampunk" science fiction. He is perhaps best known for his *The Steampunk Trilogy*: *Victoria*, *Hottentots*, and *Walt and Emily*; his Linear Cities series; and for the very wide breadth of ideas in his fiction. He is a regular reviewer for many high-profile magazines in the field and lives in Rhode Island. Learn more about his work here: https://paul-di-filippo.com/

Dominic Harman is a British illustrator whose award-winning work has been commissioned by all of the major book publishers in the science fiction, fantasy and horror fields and countless magazines. His awards include, among others, the British Science Fiction Award for Best Artwork and the Asimov's Science Fiction Award for Best Artist. His work has appeared on the cover of books by H.G. Wells, Terry Pratchet, Clive Barker, Phillip Pullman, and many others. His influences and inspirations include artists like Boris Vallejo, Frank Frazetta, Velazquez, Rubens, Caravaggio and Rembrandt, and he is a graduate of the legendary Caravaggio workshop in Florence, Italy. Under the name Emile Parks, he creates work of a different style. Check out his work as Dominic Harman at www.bleedingdreams.com and as Emile Parks at https://emile-parks.squarespace.com/

Praise for *The Village Sang to the Sea*

"*The Village Sang to the Sea* is a uniquely haunting book, unlike any novel - fantasy or mainstream - I've read in a long time. By turns touching, funny, and truly frightening, it goes its own deliberate, constantly surprising way to an immensely satisfying climax. I've no idea whether or not a critic might call it 'magical realism,' but under any official designation, it's quite simply a beauty--in the fullest meaning of the word."

- Peter S. Beagle, World Fantasy Lifetime Achievement Award winner and author of *The Last Unicorn*

"*The Village Sang to the Sea* is that rarity: a book that delicately and perfectly captures the magic we all know underlies the world, the sure knowledge that things mean more than they appear. Brad is a real American boy in a real Italian village, but he can see clearly what the rest of us must infer. In prose both precise and lyrical, Bruce McAllister captures Brad's vision and shares it richly. You will not forget this book. Not ever."

- Nancy Kress, Hugo and Nebula awards winner and author of *Beggars in Spain*

"*The Village Sang to the Sea*, like any profound work of art, works on more than one level; that is, it is more than it seems to be. It works in profound, dark counterpoint, the story concealed, then revealed like the six-part conclusion of Bruckner's Eighth Symphony. Sharp and lingering...."

- Barry Malzberg, John W. Campbell Memorial Award winner and author of *Beyond Apollo*

Lightning Source UK Ltd.
Milton Keynes UK
UKHW021809190722
406071UK00007B/198